Praise for Novels by Brandilyn Collins

Gone to Ground

"Moves along briskly. The popular novelist's talent continues to flower . . . and sales will flourish."

—*Publishers Weekly*

"High octane. Roller coaster suspense with memorable characters and intriguing plot twists."

—*CBA Retailers + Resources*

"Collins does it again with her trademark suspense that will keep readers up late into the night."

—*RT BookReviews*

"Well crafted. A page-turning suspense."

—*Examiner.com*

Double Blind

"Collins keeps coming up with fascinating, unique plots. . . . Fantastic twists will keep readers guessing until the very end."

—*RT BookReviews*

"Another suspenseful winner."

—*CBA Retailers + Resources*

"A psychological thriller with abnormal twists and turns. Be prepared for intrigue and the unexpected!"

—*TitleTrakk*

Over the Edge

"Tense and dramatic . . . a dense and compact narrative that holds its tension while following the protagonist in a withering battle."

—*New York Journal of Books*

"A taut, heartbreaking thriller . . . Collins is a fine writer who knows how to both horrify readers and keep them turning pages."

—*Publishers Weekly*

"A frightening and all-too-real scenario . . . very timely and meaningful book."

—*RT Book Reviews*

Deceit

". . . good storytelling and notable mystery . . . an enticing read [that poses] tough questions about truth and lies, power and control, faith and forgiveness."

—*Publishers Weekly*

"Solidly constructed . . . a strong and immediately likable protagonist. One of the Top Ten Inspirational Novels of 2010."

—*Booklist*

"Filled with excitement and intrigue, Collins' latest will keep the reader quickly turning pages . . . This tightly plotted mystery, filled with quirky characters, will appeal to suspense lovers everywhere."

—*RT Book Reviews*

". . . pulse-accelerating, winding, twisting storyline [that will] keep your attention riveted to the action until the very end."

—*Christian Retailing*

Exposure

". . . a hefty dose of action and suspense with a superb conclusion."

—*RT Book Reviews*

"Brandilyn Collins, the queen of Seatbelt Suspense®, certainly lives up to her well-deserved reputation. *Exposure* has more twists and turns than a Coney Island roller coaster . . . Intertwining storylines collide in this action-packed drama of suspense and intrigue. Highly recommended."

—*CBA Retailers + Resources*

"Captivating . . . the alternating plot lines and compelling characters in *Exposure* will capture the reader's attention, but the twist of events at the end is most rewarding."

—*Christian Retailing*

"Mesmerizing mystery . . . a fast-paced, twisting tale of desperate choices."

—*TitleTrakk.com*

"[Collins is] a master of her craft . . . intensity, tension, high-caliber suspense, and engaging mystery."

—*The Christian Manifesto*

Dark Pursuit

"Lean style and absorbing plot . . . Brandilyn Collins is a master of suspense."

—*CBA Retailers + Resources*

"Intense . . . engaging . . . whiplash-inducing plot twists . . . the concepts of forgiveness, restoration, selflessness, and sacrifice made this book not only enjoyable, but a worthwhile read."

—*Thrill Writer*

"Moves from fast to fierce."

—*TitleTrakk.com*

"Thrilling . . . characters practically leap off the page with their quirks and inclinations."

—*Tennessee Christian Reader*

Amber Morn

". . . a harrowing hostage drama . . . essential reading."

—*Library Journal*

"The queen of seatbelt suspense delivers as promised. Her short sentences and strong word choices create a 'here and now' reading experience like no other."

—*TitleTrakk.com*

"Heart-pounding . . . the satisfying and meaningful ending comes as a relief after the breakneck pace of the story."

—*RT Book Reviews*

"High octane suspense . . . a powerful ensemble performance."

—*BookshelfReview.com*

Crimson Eve

"One of the Best Books of 2007 . . . Top Christian suspense of the year."

—*Library Journal, starred review*

"The excitement starts on page one and doesn't stop until the shocking end . . . [*Crimson Eve*] is fast-paced and thrilling."

—*RT Book Reviews*

"The action starts with a bang . . . and the pace doesn't let up until this fabulous racehorse of a story crosses the finish line."

—*Christian Retailing*

"An unparalleled cat and mouse game wrought with mystery and surprise."

—*TitleTrakk.com*

Coral Moon

"A chilling mystery. Not one to be read alone at night."

—*RT BOOKclub*

"Thrilling . . . one of those rare books you hurry through, almost breathlessly, to find out what happens."

—*Spokane Living*

". . . a fascinating tale laced with supernatural chills and gut-wrenching suspense.

—*Christian Library Journal*

Violet Dawn

". . . fast-paced . . . interesting details of police procedure and crime scene investigation . . . beautifully developed [characters] . . ."

—*Publishers Weekly*

"A sympathetic heroine . . . effective flashbacks . . . Collins knows how to weave faith into a rich tale."

—*Library Journal*

"Collins expertly melds flashbacks with present-day events to provide a smooth yet deliciously intense flow . . . quirky townsfolk will help drive the next books in the series."

—*RT BOOKclub*

"Skillfully written . . . Imaginative style and exquisite suspense."

—*1340mag.com*

Web of Lies

"A master storyteller . . . Collins deftly finesses the accelerator on this knuckle-chomping ride."

—*RT BOOKclub*

"fast-paced . . . mentally challenging and genuinely entertaining."

—*Christian Book Previews*

Dead of Night

"Collins' polished plotting sparkles . . . unique word twists on the psychotic serial killer mentality. Lock your doors, pull your shades—and read this book at noon."

—*RT BOOKclub*, Top Pick

". . . this one is up there in the stratosphere . . . Collins has it in her to give an author like Patricia Cornwell a run for her money."

—*Faithfulreader.com*

". . . spine-tingling, hair-raising, edge-of-the-seat suspense."

—*Wordsmith Review*

"A page-turner I couldn't put down, except to check the locks on my doors."

—*Authors Choice Reviews*

Stain of Guilt

"Collins keeps the reader gasping and guessing . . . artistic prose paints vivid pictures . . . High marks for original plotting and superb pacing."

—*RT BOOKClub*

". . . a sinister, tense story with twists and turns that will keep you on the edge of your seat."

—*Wordsmith Shoppe*

Brink of Death

". . . an abundance of real-life faith as well as real-life fear, betrayal and evil. This one kept me gripped from beginning to end."

—*Contemporary Christian Music*

"Collins' deft hand for suspense brings on the shivers."

—*RT BOOKclub*

"Gripping . . . thrills from page one."

—*christianbookpreviews.com*

Dread Champion

"Compelling . . . plenty of intrigue and false trails."

—*Publisher's Weekly*

"Finely-crafted . . . vivid . . . another masterpiece that keeps the reader utterly engrossed."

—*RT BOOKclub*

". . . riveting mystery and courtroom drama."

—*Library Journal*

Eyes of Elisha

"Chilling . . . a confusing, twisting trail that keeps pages turning."

—*Publisher's Weekly*

"A thriller that keeps the reader guessing until the end."

—*Library Journal*

"Unique and intriguing . . . filled with more turns than a winding mountain highway."

—*RT BOOKclub*

"One of the top ten Christian novels of 2001."

—*christianbook.com*

DARK

JUSTICE

BRANDILYN
COLLINS

DARK

JUSTICE

PUBLISHING GROUP

Nashville, Tennessee

978-1-4336-7953-7

Published by B&H Publishing Group
Nashville, Tennessee

Dewey Decimal Classification: F
Subject Heading: ADVENTURE FICTION \
MYSTERY FICTION

Author represented by the literary agency of Alive
Communications, Inc., 7680 Goddard Street, Suite 200, Colorado
Springs, Colorado, 80920, www.alivecommunications.com.

1 2 3 4 5 6 7 8 • 17 16 15 14 13

Author's Note

While this story is fictional, it is based on the terrifying reality that terrorists could target America's electrical grid. In 2011, the consulting firm Pike Research issued a report stating that security for the electrical grid was in "near chaos," giving attackers the "upper hand" since many attacks could not be prevented. The problem centered on aging infrastructures with no built-in security. And the security that was present could be bypassed by a "$60 piece of software."

The shutdown of just one local grid could cause a "cascade effect," said Pike, causing an entire region to lose power.

I first learned this information when I saw a CNN report of an experiment conducted in 2007 by the U.S. Department of Energy. In the experiment, a replica of a power-plant control system was hacked and damaged by remote. The generator shook and released steam, and soon went out of control. The entire video lasts about a minute.

In 2010, a unique and sophisticated computer worm spread through Iran, India, and Indonesia. Named Stuxnet, the worm looked for very specific settings, then injected its own code into that system. After a few years of studying this worm, security researcher Ralph Langner concluded he was 100 percent certain Stuxnet was specifically targeted to wreak havoc in Iran's uranium-enrichment facility in Natanz. "This stuff is so bizarre," Langner told a reporter in an e-mail, "that I have to make up my mind how to explain this to the public." Later Langner said that now Stuxnet was "history," the current problem was "the next generation of malware that will follow."

That was more than enough to set my imagination running.

This novel is set in real towns, naming real law enforcement agencies. But all the characters are fictional. None is intended to even remotely represent anyone in real life. What's more, wielding the power I have as a novelist, I may have tweaked some of the policies and procedures within these agencies to allow my story to flow more smoothly. At some point, it becomes necessary to jump from the cliff of reality into the chasm of fiction.

But I will look to the LORD;
I will wait for the God of my salvation.
My God will hear me.
Do not rejoice over me, my enemy!
Though I have fallen, I will stand up;
though I sit in darkness,
the LORD will be my light.
(Micah 7:7–8 HCSB)

Chapter 1

Sunday, February 24, 2013

"When I was in fifth grade, three kids in my class swore up and down they saw a woman with a baby fly by the window."

This statement, out of the blue, from my eighty-two-year-old mother.

I glanced at her. She was looking out her car window, veined hands folded in her lap. Her ever-present Annie-Hall-style purple hat sat at a rakish angle on her white head. As usual, she wore no makeup, but her cheeks still tinged a faint peach. That coloring was a source of pride for my mother, as was her perfect eyesight.

"Interesting. Why do you suppose the kids said that?"

"Because it happened, of course."

"People don't fly, Mom."

"Well, they did that day."

Here we go.

"Maybe the woman just walked by, and the kids thought she was flying."

"Our classroom was on the second floor."

Mom had me there. "Maybe they made it up."

"Absolutely not! One of them was my good friend, Julie. She was straight as an arrow. Never lied about anything." Mom's voice carried that decisive ring that signaled she'd dug in her heels. Happened more and more often these days. Many times I just let it go. But when her words defied logic, something within me wanted to fight the dementia that had begun to nibble at her mind. My mother had always been so independent. If elderly women were supposed to wear red hats, Carol Ray Ballard's would be purple. If they attended classical concerts, she'd go to a nightclub and dance to every song—by herself.

Of all people, my mother should be able to beat this.

"Okay, maybe they were just mistaken." I kept my tone light. "Maybe a big bird flew by, and somehow the kids convinced themselves they'd seen flying people."

Mom sniffed. "Birds so often look like a woman with a baby."

My heart twinged. Now she'd descended into just plain stubbornness. Why did I insist on pushing her? It was pointless. This life-stealing illness was so powerful. Yet I kept acting as though I could beat it back. I *couldn't*. It just came on and on, a slow-rising tide. I was a fixer, but I couldn't fix this.

I should take cues from my twenty-seven-year-old daughter, Emily. She handled her grandmother far better than I did. Emily was known for speaking her mind and not taking flak from anyone. Yet she was so patient with her "Grand." So willing to just let the woman *be*.

"Honestly." My mother folded her arms and huffed. "Sometimes you act like I'm just stupid."

"Mom, no! I've *never* thought you're stupid. Not for a second."

I negotiated a curve on Tunitas Creek Road, off Highway 1, a little south of Half Moon Bay, California. We'd set out from our weekend at the Ritz Carlton on the ocean to return to our home in San Carlos. Instead of taking the more popular Highway 92 over the hills, I'd taken a detour, choosing to follow the little-used Tunitas up to Skyline, then hook up to 92.

An off-the-cuff decision that would change our lives.

It was a beautiful drive on this afternoon in late February. The weather was unseasonably warm and dry, the month known for bringing rain to the Bay Area. Mom and I wore coats, but they were much lighter than usual. We'd both dressed in casual clothes for our trip home, I in jeans and a blue sweatshirt, Mom in her pull-on knit pants and a long-sleeved blouse. Our weekend had done Mom a world of good, or so I'd thought. She'd had fewer episodes of disjointed conversation or misplacing an item. I'd hoped that could last. Maybe I just needed to get her out more. Maybe . . . something.

"Anyway, I'm sure your friends were right, Mom, the woman and baby must have flown." I tried to keep the defeat from my voice.

Mom made a point of continuing to look out her window. "You don't really believe me."

"Yes, I do."

We rounded another curve, admiring the scenery. I hoped Mom would let the subject drop. The wild pull of the ocean had given way to an open field. "We should call Emily when we get home. She'll want to hear—"

"Look!" Mom's finger jerked toward her side of the road. My gaze flicked to follow her gesture—and landed on a small gray car, gone some distance off the pavement and flipped onto its passenger side. I gasped.

"Oh, dear, there's a man!" Mom's voice quivered.

He lay on his back in the grass. Unmoving.

It happened so fast, we'd passed the scene before I could react. My foot hit the brake. I steered our car off the road and onto grass, carving to a halt. Turned off the engine and grabbed out the keys. I couldn't leave them in the ignition with my mother around. "Mom, you stay here, okay? *Don't* move. I'll run back and check on him."

I bounded out of my Ford Escort, dropping my keys in the pocket of my coat. Then I remembered my cell phone. I whirled back and opened the rear door to fish it from my purse.

"You think he's okay?" Mom was turned around in her seat, her face pinched.

"Don't know, I'll see."

My cell phone fell into the same pocket as my keys. I ran toward the man and sank to my knees beside him. He looked to be in his late seventies, his face gray. On more than one occasion a patient in the cardiologist's office in which I served as reception- ist had collapsed in the waiting room. I was used to helping the infirm and elderly. My heart ached for every one of them, even as I snapped into a no-nonsense, medical mode.

"Sir?" I placed the backs of my fingers against the man's neck and felt a pulse. "Sir, can you hear me?"

His eyes fluttered open. His mouth moved to talk, but no sound came.

"Do you hurt anywhere?" I checked down the length of his body. His legs looked normal, nothing torqued at an odd angle. Had he been thrown from his car? I glanced at the vehicle. The open window of the driver's side gaped up at the sky. Could he have been thrown out of such a small space? Maybe he climbed out.

The man's lips tremored. "M—my . . ." He lifted a shaking hand and slid it over his heart.

"Your chest?"

"Unhh." He winced.

I pulled my phone from my pocket and punched in 911. The man's hand raised, reaching for my wrist.

"Nine-one-one, what is your emergency?"

"Auto accident on Tunitas Road, off Highway 1. One victim, male, late seventies. He's outside the car, lying on his back. Complaining of chest pains. I see no other obvious signs of trauma."

"Is he breathing?"

"Yes. Trying to talk."

"All right, stay on the line, please."

The man's cold fingers fumbled for me. "Lis . . ."

"It's okay, it's okay." I grasped his hand. "Help will be on the way. I'll stay with you."

"Nnnn . . ."

"Shh, it's okay. Let's have a look at your chest."

I eased his arm toward the ground and fumbled one-handed with the buttons on his coat. His hand shot up and grabbed mine again. "Lisss!"

His strength startled me. Abject fear etched his face. I stopped all movement.

"Ma'am, ma'am?" The woman's voice came through my phone.

I held the man's hand, my eyes on him as I pulled the cell close to my ear. "I'm here."

"Is he able to move his legs?"

The man's fingers tightened over mine. "Pleease . . ."

Such fear in his eyes. I'd seen it before in a patient who knew he was dying. Did this man feel that? I tried to give him a reassuring smile, but it came out twisted. "Shh. It's all right." Into the phone I said, "I don't know. When will you get here?"

"Help's on the way from Half Moon Bay. Five to ten minutes."

The man gasped in breaths. "Raaaalll . . ." His fingers sank into my palm, his determined expression shooting right through me. He must be feeling himself slip away. Did he have a final message for someone? If so, I would move Earth to deliver it.

I knew I was supposed to stay on the phone. Report what vital signs I could. But this panicked man was alone and terrified, and I was all he had.

"I have to put the phone down for a moment," I told Emergency. I laid it on the grass without waiting for a reply.

"Raalll . . ."

With both hands, I grasped the man's fingers. Shifted my body so he could see my face more easily. "Ral?"

His head tried to nod. "Ral . . . ee."

"Raleigh?"

"Unhh." His nails sank into my skin. "In . . . Ral-leigh." The last syllable sank like a sigh.

"In Raleigh."

"Yeah." Tears sprang to his eyes, as if he couldn't believe he'd gotten it out. My own eyes watered in response. His emotion rolled off him like fog, wrapping around my shoulders. Making me shiver.

Pain crimped his face. He closed his eyes, a tear running down each temple. "F-find. Please. S-save."

Find what? "Okay." I nodded. "I will."

He looked at me once again, his gaze piercing. "Prom . . ."

"I promise."

"Im . . . port . . ."

"It's important?"

"Uh."

"Is he okay?" My mother's voice drifted from behind me.

Oh, no. I half-turned. "Mom, I wanted you to stay in the car."

She gazed down at the man, her cheeks red. Her hat was about to slip from her head. "Oh, the poor thing."

"Mom, please." Anxiety edged my voice. I couldn't trust her here. What if she wandered out into the road? I let go of the man's hand, fumbling around to face Mom, still on my knees. "Please get back to the car." How long until we saw the ambulance? The police?

"No, I want to help."

Movement from the man rustled from behind. He grasped the left side of my coat, his fingers plucking at my pocket.

"Mom, listen to me."

But my mother had no intention of listening. She slipped to the man's other side and awkwardly lowered herself to the ground. I shuffled back around to face them both. At least Mom was right in front of me.

The man's hand fell back to his chest. His mouth trembled.

"That's all right now, you'll be all right." Mom's words crooned. She placed her hands against the man's cheeks. "'In God I trust; I will not fear. What can man do to me?' That's in the Bible, you know."

He managed a tiny nod, his gaze latching onto my mother's face as if it were the most beautiful thing he'd ever seen.

"My daughter works in a big, important doctor's office. She knows what to do." Mom leaned closer to him. "She's a little stubborn sometimes, but you know children."

No response. The man was struggling to breathe.

"What's your name?" Mom asked.

"M . . . Morton."

"Hi, Morton. I'm Carol. This is my daughter, Hannah."

Morton's breathing grew worse. That scared me. I snatched up my cell phone. "Hello? You still there?"

"I'm here. What's happening?"

"It's getting harder for him to breathe. We need help now."

A pause. "They're en route and should be there soon."

I'd never gotten Morton's coat unbuttoned. He could have a wound, maybe from hitting the steering wheel. Or what if he was bleeding internally? Having a heart attack? Not that I could stop that. I threw the phone down again. "Morton, I need to look at your chest." I reached for the top button, but his arms were in the way.

He wound his fingers around Mom's small wrist. "In . . . Raleigh."

"In Raleigh?"

"Ye . . ."

She tilted her head. "What's in Raleigh?"

"K . . ."

Mom frowned at me. "What's he—"

A siren wailed in the distance. Thank God. I grabbed my phone again. "They're here, I'm hanging up." I punched off the call and dropped the cell into my deep pocket.

I smoothed Morton's hair. "Hear that? Help's almost here."

His glassy eyes turned toward mine. The gray in his face drained to white. "*Don't* t-t-t . . ." His jaw snapped up and down, uncontrolled, his voice sounding panicked. "Tell."

"Don't tell?"

His eyes closed in a *yes*. "Any . . . one." He gripped Mom's wrist harder, as if his fingers could force into her what he wanted to say.

I could feel the dire need flowing from him. I knew Mom felt it too. My mother and I glanced at each other, shaken to the core.

Mom began to cry. "Oh, you poor man." She patted his cheeks, her words spilling out as they did when she was overwhelmed. "Don't tell anyone—okay, we won't. We'll come see you in the hospital, and you can tell us all about it. Help him, Jesus, Jesus. Help this poor soul."

The siren grew loud. I pushed back on my haunches and saw a fire truck round the curve. It veered off the road a little below us and ground to a stop. The siren died away as two men jumped out. A white sheriff's department car pulled up behind it. Men from the fire truck gathered equipment kits and ran toward us.

Morton's eyes popped open. He pierced me with a final look. "Be . . . *careful*."

I pushed to my feet. My mother didn't move. "Mom, you'll need to step back now so they can work on him."

She brushed her fingertips across the man's forehead. His eyes were closed again, pain pinching his face. "I don't want to leave him."

"You'll have to." I moved around Morton's head to take her elbows.

The firemen reached us. The first fell to his knees on Morton's other side and nodded to me. "What can you tell me?" He was already reaching into his kit for equipment.

"He's still complaining of chest pains. I don't know much more. His name's Morton."

The other fireman ran around to our side.

"Come on, Mom." I pulled her to her feet. "We have to get out of the way."

With obvious reluctance she shuffled backward with me. We moved some distance away and huddled together to watch. A breeze picked up, whistling a dirge around the parked vehicles. Mom shivered. I put an arm around her thin shoulders. We couldn't see Morton's face anymore. Could only watch the back of the fireman closest to us.

A portly sheriff's deputy hurried from his car and over to Morton and the first responders. "Ambulance is on its way," he told them.

"Be careful." What did Morton mean?

The few other cars on Tunitas Road were slowing down, the drivers rubbernecking. A second sheriff's department vehicle arrived. The deputy hopped out and waved drivers on.

Mom was sniffing. "I feel so sorry for him."

I squeezed her shoulder. "Me too."

"We'll help him, won't we." It wasn't a question.

"Of course we will."

"He said Raleigh. North Carolina?"

"I guess. Maybe he's from there."

"What's in Raleigh?"

He had tried to say it. A word starting with a *K*. Maybe a hard *C*. "I have no idea."

"Someone important, he said. I think it's his daughter."

"His daughter?" The responders were taking vital signs. One reported findings into a radio. The sheriff's deputy stood over them, watching. He gave me a quick nod, and I nodded back.

"Yes," Mom said. "She's a lost soul. He hasn't seen her for the longest time. He wants to tell her he loves her."

"I see."

"So sad."

"Yes."

"We'll have to go to Raleigh and find her. Bring her back to him."

My throat tightened—for more than one reason. I gave Mom a shaky smile.

"We'll do that, Hannah, won't we? He wants us to."

"Okay, Mom."

She held onto me, her body small and vulnerable. I hugged her back, resting my chin on the top of her purple hat. The breeze blew harder, and Mom shivered more. I rubbed her arms. "You're cold. Want to get back in the car?"

"No. Morton might need me." She stuck her hands in her pockets.

She would be upset all evening. Perhaps pace the house, restless. In the morning she may have forgotten these events. Or not. If the latter, she'd latch on to every detail she could remember. Again and again she'd insist on going to Raleigh—all the way across the country—to find Morton's daughter. No amount of talking would persuade her that the daughter's existence had sprung from her own mind. That the woman may well not even exist.

Dorothy, Mom's caretaker, would have to deal with it while I was at work. I'd face it when I got home.

I hugged Mom harder, wanting to cry for her. For me. For the man we could do so little to help. How horrible this was, to see someone struggle to survive. How fragile, our lives.

"Be careful."

Another siren approached. Soon an ambulance pulled up, a man and woman jumping out. Now four voices mingled over their patient, exchanging information. Equipment clinked. What was it like to be Morton, flat on his back on the ground, looking up at unknown faces, his life in their hands?

Another vehicle engine sounded behind me. I turned to see a Channel 7 news van pull off the road.

"Oh, no." I gaped at the van. "How'd they get here so fast?" They must have been in the area already.

The sheriff's deputy gazed at a man jumping out of the van, camera up and ready. A woman followed. Looked like a reporter. The deputy mumbled something under his breath and strode past us in their direction. He threw words at me as he walked by: "Can you stick around until they're done here?"

"Yes." I knew he'd want my contact information. But I did *not* want to end up on the evening news.

The deputy hurried on. "You can only film from where you are," he called to the reporter and cameraman. "I'll need you to stay back."

I glanced at Mom. She hadn't even turned around, her gaze fixed on Morton. The first responders had moved aside, the paramedics fitting a collar around his neck.

"What are they doing?" Mom sounded protective, as if she couldn't trust them to help her new friend.

"They can't move him around very much in case he's got a spinal cord injury. The collar is to protect his neck."

"He's going to live, isn't he?"

My throat tightened. Morton could be someone's husband, father, grandfather. "I sure hope so."

One of the paramedics ran to the ambulance and readied a gurney. Next he carried over a backboard and laid it on the ground. With care they moved Morton onto it. They and the firemen lifted Morton up and began carrying him toward the gurney.

I flicked a look over my shoulder. The Channel 7 camera was filming.

"I want to say good-bye." Mom pulled away from me before I could stop her. She trundled after the paramedics. "Wait! I want to see him."

They didn't stop. I went after her.

"Wait! Please!"

From the corner of my eye, I saw the camera swing toward Mom.

The medics reached the gurney and laid Morton, still on the backboard, upon it. A young-looking man turned to my mother. "Ma'am, we need to go."

She brushed past him, determined.

"Ma'am—"

Must have been something in Mom's eyes. The female paramedic gazed at my mother, then shook her head at her colleague. "One second."

Mom reached Morton's side and bent over him. I could see his face. His eyes were still closed. Was he even conscious?

"I remember," she whispered. "We won't forget." She patted his head.

I looked to one of the men from the fire truck. "Where are they taking him?"

"Coastside in Moss Beach. It's the closest hospital."

"Is he going to make it?"

He bunched his lips. "Don't know. I don't like how his breathing sounds."

"Okay, let's go." The female paramedic nudged Mom away. I slipped to my mother's side and eased her back from the gurney. The paramedics placed Morton into the ambulance and shut the doors.

Mom clutched her hands to her chest, watching. Trembling.

The camera turned from us to the ambulance.

One of the men from the fire truck nodded to me. "Thanks for your help."

"Sure."

Another breeze kicked up as the ambulance pulled onto the highway and turned back toward the coast. The heady scent of grass and dirt swept over me. I glanced back toward Morton's small car, still on its side. How crushed it looked. The harbinger of death.

A sudden sense of doom sank talons into me. I wanted to be away from this scene of disaster and the rolling news camera. Safe and quiet in my home with my mother.

"Let's move back a little from the road, Mom." I took her elbow.

"Wait. I have to watch him as long as I can."

We gazed at the back of the ambulance until it disappeared around a curve.

"Okay." I nudged her arm.

She looked at me, her eyes still shiny with tears. "Can we go home now?" Her lips turned down, forlorn.

"Yes. Soon as we talk to the deputy."

"What for?"

"He'll probably want to get our names and phone number, since we were the first witnesses."

The firemen headed for their truck. The reporter and her cameraman made a beeline for us, microphone in her hand. "Ma'am, did you see the accident?"

I cringed and shook my head.

"Wait now." The deputy hustled toward them, his hands up. "I need to talk to these folks first."

"But if we could just ask—"

"You'll have to *wait*."

Mom looked on with round eyes. "Are we gonna be on television?"

I shuddered at the thought of such attention. "Not if I can help it."

The deputy had a few more words with the reporter, then headed our way. The camera followed him. I turned my back to it, shuffling Mom around with me.

"Remember," Mom whispered. "Don't tell."

"Well, I imagine it's okay to tell law enforcement."

"No, it isn't!" Her voice rose with immediate indignation. She grasped my hands. "We promised. We promised Morton!"

"I know, but—"

"Don't you *dare* say anything!" Her expression hardened, a precursor to her episodes. My heart stilled. One of my mother's screaming meltdowns and a rolling TV camera would be a terrible mix.

"Tell me you won't, Hannah. *Tell* me you *won't*!" She shook a boney finger at me.

"Okay, Mom, okay." I grabbed her finger and lowered it. Anything to keep this from escalating.

Since she'd come to live with me, that was how I'd learned to live my life.

The deputy came around to stand in front of us. He had broad shoulders, a big neck. Mom shot me a hard look, but said no more. The deputy eyed her. How much had he heard?

He held his beefy hand out to me. "Good afternoon. I'm Deputy Harcroft from the Sheriff's Department Coastside Patrol. I understand you were first on the scene. You called 911?"

"Yes." Mom spoke before I could. "My daughter ran to help. His name is Morton. Like the salt."

Deputy Harcroft's gaze lingered on Mom's face, as if assessing her. Then he turned back to me. "Where were you headed when you saw the accident?"

"San Carlos. Where we live."

"San Carlos? Where were you coming from?"

"The Ritz Carlton."

"Why didn't you take Highway 92?"

What was this? "I decided to take a more rural drive."

"It was lovely," Mom said. "Until we saw poor Morton."

Harcroft gazed at her again.

He pulled a small notebook and pen from his shirt pocket. "I need to take your information, if you don't mind. Your names, what you saw. Won't take long."

Tiredness surged through me, and the chilled air scraped my skin. Where had the warmth of the day gone? "Sure. I do hope it's quick. I'd like to get my mother home as soon as possible."

"No problem."

Mom shook her head at me. "I'm fine, Hannah."

"Do you want to wait in the car, Mom? I can start the engine and turn up the heat."

"Nothing doing." She gave me a look that said she had to stay here and keep an eye on me.

The deputy asked our names, address, and phone numbers for home and my work. Then took down the license plate of my car. He wanted to know what we had witnessed. Did we see the crash? Any idea how it happened? I told him what we knew, which wasn't much. Mom remained quiet. But every now and then she pinched my arm as a reminder—*don't tell*.

The deputy frowned, his eyes shifting to Morton's overturned car. My gaze followed. Not until that moment did it strike me—how strange, this accident. The car was on the side of the road we'd been driving yet was pointed in the opposite direction. Had he been going toward Highway 1 instead of away from it? And why had he wrecked in the first place? I saw no skid marks, nothing that would make him swerve. He hadn't sounded drunk. Hadn't smelled drunk. What had happened here?

An uneasy feeling slow-rolled through my limbs.

"Don't tell anyone . . . Be careful."

The deputy refocused on me. "Anything Morton told you that we should know? Maybe the name of a family member we can contact?"

"No!" Mom spoke the word with vehemence. The deputy's eyebrows rose. He looked to me, as if for an explanation.

For a moment I hesitated. Shouldn't I tell the deputy everything, regardless of my mother's reaction? My sense of civilian duty said yes. The memory of Morton's eyes cried no. He'd trusted us, total strangers. He'd *warned* us. What could drive a man to such desperation?

I tried to smile at the deputy. "My mother's pretty upset about the whole thing." I gave him a meaningful look, patting Mom's arm.

He gazed at her again. "I understand. But I need to make sure you've told me everything." The deputy locked eyes with me.

He *had* heard something.

"We told you *everything*." Mom glared at him.

For a drawn-out second the deputy and I faced off. My neck tingled. I didn't like the feel of any of this. Including the news camera aimed at my back.

I swallowed. "She's right. We have."

Harcroft's eyes lingered on me. Then he looked at his notes. "Okay. I have what I need for now. Appreciate your cooperation. If anything comes up I'll contact you."

Relief snagged my breath. "All right. Thank you."

"What happens to Morton now?" Mom asked. The wind tugged at her hat. She clamped a hand on top of it.

The deputy offered her a tiny smile. "Maybe if you call Coastside Hospital tonight they'll be able to tell you something."

Would the hospital do that, since we weren't family? But the deputy seemed to be trying to reassure Mom, and for that I was grateful. My unease loosened a little.

I lowered my voice. "Is that reporter still behind us?"

His gaze flicked beyond my shoulder. "Yeah."

"We don't want to be on camera. We just want to get out of here."

"That's fine, you don't have to talk to her. You're free to go."

"Thanks." I took Mom's arm.

She was still shivering but didn't complain. We headed toward my car—and heard sudden huffing behind us. "Ma'am!"

I turned to see the reporter awkward-jogging in her high heels, cameraman at her side. My hand flew up, my words fast and tinged with panic. "I don't want to talk."

The reporter closed the distance between us. Mom's eyes bounced from me to the reporter, uncertainty in her face. "Come on, Mom." I nudged her on.

"Look." The reporter caught up to my side. "Here's my card. Amanda Crossland. If you have something later you can call me."

I waved the card away. "No, thanks."

Amanda fell back, and I urged Mom to the car. She allowed me to open her door and help her inside. I fastened her seat belt.

As I started the engine I glanced out my window. The deputy was watching me. I gave him a quick wave. He nodded back.

I pulled out onto Tunitas Creek Road and headed back toward Highway 1. No more adventuresome drives toward Skyline for me. I just wanted to get *home*. The trip would take less than thirty minutes.

As we drove off I could feel the deputy's gaze watching my car. Did he wonder why I wasn't continuing on the rural road?

Mom was silent. I couldn't stop reliving the scene. Morton's desperate eyes. His words and gripping hands. The deputy's steady gaze. Why had I lied to him? So what if Mom would have gotten upset. I'd *lied* to law enforcement.

How was Morton right now? Were the paramedics stabilizing him?

Oh, Lord, please help him make it. I'd call the hospital tonight. Beg someone to tell me how he was doing.

Mom sighed. "'The Lord is near the brokenhearted. He saves those crushed in spirit.'"

I glanced at her. Despite the memory loss, Mom could still quote many Bible verses. And she clung to them, even if most of the time she could no longer tell you what book they were from. "Are you brokenhearted?"

"I'm sad. For Morton."

"Yes. I'm sad too."

We turned off Highway 1 onto 92, leaving Half Moon Bay. Passing nurseries and winding into the hills separating the coast from the Bay Area. Soon eucalyptus trees lined the road, their peeled bark an eerie blend of gray and white. Mom drew in a deep breath through her nose. "Smell that? Vicks VapoRub."

She'd said the same thing when we passed the trees two days ago. "Yup."

"I used to rub it on your chest when you had a cold. When you were a little girl."

"I remember."

Mom sighed. "A daughter's a very important thing."

My thoughts flicked to Emily. "You're right about that."

Mom made a satisfied noise in her throat. "That's why we have to find Morton's daughter for him."

Oh, boy. One more reason I should have come clean with the deputy. At least I'd have been able to assure Mom they would handle finding Morton's daughter.

"We'll start tomorrow." Mom's head bobbed up and down.

"I have to work tomorrow."

She waved dismissive fingers in the air. "Tell the doctor you're busy."

"Don't tell." Morton's plea drummed in my head. *"Be careful."*

If I'd had any idea what those words would mean to me, to my mother and daughter, I'd have fled California without looking back.

Chapter 2

SPECIAL HOUSE SELECT COMMITTEE
INVESTIGATION INTO FREENOW TERRORIST
ACTIVITY OF FEBRUARY 25, 2013

SEPTEMBER 16, 2013

TRANSCRIPT

Representative ELKIN MORSE (Chairman, Homeland Security Committee): Seven months ago, tragic and terrifying events pushed this country to the brink of destruction. Since that fateful day of February 25, 2013, every American citizen has had to fight his way back to recovery. Haunting questions remain. Will it happen again? How do we regain our sense of safety? Or should we try to regain it at all? It is a hard balance—between vigilance against evil, and trusting in our own resources and the God who has sustained us.

Now, after all the media stories and preliminary investigations, this committee embarks on a difficult journey—that of trying to separate fact from fiction. As we begin, I feel both anticipation and great sadness. Anticipation for what we can learn and better implement into our national security policies (a task that looms crucial). Yet sadness about the events that occurred, so many of them unnecessary and avoidable. Private citizens were put at risk. Lives were lost. Innocence was stolen.

I pray our investigation yields the truth. But that can only be accomplished if every witness who testifies will speak nothing but the truth.

We begin with the testimony of Sergeant Charles Wade . . .

Chapter 3

By the time we reached our two-bedroom house at 738 Powell Street in San Carlos, it was after 2:00. I pulled our small suitcase from the trunk of my car and followed Mom through the garage side door into our laundry area.

"Ah, home." She walked into the kitchen and spread her hands.

"Glad to be back?" Mom had lived with me for two months, and she'd raised a real ruckus about moving out of her house in San Mateo. She'd insisted she could remain on her own. But she would never be on her own again.

"Yes, it's nice." Her hat sat askew on her head, and she straightened it. "But the hotel was wonderful too. Thank you for taking me."

"You're welcome."

"Will we go again?"

"Sure, sometime." But not very soon. Even though it was off-season at the Ritz Carlton, which sat right on the ocean, I'd had to save for the weekend over a number of months. It had been worth it, though, to see Mom's face as she watched the waves.

I helped Mom out of her coat, took mine off, and hung them both in the closet. As I wheeled our suitcase to my bedroom to unpack, the phone rang. Mom picked it up. "Oh, hello, Emily!" She paused. "Yes, we had a wonderful time. Except on the way home we saw a man in an accident, and your mom tried to help. And then the fire truck came, *and* the paramedics, *and* the sheriff, *and* news people. They took the man to the hospital. Morton's his name. He was so nice but very, very upset. We have to find his daughter for him."

Silence. I flung the suitcase on my bed and headed back toward the kitchen, imagining Emily's nonplussed response.

"She's in Raleigh. North Carolina." Mom's hat sat on the counter. She was rubbing her temple. "We don't know her name."

"Can I talk to her, Mom?" I held my hand out for the phone.

Mom pursed her lips. "Here's your mother. Now don't upset her, she's had a difficult afternoon."

I took the phone. "Hi, Em." Mom picked up her hat and wandered into her bedroom.

"*What* is Grand talking about?" Concern edged my daughter's voice.

"Believe it or not, most of it's true." I told Emily the whole story.

"Wow." Emily fell silent, as if taking it all in. She wasn't speechless very often. "And you didn't tell the sheriff's deputy what the man said?"

"No."

"Why?"

"Because . . . I don't know. Your grandmother, mostly."

"Mom, don't you think they need to know?"

"Yes. No. I don't know. It's just . . ." How to explain? As much as Emily loved her grandmother, she didn't live with the woman. In fact, she lived five hours away in Santa Barbara. She couldn't know what it was like to try to keep peace at all costs—because it could so easily be broken. Besides, Morton had been so insistent. So desperate. The look on his face still rent my heart.

"Thing is, Em, he didn't give us enough information to mean anything. By now they know more about him than we do. They have his driver's license and address. They'll be calling his family members. Maybe he'll be able to speak to his family. They can help him deal with Raleigh."

Even as the words left my mouth, something inside me twisted. Morton had asked *me* to do this. I'd said I would.

Well, that was ridiculous. I'd done what I could to help him. Now he was in the hands of the doctors.

"Yeah, I guess," Emily said. "So you gonna watch the news tonight? See what you can find out?"

"Yes. And hopefully not see myself on TV."

"That wouldn't kill you, Mom."

I shivered. "It might."

The proverbial fifteen minutes of fame—that was for other people. I just wanted to live my life quietly. Go to work, and keep close to my mother and daughter. I'd lost my husband, Jeff, to brain cancer two years before. As soon as he died, Mom had started going downhill. Now I needed to take care of *her*.

There lay the irony. My life had been anything but quiet in the past few years.

In Mom's bedroom, music kicked on.

"Uh-oh." Emily laughed. "I hear Lady Gaga."

Mom's favorite. I sighed. "For the millionth time." I crossed the kitchen and into the hallway to close Mom's door. She was already swaying to the beat, one arm across her chest and the other held up and waving in the air. Her eyes were closed. She'd danced like that at Mallory's in San Mateo every Friday and Saturday night for three years—a white-haired old woman in the middle of twenty- and thirty-year-olds. The regulars at the club got to know her so well, when she was sick and missed a night they'd call to check up on her. Then Mom started getting lost while driving. Her license had to be taken away, and she came to live with me.

Every once in awhile I took her to the club and let her stay awhile and dance. She was thrilled to go. I'd emerge with a terrible headache. But it was wonderful to see how happy everyone was to see her.

I retreated back into the kitchen. "How are *you?*" My beautiful golden-haired, blue-eyed daughter had dated a man for two years and thought they were on the way to marriage. Just two months ago she learned he was cheating on her and broke things off.

"Okay. Just taking it a day at a time, you know?"

"Yeah. I know." I had to do the same thing when I lost Jeff. "And how's your job?" Emily worked in a marketing firm. Most of her projects involved creating, editing, and posting advertising videos online.

"Fine. Still working on that big project. If I can dazzle our clients, it'll earn me some great commission money."

"Of course you'll dazzle them. You're a wizard with that stuff." Not to mention Emily was aggressive. My daughter went after what she wanted.

"You're biased."

"You're right."

The music pounded. I rubbed my temple. *How* did my mother stand that noise?

"Tell me what you find out, okay?" Emily said. "About that man."

"Okay."

We hung up. I returned to my bedroom to unpack, my entire body begging for quiet. Not a chance.

At least the music and dancing keep my mother occupied.

I slid the empty suitcase into my closet—and remembered my cell phone. I'd left it in my coat pocket. At the front closet I patted the pocket of my coat, then realized it was the wrong side. I reached for the other pocket.

Wait.

Had I felt something in the bottom of that left pocket?

I frowned. Reached inside. My fingers brushed something small and hard. I drew it out.

A flash drive.

I stared at it. Turned it over. Where had it come from? I didn't own a flash drive like this.

Was it Emily's? Maybe last time she came home she wore this coat. Had she meant to show me some video she'd designed, then forgotten about it?

Emily wouldn't be caught dead in this coat.

I stared at the small black and silver thing lying in my palm. Had it been in my pocket all weekend?

A picture rose in my mind—Mom and me walking on the beach, heads down against the wind, our hands in our pockets. The flash drive hadn't been there.

I walked to Mom's room and opened the door. Lady Gaga's "I'm on the Edge of Glory" assaulted my ears.

"Mom."

She kept swaying, her eyes closed. I stepped to her CD player and turned down the volume. Mom's eyes snapped open.

I held out the flash drive. "This was in my coat pocket. Do you know anything about it?"

My voice remained light, even as I braced myself. Mom was known to pick up items and put them down . . . somewhere else. Anywhere. Half the time she didn't even remember—and would be very indignant if I pressed her on the subject. She did not relish being treated "like a child."

She peered down at the drive. "What is it?"

"It's a little thing you plug into a computer. It holds data."

"What would I want with that?"

"I don't know. I just wondered, since it appeared in my pocket."

Mom drew back her head, her lips pressed. "Well, *I* didn't put it there."

"You have any idea who would?"

She thought a moment. Her face lit at an idea. "Morton."

"Morton?"

"When I came up to you both, he was fumbling with your pocket. I saw him."

My mouth opened. I gazed at Mom, reliving that moment on the side of Tunitas Road. "You're right. He *was* doing something with my pocket." Amazing that she'd remembered that detail.

We both looked at the flash drive.

"Can it hold pictures?" Mom reached out to touch it.

"Yes."

Her eyes rounded. "Maybe they're of his daughter. The one we're supposed to find for him."

I nodded. "Maybe so."

"Let's go see! Turn on your computer."

She turned toward the door, excited. I grasped her arm. "Mom, that'll take awhile. Why don't you keep dancing? I'll let you know what I find."

Mom peered at me. A song ended on the CD, and another started. "Okay."

Before leaving her room I turned up the volume on Lady Gaga—just enough that I hoped would satisfy Mom. As I closed her door, the music got even louder.

Standing in the hall, I stared at the flash drive. *Had* Morton given me this?

"Don't tell. Be careful."

The vague unease came over me again. Part of me—a big

part—didn't want to know what this was. But what if it was important? Morton had been so insistent . . .

Maybe it *was* Emily's. Somehow I'd just missed it in my coat.

I returned to the front closet and retrieved my cell phone from my coat's right pocket. I turned it off and placed it in my purse, which was sitting in the kitchen.

I lingered at the counter, looking at the flash drive in my hand. Should I see what was on it?

What if this thing contained contaminated files? Once I plugged it into my laptop, the virus could spread into my computer. Never a good idea to connect your computer to something you weren't sure about.

"Please. It's important."

A sigh escaped me. Almost as if pushed, I found myself entering my bedroom and sitting down at the small corner desk. As my slow, over-the-hill laptop booted up I relieved the scene with Morton. The terror and despair on his face. That sense of extreme urgency, as if I were his last hope.

For what?

Before plugging in the flash drive I performed a manual backup of my files onto my external drive. It would been done automatically when I was last on the computer, but I didn't want to take chances. And if that external drive were to go down, I had a second, online backup. Anytime my computer sat idle for thirty minutes, the online backup kicked in automatically.

I picked up the flash drive and stared at it some more. As if it would speak to me, tell me its secrets. Then I plugged it in. When the "found new hardware" prompt appeared, I clicked to view the files it contained. One appeared: "video."

Something squirmed in my stomach.

How to explain my feeling at that moment? It was as if an oppressive fog had crept into my room. Dark and swirling and filled with portent. I looked over my shoulder. Nothing, of course. Everything remained the same. My queen bed with its large blue pillows—the bed I now slept in by myself since Jeff died. The old wallpaper we'd been meaning to replace for years. My long dresser against the far wall. Jeff's near the corner—now filled with my clothes. The pound-pound of Mom's music still filtered from her bedroom.

And yet . . . something.

Would I see some horrible picture on this video that I would forever try to rid from my mind?

Really, Hannah. Some imagination.

I opened the file.

Chapter 4

I leaned forward in my desk chair, eyes focused on the monitor, waiting for the flash drive to load. A rattley car passed by on the street, and somewhere a dog barked. These sounds I half registered above Mom's music.

On my screen a rectangular box appeared. In it . . . what? Looked like a huge piece of machinery. Garish green and silver, with various pipes and hoses, and two identical beige panels.

The usual start arrow sat in the middle of this picture. I took a breath—and clicked it. The video began in silence, as if it were being filmed with audio off. The machine just sat there. Then it shook. Small black pieces began to fall off it. I couldn't tell what they were. The machine rocked a second time—and more pieces fell. At the third shaking, white, black, then gray steam began pouring out. In a few seconds steam obliterated the machine.

What *was* this?

The scene changed to a somewhat blurred picture. I saw the side of a building, and next to it, toward the top of the video, giant steel legs of a massive tower. Other steel girders with round parts filled the picture. What were they? The video wasn't clear enough to tell. In the back of my mind the array of steel felt familiar. A large black tank sat on the ground, with a fat pipe bending from one end toward the sky.

In the next second, black smoke spewed from that pipe. White smoke billowed up from some other area, but I couldn't see where. Equipment in the foreground blocked my view. The black smoke stopped, but the white kept spewing until the building and half the legs of the tower disappeared.

The video ended, the last frame freezing on my screen. It had taken one minute, five seconds.

Frowning, I eased back in my chair. What did any of this mean?

I watched it again, trying to separate the details.

How was the first piece of equipment related to the second scene? That first machinery had looked like it was breaking apart, causing steam to rush out. Was that machinery connected to the black tank I later saw? But the green and silver equipment was nowhere in that second scene. So if they were connected—how?

Why would Morton give this to me?

I folded my arms. Maybe he hadn't. Mom could have invented the whole scenario based on seeing the man's hand pull at my coat. Just as she'd extrapolated on his words to invent his long-lost "daughter."

But then—where would the flash drive have come from? And I *had* felt Morton's hand fingering my left pocket.

I enlarged the video to full screen and watched it a third time. And a fourth. Each time the array of steel in the second scene seemed familiar. But I couldn't put my finger on it, and the picture remained too blurry.

In Mom's room Lady Gaga played on. I hoped Mom had forgotten about the flash drive and its "pictures of Morton's daughter."

One more time I watched the video, memorizing its sequences. Still I had no idea what it was.

"Don't tell anyone."

More strangeness trickled through me. I needed to ask Morton about this. Maybe we could visit him in the hospital in a few hours. He would be stabilized by then.

I glanced around at the digital clock on my nightstand. Almost 3:00.

Mom's music stopped.

I sighed relief into the blessed silence. She'd be tired from all the dancing. Time for her nap.

Giving up on the video, I unplugged the flash drive from my computer. I'd return it to Morton. Or at least find out to whom I should mail it. As long as it remained in my possession, his pleas would haunt me. I didn't want to do whatever he so needed. Didn't I have enough to handle in my life? I wanted to be rid of this . . . whatever it was. All of it.

I set the flash drive on my desk.

In the kitchen I pulled my phone book from a drawer. Would the yellow pages have a listing for the Moss Beach hospital, where they'd taken Morton? That area was far outside the white pages coverage. I stared at my tile counter, trying to remember the hospital's name.

Coastside.

I flipped to the yellow pages and checked. No listing.

Showed my age—using the yellow pages at all. Emily would have looked it up online.

Back at my computer I Google-searched the hospital until I found the phone number. I picked up my bedroom receiver and punched in the numbers. When the receptionist answered I asked for the emergency room. The line clicked.

"Coastside E.R." The female voice sounded very efficient.

"Hi. My name is Hannah Shire. I'd like to check on a man that came into your department less than two hours ago. His first name is Morton."

"Last name?"

"I don't know. I . . . we were the first ones to see him at the car accident. I called 911. Just wanted to see if he's okay."

"You said Morton?"

"Yes."

A long pause. "Ah."

What did that mean?

"Hold a minute, please."

I waited, pacing my small bedroom, right hand cupping my left elbow. In my mind I felt the wind on Tunitas Creek Road and smelled the open field. Remembered the surprising strength of Morton's fingers as they sank into my arm. *"Please. Important."*

"Ma'am?"

I jumped. "Yes?"

"What did you say your name was?"

"Hannah Shire."

"Are you a relative of the patient?"

"No."

Another pause. In the background I could hear a doctor's name being called.

"I'm sorry I can't give you any information."

"Why? Do you know how he's doing?"

"I can't give you any information."

"I'd just like—"

"Sorry. I suggest you call the sheriff's department if you'd like to learn more."

Sheriff's department?

I ended the call and stared at the receiver. This could be normal policy for the hospital. All the same, it unnerved me.

The front door bell rang. I jumped again—a sign of nerves on edge. Who could that be? Neighbors and friends didn't tend to just show up at my door.

I shoved the phone into its holder and hurried toward the entryway, hoping the sound hadn't awakened Mom. At the living room window I leaned to one side, trying to glimpse who stood on the porch. I caught the partial side of a man in a dark suit.

Great. Religious solicitors.

"Mrs. Shire?"

The muffled voice came through the door, followed by a harder knock. I jerked back from the window.

"Mrs. Shire?"

I edged toward the door and leaned in. "Who is it?"

"We're with the FBI, ma'am." The accent was a Southern drawl. "We need to ask you a few questions."

FBI? "What about?"

"The accident you saw today."

The answer hit me in the gut. I drew back, nerves shimmying. What was this? That deputy knew I'd lied to him, and now the FBI was at my door? What had I *done*?

What had Morton done?

Rationality pulsed through me, pushing back the paranoia. "Just a minute."

I unlocked the door and opened it a couple inches. Not one, but two men, stood on my porch. They both reached inside their coat pockets and drew out folded black holders. Inside each was a gold-colored FBI badge and a picture of the man with his signature.

I pulled back the door. "Please come in."

With tight smiles, the two men stepped inside. They were of equal height, about six feet. The one with the accent was quite young—early twenties, maybe? He had a lanky build, a buzz cut, and a stern, hard jaw. The other was a good ten years older, with a shaved head. The latter's chest and arms were huge. I focused on him, taking in his steel-gray eyes. "What can I do for you?"

I couldn't help but glance toward the hallway. Mom could be quite rattled if she saw two strange men in our living room. On the other hand, she might be delighted and offer to play one of her CDs for them.

The younger one spoke up. "I'm Special Agent Rutger, and this is Samuelson. We're sorry to barge in on you like this. We just need to ask you a few questions regarding the auto accident you witnessed today."

"I didn't see the accident. We came upon the scene after it happened."

"We . . . ?"

"My mother and I."

"Is she here?"

"She's napping." I spoke abruptly, as if protecting a child. I could feel the eyes of both men boring into me. "She struggles with dementia. She wouldn't be able to help you anyway."

"I see."

Rutger glanced around. "Mind if we sit down?"

I extended my arm toward the couch. The men took opposite sides of the sofa, sitting forward, legs spread. Samuelson withdrew a small notebook and pen from his inside coat pocket. I sat facing them in Mom's old cane rocker, furniture that had been handed down from her mother. Mom had left her favorite red-and-blue crocheted blanket hanging over one arm of the chair. I rubbed it absently. "Can you tell me how the man is doing? I only know his first name: Morton."

Rutger looked down and nodded. "I understand you called 911."

"Yes. How is he?"

Rutger's lips pressed. "I'm sorry to say he didn't make it."

My eyes widened. "He's . . . *dead?*"

The agent nodded.

The news hit me in the chest. I leaned back in the chair, gazing around the room. As bad as Morton had looked, it was still hard to believe he was dead. Poor man. And I'd had high hopes that he would make it. Could I have done something more? My thoughts turned to the words he'd spoken. Now he could never explain them to me. Did he have the chance to tell someone at the hospital?

I'd never be able to ask him about the flash drive.

"How did he die?"

"Why would you ask that? You saw he was in an accident." Samuelson spoke in a light enough tone, but something lay beneath. I frowned at him.

"I knew Morton was in pain, and I think unconscious when they put him in the ambulance. But I just thought . . . When he said his chest hurt, I feared internal injuries. Is that what happened?"

"You could say that."

Both men regarded me, unblinking. Why weren't they answering directly? As if they toyed with me. Something in the air shifted. My muscles tightened, and for a split-second my breath held. These men no longer seemed harmless. They were too caught up in the power of their badges, the federal government behind them. What did they want?

My mind flitted to Mom, sleeping in her bedroom. So vulnerable. So needy.

I sat up straighter, allowing my expression to harden. I stared back at Samuelson. "Why are you here? What do you want from me?"

A beat passed. The three of us faced off.

"His name was Morton Leringer." Rutger spoke up, his accent drawing out the name. "You know who that is?"

"No."

"He's a billionaire financier from this area."

Driving such a nondescript car? "What was he doing on that little road?"

"He owns an estate—one of many across the country—up on Skyline. Overlooks the ocean."

He'd been so close to home. The thought saddened me more.

"So what do you want from me?" The two men still stared, and I glared right back. They were leading up to something, I could feel it. And I didn't care for their games.

Samuelson's head moved, just the slightest. "Mrs. Shire, Morton Leringer did not die as a result of wounds sustained in an accident."

"No?" I frowned at him.

"Not at all." Samuelson laser-focused on my face. "The man was murdered."

Chapter 5

Murdered? Air left my lungs. "What? How can that be?"

Samuelson's stare was unyielding. "Leringer was stabbed in the back."

"When? You mean at the hospital?"

"No."

I waited for more, but they sat like stone. "*What* then?"

"He was stabbed before the ambulance arrived, Mrs. Shire." Samuelson's tone was flat.

I blinked. "You mean, when I was with him, he'd been stabbed?"

Samuelson nodded.

Coldness trickled through my veins. All that time I'd been with Morton, he had a *knife wound* in his back? "I . . . can't believe it. Why didn't he tell me?"

"We thought he may have."

"No. He never said . . . I just can't believe this. When was he stabbed? Who could have done it?"

"It was a single wound. It hit his pericardium—the sac around the heart."

My head lowered. After all my years of working in a cardiologist's office, I knew what that meant. Morton's pericardium would have filled with blood while causing little external bleeding. No wonder he'd had such trouble breathing. He'd have gone into shock. Meanwhile the paramedics, fearing spinal injury, couldn't move him enough to find the wound.

I focused on my lap, trying to choose between a dozen questions to ask next. "Did he make it to the hospital?"

"He died in the E.R."

This was beyond sad. "The doctor must have discovered the stab wound."

"Yes. But it was too late."

In Raleigh . . . Find. Morton had known he was dying. Struggling to breathe, in terrible pain, he'd chosen those final words, rather than tell me he'd been stabbed. Or who had done it.

How could that message be more important than his own life?

I raised my head. "I didn't know. He didn't tell me or give any indication."

"Did you see anyone in the area?"

My mind fled back to the scene. The car overturned, driver's window open. I'd assumed Morton had crawled out of it. Had someone dragged him out, then killed him? "No. Just him. And his car on its side."

Samuelson jotted in his notebook.

"How long had he been lying there before I came?" The E.R. doctor might have some idea of the time it would take for that kind of wound to lead to death. "Long enough for someone to drive away?" It chilled me to the bone to think a killer had been in the area while Mom and I were there.

Samuelson shook his head. "It appears the stabbing occurred shortly before the ambulance came."

In that instant their taciturn expressions made sense. My fingers curled around the rocking chair's arm. For a moment the words wouldn't form on my tongue. "Are you saying you think *I* did this?"

"Did you?" Samuelson's tone signaled his suspicion.

"No! Are you—" I leaned forward, hands spread. "You have got to be kidding me. I work in a doctor's office. I help save people."

"Then what were you doing there?"

"I saw an accident! I stopped to help."

"Did you know Morton Leringer?"

"No. I still don't know anything about him." My voice rose. "Besides, I had my mother with me. In her state I have to be careful not to upset her. There is *no way* I'm responsible for this."

My vehemence ran out. I flopped back in the rocking chair.

The men's expressions did not change. Then Rutger gave a slow nod. "We may be inclined to believe you. *If* you tell us everything that transpired between you and Leringer."

"What have we here, company?" My mother's voice, laced with childlike excitement, came from behind me. "How nice." She came into the living room, hand extended. One side of her hair stuck out, a crease in her cheek from her pillow.

I jumped to my feet. "Mom, maybe you should—"

"I'm Carol Ballard." She smiled at Samuelson.

He shook her hand but didn't rise from the couch. "Samuelson."

Mom shook Rutger's hand next. He didn't bother to rise either. Such rudeness.

"Goodness, you have nothing to drink." Mom turned to me. "Have you offered them something?"

"It's okay." Samuelson raised a hand. "We're fine."

"Mom, you want to go back to your room?" I reached for her arm. "We'll be done here soon."

"No, I want to stay." She looked around for a place to sit, then lowered herself onto an ottoman near the small fireplace. Mom looked at the three of us expectantly. "What are we talking about?"

I hesitated, wishing I could persuade her to leave, knowing she wouldn't budge. "You want to sit in your chair, Mom?"

"No, no, this is perfect." She patted the ottoman.

With reluctance, I sat back down in the rocking chair.

Samuelson eyed Mom as if sizing her up. Or should I say— down? His lip curled. I shot him a disdainful look. How dare they treat my mother like this! FBI or not, I wanted them out of my house—*now.*

Rutger caught my glare. He raised his chin, eyes narrowing. "As we were saying, Mrs. Shire—"

"I remember very well what you were saying." I pushed to my feet again. "I want you to leave."

Mom gasped. "Carol, how impolite you're being." She turned to the men. "I apologize for my daughter. She's had a hard afternoon. We were driving and saw a—"

"They know, Mom. That's why they're here."

"Oh, really?" Anticipation flitted across Mom's face. "How *is* Morton, Mr. Samuelson? Can we go see him?"

I shook my head at Samuelson—*don't tell her.* He ignored me, focusing on my mother. "Mr. Leringer died in the hospital."

Mom's expression froze. "He . . . *died*?" She turned to me, her eyes filling with pain. "He's dead?"

I wanted to strangle the FBI agent. What was *wrong* with him? "I'm sorry, Mom."

Her hands laced together tightly. "Oh. Then we can't . . ." She caught herself, and her face shuttered.

Rutger honed in on her. "Can't what?"

"Nothing." Mom placed both hands on the ottoman, struggling to rise. Her sudden blank look and open mouth signaled how upset she felt.

I helped her up. "You want to go to your room now, and we'll talk about this later?"

"We need to question her first," Samuelson said.

I swiveled toward him. "You're not questioning her at all."

Mom waved a weak hand in the air. "Yes, Hannah, I'll go . . . lie down."

Rutger shook his head. "She needs to stay."

"No, she doesn't." I didn't even try to keep the anger from my voice. "I'm going to take her to her room, then I'll bring you what you clearly came for." Anything to get rid of these two ogres.

Mom allowed me to lead her out of the living room. "What do they want, Hannah?" Her voice sounded plaintive, wavery.

"I don't know. Let me find out while you rest." In her room I pointed to her bed. "You want to lie down?"

"I'll sit in my chair." She made her way to her stuffed armchair in the corner. "It's where I . . . deal with things, you know."

"I know."

"'Those who mourn are blessed, for they shall be comforted.'"

Leaving her room, I shut the door behind me. Anger still fueled me. I hurried to my own bedroom to get the flash drive, then stilled as I saw it sitting on my desk. For a long second I stared at it. Why had I been so quick to tell those men I had something for them? Their attitudes, most of all toward my mother, didn't warrant me giving them anything.

But—too late.

Would Morton have wanted these men to have the video?

"Don't tell . . ."

On impulse I yanked open my desk drawer and snatched up one of my own, empty flash drives. I inserted it and the original drive into two ports in my computer, and copied the video file over. Then I carried the copied version out to the agents. "Here." I thrust the drive toward Samuelson, my voice still edged. "I found it in my coat pocket when I got home. Morton must have put it there when I was trying to help him."

Samuelson took it from me. "What's on it?"

"I have no idea."

"You didn't look at it?"

"No. I've been too busy trying to keep my mother calm since we got home."

God, forgive me for the lie.

Both men eyed me.

"You have what you want. Now leave."

Samuelson put the flash drive in his jacket pocket. "What did he say to you?"

"Very little. He could barely breathe."

"I think he said something."

I disliked these men more by the second. "Whatever would make you think that?"

"Why would your mother say to him, 'I remember. We won't forget.'"

I stared down at Samuelson. So they'd known about my mother before they ever came here. They'd acted like they didn't know she'd been with me at the scene. They'd even talked to the paramedics.

"My mother felt very sorry for Morton. He was trying so hard to speak. To breathe. When they put him in the ambulance, she wanted him to know she'd remember him."

"She said 'we.'"

I shrugged. "I was there too."

Rutger unbuttoned his jacket and leaned back against the sofa, stretching one arm across its back. Allowing me a clear view of the holstered gun around his waist.

My breath hitched. Rage and fear swirled through me. The rage won. Now these men were *threatening* me? What if he'd showed that gun in Mom's presence?

I knew my rights. I didn't have to talk to any law enforcement if I didn't want to. "Get out." I stepped back and pointed toward the door.

Rutger tapped a finger against his knee. "We think you know something else, Mrs. Shire."

"I don't know *anything*. And I told you to leave."

"If you—"

"I want a lawyer." My eyes locked with Rutger's. "I refuse to talk to you anymore."

"Why would you think you need a lawyer?"

"Because I no longer want to talk to *you*." I'd tell some other FBI agent what Morton had said. And give them the original flash drive. But I was through with these two. "Now *leave*."

The agents stared at me, faces like granite. I didn't budge.

Rutger let out a long breath. Then made a show of rebuttoning his jacket. His head tilted. "As you wish, Mrs. Shire." His Southern drawl now sickened me. "But if you've withheld anything from us, I can assure you we'll be back."

A lot of good it would do them. I would never open my door to these men again. What I *would* do is inform their superior of how they'd treated me.

The two men stood. I strode to the door and opened it wide. They stepped through it without a word. The minute they were out I shut the door and drove home the lock with a loud *click*. A sound I knew they heard.

Through the living room window I watched them head for their vehicle. Not until then did I realize how hard my heart was beating. I leaned against the wall, eyes closed.

Outside two car doors slammed. An engine started. The agents drove away.

Weak-kneed, I sat down hard on the couch, waiting for my pulse to slow. A minute, maybe two ticked by. Then with a deep breath, I listed in my mind what I had to do. Comfort Mom. Call the nearest FBI office and complain—loudly—about the two men. Offer the further "Raleigh" information to another agent who'd show some respect. Make dinner. In that order.

I rose to head toward Mom's room—and the phone rang. I veered into the kitchen and picked up the receiver, too distracted to check the ID. "Hello?"

"Mrs. Shire, this is Deputy Harcroft from the Sheriff's Department Coastside Patrol. We met this afternoon at the scene of the accident."

Great, the man I'd lied to. Now I'd have to fix it. Maybe in the midst of his accusing me of murder. "Yes, I remember. Two FBI agents just left here. They told me Morton died at the hospital. That he was stabbed. I don't know anything about that."

Silence pulsed over the line. "FBI agents?"

"They weren't nice at all, I can tell you that. I had to practically throw them out of my house."

"What were their names?"

"Samuelson and Rutger. They didn't give me first names."

"Did they show you badges?"

"And name tags with their pictures on them."

"What did they want?"

"They demanded to know what I'd seen at the accident. What Morton had told me, if anything."

Harcroft paused. "I need to check this out and call you right back. Will you be home?"

Good grief, what now? "Yes. Okay."

I hung up the phone—and heard Mom calling my name. She sounded distraught.

"Coming!" On the way to her room I pushed aside my own feelings. No need to upset Mom more. I nudged open her door and found her still sitting in her chair. "You all right?"

She nodded. "Just sad."

"I'm sad too."

"Now we can't visit Morton in the hospital."

"No, afraid not."

"Now we have to find his daughter all by ourselves."

Oh. I was hoping she'd forgotten. "We don't know he was talking about a daughter, Mom."

"Of course we do. He said so."

"He only said—"

"She lives in Raleigh. North Carolina."

I sighed. "Yeah. I know." Maybe by tomorrow morning she'd forget this.

She pushed up her lower lip. "I'm getting kinda hungry."

"I'll make dinner, okay?"

"Chicken sounds good. And some potatoes. A good potato always make me feel better."

I managed a smile. "I know."

The phone rang. The deputy? "Sorry, Mom, I need to answer that."

Back in the kitchen I snatched up the receiver. "Hello."

"It's Deputy Harcroft." He sounded grim. "Did you see what kind of car those men were driving?"

"Some kind of brown sedan."

"Any chance you noticed the license plate?"

"No. Not at all."

"And you said they showed you official badges."

The deputy's tone unsettled me. "Yes. Why, what's going on?"

"Mrs. Shire, we need to bring you in right away and talk to you about this. Mr. Morton was a very important man. I have no idea who those two men who came to your house are, but they're not FBI agents."

Chapter 6

I dropped the receiver into its cradle and sagged against the counter. *"Not FBI."*

Then who were they?

I should have known. The way they acted, forceful and menacing. Rutger—or whatever his real name was—wanting me to see his gun.

I'd given them a copy of the video. They seemed to see right through my lie that I'd never watched it. Would that somehow put me in danger? And Mom?

An even worse thought hit me. What if those men had killed Morton? What if they'd come here to learn if I'd seen something? If Morton had told me about them.

Had I convinced them I didn't know anything?

"I can assure you we'll be back."

Dear God, help us.

Before I'd hung up from Deputy Harcroft's call I told him about giving the men a copy of the flash drive. And I told him about Rutger's gun and threats. At that, a long pause followed.

"Tell you what." Harcroft's voice remained calm, but I could hear the underlying concern. "Rather than you driving to the substation in Half Moon Bay, let me send someone over to pick you up. You'll need to bring that original flash drive to us. Deputy Gonzalez will come to get you. He'll be in uniform."

On rubbery legs I hurried into the living room to peer out the window. No sign of Rutger and Samuelson lurking on the street.

What if this Deputy Gonzalez was a fraud too? Maybe the man on the phone hadn't been Harcroft. I closed my eyes, comparing that voice to the deputy's on the scene. Couldn't decide whether they were the same man or not.

I returned to the kitchen and pulled paper and pen from a drawer. Dialed Information for the number of the Coastside Patrol division of the San Mateo County Sheriff's Department. I wrote down the number and compared it to the digits showing on my receiver from the last call. They didn't match.

But there must be many individual lines going into that substation. The number from Information was just the main one.

I dialed that number. A female answered. "Coastside Patrol, Half Moon Bay."

I asked if a Deputy Harcroft worked there.

"Yes. Would you like to speak with him?"

"How about a Deputy Gonzalez?"

"We have two. Do you know which one?"

"No. I . . . It's okay, thanks." I hung up.

This had to be pure paranoia. It would be far easier to flash some fake badge than to show up with an official car and uniform.

Wouldn't it?

"Hannah?" Mom appeared from the hallway.

"Hi." I smiled at her, heart in my throat. What would I do with her while I talked to the deputy? What could I tell her?

"Let me help you make dinner." Mom's face looked worn. She shuffled into the kitchen.

"Still sad?"

She nodded. "Life is hard sometimes."

Yes, it was.

"Listen, Mom, something's come up. We have to go back to Half Moon Bay and talk to the Sheriff's Deputy about Morton. Someone will be here to pick us up soon. I'm going to make you a sandwich, okay? You can take it with you. It may be awhile before we get back for dinner."

Mom's eyebrows knit. "No potato now?"

"I'm afraid it will have to wait."

"You can't tell them our secret. We promised Morton."

"I know."

"Now he's gone. We *really* have to keep our promise."

"Yes, okay." I squeezed her shoulder. "Would you like turkey or ham on your sandwich?"

"Why do they want to talk to us?"

"I'm not sure. Except Deputy Harcroft said Morton was an important man. And he just wanted to hear our story one more time."

"Of course Morton was important. Everyone is important."

"That's true." I turned toward the refrigerator. "Will ham be okay?"

"I don't want to go back and talk to that deputy man. I don't like him."

"I know. But we have to."

"No, we don't." Mom's jaw set.

Uh-oh. I laid a hand on her arm. Kept my voice quiet, calm. Too many upsetting things had happened today. "Mom, we do need to go. It's important. It's for Morton."

"He *told* us not to talk to anyone." Her voice rose.

"Yes, but—"

"Now you're going back on your word. How can you do that?"

"I wasn't—"

Mom jerked her back straight and raised her chin. "I'm *not* going." She turned on her heel and headed toward her room.

Please, God, not now.

I followed after her. Touched her again—a mere gentle finger on her wrist. "Mom—"

"No!" She whirled on me, face reddening. "I don't want to go. I. Won't. Go!"

"I'm sorry. We have to." Even as I said the words, I knew.

My mother locked her mouth tight, hard breaths whooshing from her nose. Both arms stiffened, and her fingers splayed. Her eyes squeezed shut, then popped open. She glared at me. When her jaw unhinged and her lips pulled back, I braced myself.

Mom shrieked. That high, piercing, primal sound that weakened my knees and curled my shoulders inward. The first time it had happened after she moved in, my neighbors called the police, convinced someone was being tortured.

My mother screamed again, and I could swear the walls rattled.

"I'm not goiiiiingg!" The last word ended in a third screech. Then another. And another. I stood there, helpless, hopeless, swallowing hard. Nothing I did would stop this now.

Mom kept at it. And at it. Until her voice hoarsened, and she wound down.

The yells stopped. The final one hung plangent in the air, roughening my ears.

Mom swiveled toward her bedroom and stalked away. The slammed door pummeled the air from my lungs.

For a moment I swayed there, an abandoned puppet. Then I leaned against the wall and cried.

Lady Gaga kicked on.

Why had my life come to this? I didn't want to take care of my mother, a two-year-old in an old woman's body. I didn't want to be a widow, without my Jeff. I wanted him here beside me, our old life back. I wanted to feel his arms around me, see his smile, smell him, touch him. He died far too young. What was I doing a widow at fifty-five?

And now this new mess. I didn't want to deal with the police. And a murder. And fake FBI agents who threatened me.

The tears came hot and welcome. Needed. But the crying didn't last long. Never did, since Mom had moved in. There was always too much to take care of. I lifted my head and dragged in a shaky breath. Dried my tears. A few more came, and I wiped them away, straightened my back.

Like a worn soldier, I headed into the kitchen.

For Mom's dinner, a ham sandwich would have to suffice.

By rote I made the sandwich, my sodden thoughts turning to my next challenges. First, I still had to convince Mom to leave the house with me. When we reached the station I would have to tell Deputy Harcroft everything. Including how I'd lied to him the first time around. That wouldn't be fun.

I wrapped the sandwich and put the ingredients back into the refrigerator. Went into my bedroom to pull the flash drive out of my computer. My hand stopped just as I touched it. I stared at the rolling pictures of my screen saver, biting my lip.

Did I really want to give away my one copy of the video? Why I would ever need to see the thing again, I didn't know. But too many strange things had happened already . . .

With a sigh at my own doggedness, I copied the video onto my computer's hard drive.

Mom's bedroom door opened, her music still on. She walked into my room, purple hat on her head. Her face looked worn, as it always did after one of her episodes. Did she even remember it had happened?

She might be placid now, though more from exhaustion than anything.

She spread her hands. "I'm hungry."

My head nodded. "I made you a sandwich. We need to take it with us to see the deputy, remember?"

"What for?"

"We have to talk to them about Morton."

Mom's expression softened. "He died."

"Yes. I'm sorry."

"What do they want?"

"They want to hear from you what a good friend Morton was."

"Oh." Her gazed wandered across the room. "Okay."

I gave her a weary smile.

"When do we go?"

"Soon as a deputy gets here to drive us."

"I'm ready now. Well, maybe I should comb my hair."

"Okay. Then you can sit in your chair and wait."

Mom fussed with her hair, then settled into her rocking chair.

A short time later the doorbell rang. "He's here!" She headed for the door. In the kitchen I snatched up her sandwich, some napkins, a bottle of water, and my purse.

"How nice to meet you," I heard Mom say. So polite. So in control. "I'm Carol Ballard. My daughter's almost ready. She always has so many things to do."

Deputy Gonzalez stood in the doorway, a short man with thick, dark hair. "Mrs. Shire?"

I gave him the once-over. Beyond him at the curb sat a white car marked "San Mateo Sheriff's Department."

"Hannah, say hello." Mom frowned at me.

The deputy tipped his head to me. "You ready to go?"

His question reverberated. Not an hour ago I'd faced two other official-looking men, believing everything they said. Now I was putting myself and my mother in the car with this man. I should have said no to Harcroft. Told him I'd drive myself.

"Hannah." Mom's tone reprimanded.

Again I stared at the car—and my worries about Gonzalez spritzed away. This was real law enforcement, for heaven's sake. I should be glad he was here—and that my mother was willing to get into his car. I'd tell Harcroft what he needed and be done with this. As for those fake FBI agents—if they hadn't been satisfied with my answers, they wouldn't have left. They knew I was just some woman who stopped at a car accident. I'd given them what they wanted. They were done with me.

Tomorrow, all of this would be behind us.

"Sorry." I managed a weak smile. "It's been . . . a lot has happened today."

"I understand." Deputy Gonzalez stepped out onto the porch, holding the door for Mom.

In the back seat of the deputy's car I offered Mom her sandwich. She waved it away. "Two other men visited us just a while ago, did you know that?" She leaned forward, aiming her words at Gonzalez. "They were very nice. But they told us Morton had died."

"Yes, I know." Gonzalez nodded.

"It made me very sad. He was my friend."

I remained silent, watching houses go by. Soon we turned onto Edgewood Road, headed toward Freeway 280. A sudden wave of grief for Jeff rolled over me. If he were alive, he'd know how to handle this. Two years after his death, the world could still threaten to overwhelm me. For thirty years I'd faced life's challenges with him by my side.

We wound our way past the eucalyptus trees on Highway 92, Mom again breathing in deep and saying, "Vicks VapoRub." In Half

Moon Bay, we turned onto Kelly Street and parked at the substation. I breathed a sigh of relief.

Inside the building, Gonzalez ushered us to a small windowless room with a table and three chairs. Looked like a place where they'd interrogate suspects. My skin prickled.

"Hello, Mrs. Shire." Deputy Harcroft approached, another man by his side, this one tall with gray hair and steel-blue eyes. A no-nonsense air hung about him, an air that exuded the power and confidence of law enforcement. "Thank you for coming," Harcroft said. "This is Sergeant Charles Wade."

Wade held out his hand, and I shook it. *This* was the man I'd have to tell that I'd lied to Harcroft?

A far worse thought nipped at me. What if I hadn't lied? Could the doctors have saved Morton? If they'd known that something beyond the car accident was wrong . . . If they'd thought to look for a wound . . .

But nothing Morton said made me think he'd been attacked.

Wade looked me straight in the eye, as if he could see the thoughts swirling in my head.

I managed a little smile. "This is my mother, Carol. She has a sandwich to eat. Maybe she could—"

"Oh, I'm not going to eat now." Mom's voice carried her what-are-you-thinking tone. "I need to find out about Morton."

A female deputy rounded the corner, a cute young woman with sandy-blonde hair. Smiling, she introduced herself to Mom as Nance Bolliver. "Way cool hat."

My mother tilted her head. "Thank you. I want to know about Morton."

Nance nodded. "That's what I'm here for. Let's go somewhere so we can talk, okay? It's too crowded in this bare little room. I understand you brought a sandwich? Time for me to eat too."

Almost before I knew it, Nance was whisking my mother away, sandwich and water bottle in hand. I watched Mom go, anxiety pinging in my chest. We'd just gotten here, and already every move seemed orchestrated.

Why had I taken Tunitas Creek Road? Why hadn't I just driven straight home?

"Please. Have a seat." Harcroft indicated one of the straight-backed wooden chairs. I chose a seat at one end of the rectangular table and set my purse on the floor. Harcroft sat on my right, Wade straight across from me at the other end. In the top corner of the room hung a camera. Was it recording? Isn't that what they used for suspects? My frightened eyes flicked from it to Harcroft.

"Don't worry about the camera, just standard procedure."

"For what?"

"For interviews. We don't want to forget anything you tell us."

Understanding hit. That nice young female deputy wasn't just sharing a sandwich with my mother. She was questioning her—alone. With her own camera running.

"I want my mother back in here right now."

"She's fine, she's fine." Wade held up a hand. "Nance'll take good care of her. She's very good with the elderly. When she heard you and your mother were coming in, she asked to help."

"Help, using one of *those*?" I pointed to the camera.

"Really, your mother will be okay."

"I don't want you interrogating her. She's easily upset. She's *already* upset about Morton dying. You don't know how to handle her like I do."

"Mrs. Shire, we understand." Harcroft sat forward, forearms on the table. "We'll take good care of her. Trust me in that."

I pressed back in my chair. Managed a reluctant nod.

"Okay," Harcroft said. "We didn't have long to talk at the scene of the accident. The reporter was there, and you needed to get your mother home. We wanted to go over everything again with you in light of what we now know."

"Am I a suspect?"

Harcroft spread his hands. "We just need information from you, including that flash drive you told us about. And we need to hear about the two men who came to your home."

He hadn't answered my question.

"It's vitally important that we find those men."

Yes, it was. Something inside me relaxed. A little.

Sergeant Wade ran a finger along his jawline. "Let me ask you this first—why were you on Tunitas Creek Road?"

Hadn't Deputy Harcroft asked me this already? I shrugged. "I don't know. It was just a different way to go home. A scenic route. My mother loves pretty scenery. And we weren't in any hurry."

"Have you ever been on that road before?"

"I guess. I can't remember when. But I somehow knew it intersected with Skyline, which would take us over to Highway 92."

The two men seemed to digest that.

I bent over and rustled through my purse, my fingers closing on hard plastic. "Here's the flash drive you want." I set it on the table.

Wade pulled a handkerchief from his pocket and used it to pick up the drive. Too late I realized it had my fingerprints all over it. "What's on the video?" Wade asked.

"I don't know. Some big machine."

"Machine? What's it doing?"

I shrugged. "Falling apart, maybe?"

Wade stood. "I'll go get a laptop."

Harcroft waited until Wade had closed the door behind him. "So this is the original. You gave a copy to those supposed FBI agents. Right?"

"Yes."

"Did you keep a copy for yourself?"

I froze. Why had he thought to ask that? I locked eyes with the deputy, not wanting to admit the truth. Knowing I couldn't lie again.

"Yes. On my laptop."

"Why?"

I focused on the table. "I don't know. Curiosity, I guess. And because I knew it was important. Morton must have struggled to get it into my pocket. So I figured I'd better back up the file. I knew I'd be giving the original to you."

Deputy Harcroft gave me a long look. "When you get home, erase it. Now that you've put the original in our hands, we'll worry about backing it up."

"Okay."

The man's eyes lingered on my face, as if he wasn't sure he believed I'd follow his orders.

"Did Morton Leringer say anything to you about the video, Mrs. Shire?"

Here it came. "No. But he did say some things. Nothing that made much sense."

"Things you didn't tell me about?"

"Yes. I'm sorry. It's just . . . my mother was upset. And I thought what he'd said was personal, perhaps something I could talk to him about later when we visited in the hospital. But then I found the flash drive. And two men showed up at my house. Now I think it all must be connected."

The door opened. Wade strode in, carrying a small computer, already running. He set it on the table and stood beside Harcroft. "Let's see what this is." He pulled on a latex glove and plugged in the drive. Started the video.

I leaned over to see the monitor. We watched in silence. When it was done, Wade played it a second time, then hit pause as the video ended, keeping the picture of the machine on the screen.

The two men looked at each other.

I studied their faces. "What is that machine?"

Wade frowned at the frozen picture on the monitor. "A generator of some kind."

"The last scene looked like a power plant." Harcroft narrowed his eyes at the video.

Of course. The steel structures that seemed so familiar. The kind I'd seen from certain freeways in the Bay Area.

In the same second a realization rippled the expressions of both men. The air stilled. I watched them exchange silent, grim messages. Fear—of what?—rooted me to my chair. The moment stretched out, a taut rubber band.

The band snapped. A mask slid over their faces.

Harcroft turned to me. My throat felt tight, pressed in by the atmosphere of the room.

Wade pushed the computer to the side and sat down. Took off his glove. "The two men at your house. Did they seem to know about this video before you mentioned it?"

I blinked, trying to rip my mind from its questions of what had just occurred. Hugging my arms to my chest, I tried to think back. "I don't know. I don't think so. But I'll tell you one thing—they knew what was said at the ambulance, just before Morton was put inside. They must have gotten that out of the paramedics." I related how the men had repeated my mother's words to Morton: *"We won't forget."*

"When the men asked me about it, I told them it was just Mom's way of saying we'd remember Morton."

"But it was something else?" Harcroft raised his eyebrows. "You said Leringer talked to you."

"Yes." I told them every word I could remember, focusing on Harcroft. Wade listened, silent, his expression unchanging. When I was done no one spoke for a moment. "Again, I'm sorry I didn't tell you."

Harcroft nodded. He sat back in his chair, narrowing his eyes at the wall. "Raleigh." He looked to Wade. "North Carolina?"

"Maybe."

"Was Morton from there?" I asked.

A beat passed, as if the men hadn't heard me. Harcroft shrugged. "We're still learning about him."

Wade asked me about the scene of the accident. Had I seen anyone else nearby? Any cars? Had Leringer given any clues as to who stabbed him?

Not a word, I told them. "The things he did say seemed more important to him."

Wade consulted his notes for a moment. "Do you know a man by the name of Nathan Eddington?"

I repeated the name. "No."

"Never heard of him."

"No. Who is he?"

"Did Morton Leringer say anything about him?"

"No. I don't think so."

Wade nodded. He tapped his finger against the table and focused on Harcroft.

Was that finger tap a bad sign?

"Okay." The sergeant leaned forward. "Let's go through this again. Tell us everything Leringer said to you."

"Why? I told you everything the first time."

"We'd like to hear it again."

For the second time I told them Morton's words. When I finished I was tired, but they wouldn't let up. They wanted to hear a third round. I glanced at the camera. Were they trying to trip me up? Or just make sure I hadn't forgotten anything. With each question my muscles tensed more, and my head started to pound. What was all this about? Had I stepped on some sort of land mine? The thoroughness of these two men, their intense body language made me more frightened as each moment ticked by.

After an interminable time their interrogation slowed. I pressed my hands to my temples. My stomach was empty, my nerves shot. I needed to eat. "Where's my mother? I want to know if she's all right."

"I'll check on her." Wade left the room. I had the distinct impression he left to do more than just see about my mother.

In Wade's absence I faced off with Harcroft. "What's happening? I want to know what this is all about."

He shook his head. "We're not sure."

"Who do you think those fake FBI men were?"

"Don't know. Wish we did. We'll bring in a forensic artist before you leave. We need a sketch of their faces."

My shoulders sagged. How long would *that* take? "Well, at least give me a good guess as to what this is about."

He took a deep breath. "Afraid I can't do that. We just don't know enough yet."

Didn't know enough—or wouldn't tell me?

"Look." My voice toughened. "I'm in this whether I like it or not. Those two men know where I live. Where my *mother* lives. They had guns. And now you won't even tell me anything. How can you know they won't come back? They threatened to do just that!"

He gave a slow nod. "We can't be sure about that. So we're going to put someone on your house."

The news sucked air from my lungs. "You mean put it under surveillance?"

"Yes."

"By whom? San Carlos Police?" Like Half Moon Bay, my town contracted with the San Mateo County Sheriff's Department for its police services. But how subtle would that be—a marked car sitting at the curb?

"Wade will set it up with plainclothes detectives. From which department, I'm not sure."

My house, staked out by plainclothes deputies. Extra time and expense for some department. Why would they do that unless they thought chances were good those men would return?

"You think they're coming back. Don't you." I had to push the words out.

"You will be safe, Mrs. Shire. You'll be under watch."

Really. "Those men are smart. You think they won't spot an unmarked car?"

"Mrs. Shire, we're going to do all we can to protect you."

My nerves were vibrating. "'All you can' means telling me what you know. I need to understand what I'm dealing with here."

"We'll keep you informed as we learn more. I can tell you we're already working hard on this case."

I eyed Harcroft. Would he really "keep me informed"? The doubt wound my muscles tighter. If I couldn't even trust law enforcement . . .

Who was Nathan Eddington?

Wade returned, declaring my mother was having a wonderful time talking to Nance. "I asked if she wanted to see you. She insisted, 'Oh, no, I'm sure my daughter's fine.'"

His words stabbed through me. I could almost envy Mom's ignorance of what was happening.

Wade and Harcroft moved me to a bigger room where a third man joined us—a forensic artist with the wild name of Bob Smith. For the next hour and a half I struggled to remember the faces of Rutger and Samuelson as the artist scratched pencil against paper. In the end we produced two good likenesses of the men. Wade and Harcroft studied them. Wade shook his head. "Recognize either one of them?" he asked Harcroft.

The deputy turned his hands palms up.

By the time we were done it was after 8:00. I so wanted to go home—and yet I didn't. How would I ever sleep, knowing my house was under surveillance? Wondering if those men would return. What if they got past the plainclothes deputy and into the house?

What if they slipped into Mom's room?

Chapter 7

**SPECIAL HOUSE SELECT COMMITTEE
INVESTIGATION INTO FREENOW TERRORIST
ACTIVITY OF FEBRUARY 25, 2013**

SEPTEMBER 16, 2013

TRANSCRIPT

(Continuation of testimony following noon break)

Representative ELKIN MORSE (Chairman, Homeland Security Committee): Sergeant Wade, you again take your seat to testify regarding your actions as lead investigator of the murder of Morton Leringer and subsequent events. As you are well aware, those actions have raised much suspicion. This morning you took an oath to be truthful, sir, and we will expect no less of you as we continue.

Sergeant CHARLES WADE (Sheriff's Department Coastside): You will receive no less.

MORSE: So I will resume our questioning by asking: did you know about the FreeNow organization before these events?

WADE: No.

MORSE: Never heard of them?

WADE: Never.

MORSE: Really. Is it not true that law enforcement professionals have a sixth sense, a gut feel about people and situations?

WADE: Often, yes.

MORSE: Haven't you spoken about your own gut instincts regarding various former cases to your colleagues?

WADE: Yes.

MORSE: Have those instincts proven right?

WADE: Most of the time.

MORSE: Then how is it, Sergeant Wade, that you missed this powerful terrorist faction right under your own nose?

WADE: A gut instinct is about something that *happens*. Until the days in question, no events had occurred that would lead me to suspect the existence of FreeNow.

MORSE: Frankly, I find that hard to believe.

WADE: I would ask you to remember, Chairman Morse, that you are forming your opinions and today's questions based on hindsight. Of *course* it's easy to look back and see things differently. But I am testifying about that day as I saw it unfold, moment by moment. You have to look at my actions as based on what I knew at any given time.

MORSE: We will move on. Tell me, what was your impression of Hannah Shire? As she left the substation, did you believe she'd told you the truth?

WADE: I wasn't sure. I did take the cautious approach and order surveillance on her home. But I was concerned at her admission that she'd initially lied to Deputy Harcroft. She'd changed her story. Sometimes people change their story because they're coming clean. But all too often, a story changes in order to hide something.

MORSE: And what did you think she might be hiding?

WADE: I didn't know. Perhaps having some involvement in the death of Morton Leringer. Or at least knowing more about his death than she was telling us. What I did know was there were two strikes against her. She'd lied to Deputy Harcroft when there seemed no reason to do so. And she was the last person to be with the victim of a stabbing that proved fatal. And one more thing. Her story about why she was on Tunitas Creek Road didn't ring true. That's a very unusual route to take from Highway 1 to San Carlos.

MORSE: I assume Deputy Harcroft shared your suspicions?

WADE: Yes. He told me he'd questioned Mrs. Shire about her presence on that road.

MORSE: Would you say Harcroft's suspicions helped form your negative opinion of Mrs. Shire?

Sergeant Wade?

WADE: No.

MORSE: So these gut feelings were your own.

WADE: I've already told you why I had suspicions regarding Hannah Shire.

MORSE: Yes, you have. But you've also told us your instincts are usually right. In this case you were wrong.

Have you nothing to say to that? I remind you again you're here to tell us the truth.

WADE: And I remind *you*, sir, that you're here to believe the truth when you hear it.

(Pause in testimony as committee confers.)

MORSE: Sergeant Wade, we now want to turn to the video. In order for us to understand the chain of command—what did you do with the flash drive that evening?

WADE: I bagged it as evidence in the homicide of Morton Leringer. It was around 8:30 p.m. on a Sunday. I knew that on Monday morning a deputy with technical knowledge would be on duty. I planned to have him look at it.

MORSE: You saw no need for more immediate action?

WADE: Nothing I saw on the video made me think immediate action was needed.

MORSE: Yet you have testified you recognized the machine on that video as a power generator. And you and Deputy Harcroft discussed the possibility that the video might signal some kind of terrorist attack.

WADE: We discussed it, yes. But Harcroft's emerging opinion was that it just showed a generator going haywire. Beyond that we had no evidence or any indication whatsoever that it was connected to a terrorist attack.

MORSE. It certainly seemed to be an important video. It was slipped into the pocket of a woman by a dying man. And two men posed as FBI agents to gain possession of it.

WADE: At the time we didn't know those two men were in pursuit of the video. In fact, evidence pointed to the contrary. According to Mrs. Shire, they didn't say anything about it when they were at her house. She was the one who told them about the video.

MORSE: All right. So you entered the flash drive as evidence. Did you continue to view it, looking for more clues as to its meaning?

WADE: I looked at it quite a number of times but saw nothing more than I'd seen the first time. At that point I was interrupted. I received a call that a deputy had made contact with Cheryl Stein, the daughter of Morton Leringer. Ever since we'd learned Leringer had been stabbed, we'd been trying to locate Mrs. Stein to gain entrance to his home. We needed to search the premises for possible evidence. I had to leave right away to meet Mrs. Stein at Leringer's house. She had a key and the code for his alarm system.

MORSE: Where is Morton Leringer's residence?

WADE: On Skyline near its intersection with Tunitas Creek Road. It's a large home overlooking the ocean.

MORSE: You mentioned Mrs. Stein had the code to her father's alarm system. When you entered the home, was the alarm on?

WADE: No. Which surprised Mrs. Stein, who informed me her father always turned it on upon leaving the house. She surmised he'd left in a hurry. Her theory fit with the unexpected scene we were about to discover inside that home. A scene that would make me suspect Mrs. Shire even more.

Chapter 8

Sunday, February 24, 2013

On the way home in the backseat of Deputy Gonzalez's car, Mom talked a blue streak about her "new friend Nance." I sat beside her, numb, managing once in awhile to interject an "uh-huh" and "that's nice." My mind could not dwell on her chatter. I couldn't shake thoughts of the two FBI frauds in my living room, warning me they'd be back if I hadn't told them everything. Which I hadn't.

But how would they know that?

"Nance." Mom half sang the name. "Rhymes with *dance*, you know. And *fancy pants*."

"Yeah." I patted her hand.

"She told me all about her childhood. Had six sisters growing up. Can you believe that? *Seven* girls in one family."

"That is a lot."

"Said they drove her father crazy." Mom adjusted her hat. "Your father had a hard enough time just dealing with you and me."

My father had always been distant. Not like Jeff, who'd doted on me and Emily. A pang shot through my chest. He should be here with me. If he were here, I wouldn't be afraid.

"Did Nance ask you about Morton, Mom?" Interesting how the woman had used her first name with Mom instead of calling herself a deputy. Made her sound more friendly.

"Oh, yes." Mom aimed a sly look at the back of Gonzalez's head. "I told her he seemed like a very nice man. Then I asked her more about her family."

I had to smile at the enigma of my mother's brain. She'd lost so much short-term memory, yet the facts that did remain cemented themselves there. At least for awhile. And she still had the smarts to work against the wiles of law enforcement.

We reached our house. I stared at it, my gaze drifting over the door and across the front windows of the living room on the left, Mom's bedroom on the right.

"Thank you," I told Deputy Gonzalez as he opened the back door of his car for us.

"Yes, thank you, young man." Mom gave him a sunny smile.

Young man? The deputy and I exchanged an amused look. Gonzalez had to be in his midforties.

I ushered Mom into the house and locked the door behind us. Stood there listening. Feeling the silence of the house.

Mom yawned. "Oh, my, what a day. I think I'll go to bed." She kissed me on the cheek. "Goodnight, Hannah." She headed toward the hallway. Apprehension kicked up my spine.

"Wait, Mom." I caught up to her. "Let me just . . . check your room first." I slipped past and went into her bedroom. It looked the way she'd left it. Purple blanket draped over her armchair, the bed made. Family pictures on her dresser. I rounded the corner into her private bath. Empty. Pushed back the shower curtain. Nothing. I strode back to her closet door and threw it open. Just Mom's clothes and shoes, boxed knickknacks on the shelf.

"What are you looking for?" Mom stood in her doorway, frowning.

"Nothing. Just . . . nothing."

She shook her head. "I think you're tired too. You need to go to bed."

"Okay." I hugged her, my heart tripping. "But first I need to give you your medicine."

Ten milligrams of Aricept, taken every night at bedtime. Mom had started out with five milligrams, then graduated to ten after six weeks. At first she'd had some nausea, but that side effect seemed to have gone away. In a couple months, the dosage would likely increase to twenty-three milligrams. At this point I wasn't sure I'd seen any improvement from the medication.

Mom took her pill like an obedient child. I gave her one last hug and left her room. Closed the door behind me.

I wiped a hand across my forehead. *Really, Hannah.* What would I have done if I *had* found someone?

Jeff's gun.

For years it had sat in our nightstand, unloaded, bullets nearby. When Mom came to live with me I'd moved the weapon and bullets to a box in my closet. Tonight I'd load the thing. Sleep with it by my bed. In the morning I would put it away.

For now I couldn't stop with Mom's bedroom. I checked my room, bath, and closet. Then the closet in the front hallway. The kitchen and laundry room and garage. I even peered through the windows of my car. No one lurking in the backseat.

No one else anywhere. Just me and Mom.

Going through the house again, I closed all the curtains.

I stood in the kitchen, hands on my hips and pulse still high. I needed to eat. And I wanted to find out just who Morton Leringer was. Did he own an electrical power company? One tied to that video on the flash drive?

The phone rang. I leaned over to peer at the ID. Emily.

"Hi, Em."

"Where have you been? I've been trying to call you forever."

"At the sheriff's department."

"What? Why?"

I told her all about it. The video, the FBI agents, Harcroft and Wade. Right down to the fact that a deputy would be watching our house.

When my words ran out, Emily was silent, as if she didn't know what to say. "Mom, this is really scary."

"I know."

Another pause. "You said you gave those fake FBI agents a copy of the video. Not the original."

"Yes."

"You're sure."

"Yes. Why?"

"Because . . . nothing."

"There's something. I hear it in your voice."

Emily sighed. "Look, those guys probably won't bother you again. At least they have the video, for whatever it means to them. They should leave you alone now."

Of course they should. Her words sounded so reasonable. But they also sounded almost as if she was trying to convince herself.

"I'm going to research Morton Leringer," I said. "We never got to watch the news. I don't know if the story made it on TV or not."

"I want to see that video. Can you send me a copy?"

I hesitated. "I don't want you involved in this."

"Mom, just looking at it won't hurt anything. I might see something in it that you didn't."

"Could be. Still, I don't want you involved. Look what's

happened to me. I don't want fake FBI agents showing up at your door."

"Now you're just being paranoid."

Maybe, maybe not. "Emily, I'm not sending it. And I'm going to go erase it from my own computer. It's in the hands of the sheriff's department now."

"You're stubborn, you know that?"

"No. Just cautious. Especially when it comes to you. And Mom."

"Well." Emily's voice softened. "That's true."

For a moment neither of us spoke.

We talked a few more minutes. I had the impression Emily didn't want to let me off the phone. The worry would not leave her voice. In the end I said I needed to go.

"Okay, Mom." Her words remained tight. "Stay safe. And call me anytime tonight. It's not like I'm going to sleep anyway."

I winced, sorry that I'd concerned my daughter. Maybe I shouldn't have told her any of this. "We'll be fine."

"If anyone comes around, just tell Grand to put on her music real loud. That oughtta keep 'em away."

I managed a laugh. "You're right about that."

We hung up and I lingered at the counter, thinking. So much to sort through.

My stomach growled.

From a cabinet I pulled a can of vegetable soup. Dumped it in a bowl and slid it into the microwave. As it heated I slipped into the living room without turning on the lights and peeked through the front drapes. No parked car in sight. I leaned over to see down the street to my left. No car. Peered to the right. Some distance down, on the other side of the street, sat a van. It was as far from a streetlamp as possible.

Was anyone inside?

Deputy Harcroft had given me his cell number to call. So had Sergeant Wade. "Anytime you need us," they'd said, "day or night." I found Wade's number in my purse and punched it in. He answered immediately.

"Mrs. Shire, you okay?"

"Did you send a car to my street?"

"It's there."

"I see a van, but I'm not sure anyone's inside."

"That's it. We can't be obvious."

"Okay. I know."

"You all right?"

No. "Yes. Fine. Good night."

I hung up.

The microwave was beeping. I ate the soup by rote, not tasting. Drank a glass of water and headed to my computer.

At Google I searched for *Morton Leringer.*

The Wikipedia site for Morton came up near the top. I clicked on it and found a long article, split into sections. Leaning forward, I read.

Morton was born and raised in upper state New York, the son of a factory worker. His mother died when he was a teenager. At twenty-one he started his first company, selling homemade bread to the neighborhood. That business grew into the present-day Leringer's, a 500-million-dollar company.

Of course, Leringer's. Various foods and spices found in gourmet and organic stores. I'd eaten their bread for years.

I read further.

Morton later diversified, starting and buying more and more businesses under his umbrella company, ML Corporation. That, I'd never heard of. But I was familiar with some of the companies it owned—and they were numerous. Companies in the tech field, security, finances, consulting, food and beverage, the housing market, and appliances, and widgets, and carpeting/flooring. Nurseries, and furniture, and steel. What business *wasn't* Morton into?

But no electrical company.

And nothing in his personal life that seemed to connect with Raleigh, North Carolina.

Morton's wife had died from a stroke two years ago. They had two children, Cheryl and Ben. Both now in their forties. I couldn't tell where they lived, or what Cheryl's current last name was. If she ended up living in Raleigh, North Carolina . . . I shook my head. Mom would just say, "I *told* you."

Where to go next? Find out more about Cheryl and Ben?

First I searched *Raleigh*. All the hits on the first few pages were for businesses of that name or the North Carolina city. I tapped my desk, unsatisfied. Opened a new tab and went to weather.com. Typed in *Raleigh*. Up came additional choices for cities in Illinois, Mississippi, North Dakota, and West Virginia. And one in Canada.

I sat back and looked at the clock on my desk. Almost 10:00. Tiredness crept over me, but I knew I'd never sleep.

The gun.

I pushed away from my desk and took the small metal box down from my closet shelf. Inside sat a Chief's Special Model 36. Easy to shoot, holding five bullets. Years back Jeff took me to a shooting range. He explained about the gun's double action—how it didn't need to be cocked to fire it. I'd never held a gun before and didn't like them to this day. But I'd learned to shoot—sort of. "Well," Jeff had said with his dry humor, "if a bad guy with two heads breaks into the house, you're bound to hit one of them."

Wincing at the task, I loaded the gun. The box went back on the shelf. The weapon I laid beside me on the desk.

I returned to my research.

For the next two hours I ran down the websites for each of Morton's companies. I read about each one—where it was located, what its services or products were. I was looking for a connection between any of them and one of the Raleigh cities.

I found none.

Next I looked up each Raleigh. The Illinois town was tiny, with 700 people in the 2010 census. The Raleigh in Mississippi was the county seat of Smith County, with a population of 1,462. Raleigh, North Dakota, counted a mere 92 people in the last census. The Raleigh in West Virginia turned out to be a county, with a population of close to 80,000 living in cities with names such as Lester, Mabscott, and Rhodell. I'd never heard of any of them.

Raleigh, Canada, was a tiny place on the far eastern edge of the country. The population was somewhere in the 200s.

All small areas. Not places you'd think a large company would be headquartered.

I leaned back in my chair and closed my eyes. Exhaustion spread through my limbs. The Raleigh that Morton mentioned most likely referred to the North Carolina city. Still, none of his companies seemed to have ties to that area.

My mind chugged, unable to think anymore. My body began to relax . . .

My head fell forward.

I jerked up. Threw an anxious look over my shoulder, but saw mere empty house. Mom was quiet. Sometimes, even with her door closed, I could hear her snore. Not tonight.

Was it my imagination, or did the night . . . vibrate? I ran both hands over my face, as if to scrub clear thinking back into my brain. My gaze landed on the gun. Scary thing. Why had I taken it out of its box? Men with weapons had come to my house, yes. But I'd given them the flash drive—and they left. If they wanted anything more, if they wanted to hurt me, they'd have done it right then.

But what if those two men had watched my house and seen me and Mom drive off in a deputy's car? They'd wonder why we'd talked to law enforcement. If we'd told the sheriff's department something we hadn't told them.

Would Samuelson and Rutger come back to find out?

I flexed my shoulders, rolled my head from side to side. My muscles wouldn't loosen.

An intense desire to hear Emily's voice swept over me. I glanced at the clock. Past 1:00 a.m. Too late to call, despite what she'd told me. Besides, I couldn't let her know how scared I felt. No need to frighten her more than she already was.

The sheriff's surveillance car. Was it still outside?

In the darkened living room I edged back a curtain and looked down the street. The van I'd seen hours earlier was still there.

I wandered to the middle of the room and stood there, one hand to my neck. This couldn't go on—I needed sleep. Another full workweek began just hours from now. Did I think I could do this night after night?

Dorothy. I'd have to tell Mom's caretaker everything when she arrived. She'd need to be extra careful, on the lookout. I would give her Harcroft's and Wade's numbers.

Really, Hannah, you're making too much out of this.

How was I supposed to work, worrying about Mom here at home?

A prayer flitted through my head—for the sheriff's department to catch those two men soon. Then everything would be back to normal.

I found myself again in my room, staring with longing at my bed. The computer monitor scrolled through old pictures. I couldn't find the energy to turn the thing off.

My feet took me toward the bed, then of their own accord veered to the desk. I picked up the gun. Carried it to the living room. Only my bedroom desk lamp remained on in the house. In the near dark, I pulled Mom's blanket off her rocking chair. Laid my gun on the table beside the sofa. I lay down on the couch and covered myself with the blanket.

If anyone skulked through the front door, or the back, I'd hear them before they got to Mom's room.

My eyes drifted shut, my brain fuzzing. The unstable world shifted . . . fell away . . .

In the last moment of consciousness I convinced myself we had nothing to worry about.

Chapter 9

The phone in his pocket buzzed. A high-tech device unknown to the masses, designed by the precise and skilled engineers of FreeNow, the organization he led. Calls untraceable. A mere chosen few had the number. Alex Weyerling, known as Stone by those in the FreeNow organization, pulled out the cell and checked the ID. It was Roz—"Agent Samuelson."

Stone put the cell to his ear. "Yeah."

"There's an issue."

He stiffened. "What now?" As if a traitor in their midst—on today of all days—wasn't enough. And not just any traitor.

"The video. She gave us a copy."

"How do you know?"

Roz told him.

Stone swore. "Why didn't you get the truth out of her before you left her house?"

"You know why. She told us to leave."

"She *told* you? The big guys with the guns?" Not to mention they were two of his men with badges. Stone had badges across the country—fake and real. "So you and Tex just *crept* out of there like mice?"

"You said not to blow our cover."

"I also said not to come out of there without everything we needed!"

Silence.

Stone swore again. "Why, Roz? Just why do you think she would make the choice to keep it?"

"I don't know."

Stone punched the wall hard. There was only one reason. She knew something. "You told me she insisted Leringer didn't tell her anything."

"She did!"

"Guess what, Roz. She *lied*!"

"Yeah. Apparently. But we're fixing it."

"How fast, Roz? How fast?"

"Now. I'm going back. I'll get her computer, any backup drives, whatever I can get. I'll take care of it, Stone, I promise you."

Stone rubbed his shaved head. His gaze drifted over the cluttered apartment. How he hated the place, surrounded by sounds of traffic and neighbors. His fellow Americans going about their futile business, so unaware of what their country had become. Of how the government had taken over every aspect of their lives. Just when their two-year plan was about to change it all, *everything* was going wrong.

"You listen to me, Roz, you'd *better* take care of this." Stone slitted his eyes. "We're running out of time. And don't you leave that house again without finding out what that woman knows and who she's told. Then take them both out."

Roz hesitated. "One of 'em's just an old lady. Doesn't know half of what she says."

Stone's voice turned to steel. "Your point?"

"Nothing."

Stone gripped the phone, his back hunched. Over a year of engineering. Planning timed to the second. All for the organization now to be at the mercy of a betrayer and a series of wild mistakes. First FreeNow's computer security specialist, Eddington, had turned traitor at the last minute and rushed the crucial video to Morton Leringer. Then Nooley, sent to intercept Eddington and Leringer before it was too late, failed to get the video back. Now it was in the hands of some woman. And spreading further by the minute.

"Want to know what happened to your friend Nooley, Roz? He's *dead*. Got a bullet between the eyes."

Silence.

"That's what happens to men who fail me. Who fail FreeNow."

"I hear you."

"I hope you do. I hope you hear me loud and clear. Because I expect you over here in ninety minutes. I'll call in one of our techs. He'll go through that woman's computer and make sure she hasn't sent the video anywhere."

"Yeah, okay." Fear had crept into Roz's voice. "Ninety minutes."

Stone punched off the call and threw his phone on the table.

Chapter 10

**SPECIAL HOUSE SELECT COMMITTEE
INVESTIGATION INTO FREENOW TERRORIST
ACTIVITY OF FEBRUARY 25, 2013**

SEPTEMBER 16, 2013

TRANSCRIPT

Representative ELKIN MORSE (Chairman, Homeland Security Committee): So you entered the home of Morton Leringer along with his daughter, Cheryl Stein—and found that his alarm was not on. What did you then discover in that home?

Sergeant CHARLES WADE (Sheriff's Department Coastside): Let me backtrack a little. There is a semicircular driveway in front of the house. As Mrs. Stein and I approached and went up the porch steps, I noticed drops of what appeared to be blood. When we entered the large foyer I saw more drops leading to an office to the right of the foyer. In that office I discovered the body of a man lying on the floor. He'd been beaten and stabbed. We later learned the identity of the victim. Nathan Eddington, a security technician at StarrCom, a company owned by Leringer's ML Corporation. From that point I declared the house a crime scene, which would entail taping off the property and calling in techs to go through the house thoroughly.

In the meantime I escorted Mrs. Stein through the rest of the house so she could look for anything out of order or missing. I also checked windows and doors. A rear door to the garage had been broken into. It stood ajar, its lock mechanism bent and forced. There did not appear to be anything missing from the house. Other than what I've already noted, plus signs of a struggle in the office, it looked as if nothing had been disturbed. Morton Leringer's car, a Mercedes sedan, still sat in the garage.

MORSE: What did you surmise from this evidence?

WADE: My best theory at the time was that someone had broken into the Leringer home while Leringer and Eddington were meeting in the office. The perpetrator may have surprised the two men. Judging from the defense wounds on Nathan Eddington, I'd say he put up a fight. Leringer was stabbed, but managed to escape. Perhaps he had time to get away while the perpetrator fought with Eddington. Leringer would have been running for his life, but he was already seriously wounded. Rather than head across the large house to his garage for his own car, he chose to go down the front steps to Eddington's car and drive away. He managed to get some distance down Tunitas Creek Road before wrecking the car.

MORSE: In previous testimony you told this committee the car Morton Leringer was driving at the time of his accident belonged to Nathan Eddington. Correct?

WADE: Yes. We ran the plates after towing away the car.

MORSE: And that . . . Let me check my notes . . . You called Nathan Eddington's home and spoke with his wife, who confirmed he'd driven the car to work.

WADE: Yes. When I tried to reach Mr. Eddington at his work—StarrCom—I was informed he'd left the office in a hurry and hadn't told anyone where he was going. That's the last we knew of his whereabouts until discovering his body. So our theory of a meeting between Eddington and Leringer at Leringer's house, that meeting being interrupted by the perpetrator, and Leringer escaping in Eddington's car—it all seemed to fit.

MORSE: How did you explain Leringer's having Eddington's car keys?

WADE: Actually that detail points to the crucial, hurried nature of the meeting between Leringer and Eddington. I surmised that in his rush to get into the house, Eddington had left the keys in his car.

MORSE: How would Leringer know they'd been left there?

WADE: I don't know. Maybe he didn't. Maybe in his pain and fear he chose to run down the front steps and discovered Eddington's keys in the car.

MORSE: Mere coincidence in this crucial moment, you're saying.

WADE: Coincidence, providence—whatever you want to call it. That's not so unusual. What would be more unusual is Leringer asking Eddington for his car keys while the man was being fatally attacked.

MORSE: My question did not invite sarcasm, Sergeant Wade.

WADE: None was intended.

MORSE: I'll take that at face value.

Now, circling back to Mrs. Shire. What did the discovery of Nathan Eddington's body, and your theory of the crime scene, lead you to believe regarding Hannah Shire?

WADE: She'd already given a questionable excuse for being on a rural road where a man lay dying from a stab wound. Now we knew that road led to a house where a break-in and a deadly attack occurred, resulting in the deaths of *two* men.

MORSE: So it's your testimony that you grew more suspicious of Mrs. Shire.

WADE: Yes.

MORSE: Rather than seeing the evidence as backing up her story.

WADE: The body count had just doubled, Mr. Chairman.

MORSE: Indeed. And with that video being in law enforcement hands, so had the problems for FreeNow. Unless the video was ignored.

WADE: If you are insinuating I purposely ignored that video in order to help FreeNow succeed in their terrorist plot, I categorically deny it. And I resent the accusation.

MORSE: Then explain this: *How* did it not occur to you that the sudden meeting between Leringer and Eddington—and their subsequent murders—may have been related to the video? That Leringer managed to escape with the flash drive from his attacker? And that as he lay dying he struggled with his last breaths to tell a woman who'd come upon the accident about the planned terrorist attack—and even managed to slip the flash drive into her pocket?

How would this not tell you, Sergeant Wade, the importance of that video?

Chapter 11

Monday, February 25, 2013

A creak woke me.

My eyes flew open. For a moment my brain failed to remember where I was.

The couch. Gun behind my head on the table. I reached for it.

I lay there, body stiff as lead, head raised. Listening. Maybe I'd just heard Mom.

A horrible vision of shooting her by mistake swept through my mind. Followed by Jeff's voice: "Don't hesitate. Or the other guy might get you first."

Another sound. Coming from my bedroom. A moving of . . . something.

I sat up.

My heart pounded so hard I could not breathe. I dropped my mouth open, struggling to pull in air. The gun in my hand shook.

If someone was in that room, I had to stop him there. Before he moved to Mom's room.

How did he get in? Not the front door. Had to be the back. Unseen by the sheriff's deputy out front.

With sheer willpower I stood, legs trembling, knees watery. Both hands gripped the weapon. One step at a time, I eased forward. At the edge of the living room, I stopped. I peered down the hall, through the doorway to my room. It was dimly lit by my desk lamp. I could see the nightstand by my bed, the edge of a bookcase along the wall.

Another sound.

My limbs froze. What to do? Rush in, pull the trigger as fast as I could? What if both of those men had come back? I might hit one, but the other would kill me. Leaving Mom in the house alone— with them.

Fierce protection surged through my veins. I turned on one heel and edged toward Mom's room. It couldn't have taken more than a few seconds, but it felt like hours. At her door, I hesitated. Once I opened it, they'd hear. Would I have time to jump inside and lock it?

Maybe they'd take what they wanted and just leave. I'd rush for my phone and call Wade.

What did they want?

A footfall.

I tore open Mom's door and leapt inside the room. Slammed it shut and locked it.

"Oh!" Mom cried, woken from sleep.

Hard steps sounded in the hall. My left hand scrabbled across the wall, seeking a switch. *There.* I flicked it on.

Light flooded the room. My eyes squinted, blinked. In a split second I took in Mom, rising up in bed, fright tearing her face.

The footsteps stopped outside the door. I spun toward the sound, both hands on my gun.

A kick—and the door burst open.

Mom screamed.

A man hulked in the threshold.

My finger yanked the trigger. One, two, three times. The shots clanged in my ears.

A strangled cry. The man listed sideways. Where had I hit him?

Something heavy hit the floor. My eyes jerked down to see a big gun with a very long barrel, dropped from the man's fingers. Was that a silencer?

"Hannah!" Mom shrieked.

The man staggered. Cradled under his left arm were my laptop and small backup drive. He pressed them to his side. Bent down, fumbling for his weapon.

I saw the top of a bald head.

I fired again. Saw the bullet hit his right hand.

"Unngkk." He straightened and looked at me, stunned and unsteady. For one terrifying moment our eyes locked. It was Samuelson.

I couldn't move.

He dragged in air. For the first time I saw a patch of red spreading on his chest. A bullet hole.

His eyelids drooped. "We're both dead." The words ground from him like gravel.

Samuelson turned and stumbled away.

I stood rooted to the spot, gun wavering in my hands. As Mom wailed behind me, Samuelson's heavy treads headed through the kitchen. The back door opened and slammed.

A dozen thoughts screamed in my brain. *"We're both dead."* Why? What had I done? And—the man had come for my laptop? Why?

"Haaannaaaah." Mom sounded like a petrified child.

I whipped around, laid my gun on the dresser. Ran to hold her. "It's okay now, he's gone."

"What happened, why did he—"

"Shh, it's okay." Tears streaked her face. I wiped them away.

My computer. The truth hit home.

God, tell me this isn't true.

Mom held onto me and cried. "You had a *gun!* You *shot* him."

My throat tried to close. "I know, I know."

"Is he gone now?"

"Yes. But he might be back."

"Call the police!"

I wanted to. How I wanted that. But I couldn't trust San Carlos police now. They were part of the San Mateo Sheriff's Department. As were Harcroft and Wade. And no one had come to our aid. The officer outside, our supposed protection, *had* to have heard the gunshots.

"We have to leave. Right now."

"Leave?"

I yanked the covers off her legs. "Come on. *Hurry.*"

"Where will we go?"

Yes, *where?*

"Come on, get up." I swung her legs over the edge of the bed. My heart still galloped, adrenaline zinging my nerves. Thoughts whirled in my head. No time to sift through which ones were crazy and which made sense.

My laptop. And my backup drive.

Thank goodness I was still dressed in my jeans and sweatshirt. I flew around Mom's room, yanking out clothes and throwing them into a suitcase I dragged from her closet. Threw her medicine in as well. Mom's eyes were wide, her gaze jerking around the room. Her hands flailed in the air, seeking what to do.

"Here, put these on." I thrust blue knit pants and a green shirt into her hands.

"What about under—"

"Here." I threw a pair of panties on the bed.

How long had passed since Samuelson left? Two minutes? One

more, and we had to be out of there. I pulled a coat for Mom off its hanger, told her to put it on.

His gun. I spun around and spotted the large weapon still lying on the floor near the wall. What to do with it?

I kicked it into the hall. Couldn't leave it loaded in the room with Mom.

"What are you doing?" Mom wailed.

My own gun lay on the dresser, with one bullet left. I scooped it up.

In the hall I kicked Samuelson's gun again, toward the kitchen. When it was far enough away from my mother, I ran to get a plastic grocery bag. Set my own gun on the kitchen counter. Without touching the man's gun I scooped it inside the bag and wrapped it up, then darted to my room and shoved it in a drawer.

Wait. I yanked the drawer open. What if they came back and ransacked my house? I couldn't leave the gun here. If it contained fingerprints, it was evidence.

From my closet shelf I pulled down a tote bag and shoved the wrapped gun inside. Thrust the bag over my shoulder. Hustled back to the kitchen and threw my gun inside the tote as well.

"Let's go, Mom." I ran into her room and pushed her toward the hall. Picked up her small suitcase.

"Wait, my hat!"

"There's no *time*." I thought my heart would burst.

"I'm not leaving without my hat!"

My head snapped back and forth, looking for it. There—on her dresser. I grabbed it and stuffed it in her coat pocket.

I took no clothes from my room, just the box of extra bullets. These, too, I dropped in the tote bag. I snatched up the coat I'd worn earlier that day from the front closet, and my purse. Clutching Mom's hand, I steered her through the kitchen and into the garage. Pushed her into my car and belted her in. Her suitcase and the tote bag I threw in the backseat. I kept my purse up front. My cell phone was in it.

Wait. Shouldn't I have my gun close?

I grabbed it from the tote bag and stuck it in my purse. Mom was so confused she didn't notice.

In the car I pushed the button for the garage door. My pulse whooshed in my ears. Would we get out? They could be sitting right out there, waiting for us . . .

I'd shot a man. Pulled the trigger *four times*. What if he *died*?

The door rolled open. I screeched out of the garage and driveway. On the street I threw a wild look at the sheriff's van. Wouldn't the deputy inside follow once he saw me rush out of there?

I punched the garage door shut and took off down the street, passing the van.

It didn't move.

"Hannah, you're driving too fast." Mom clutched her seat. "Where are we going? I want to go home."

"We can't."

At the first corner I hesitated. Which way? Where on earth could we go?

I turned left, heading for Edgewood Road. From there I gunned up to 280 and turned south.

Mom was crying. "What's happening, where are we going, who was that man?"

I hunched over the steering wheel, my back like granite. "That man tried to kill both of us."

"*Why?*"

"Don't know. I just know I need to get you somewhere safe." Someplace where I could stop and rest. Think this through.

"We should call the *police!*" Her voice bent upward.

I said nothing, my throat tight. We couldn't call law enforcement. It was clear Samuelson had come to my house for two reasons.

First, for my computer and backup drive. Second, to kill me. Maybe Mom too. The only reason he'd want to take my laptop and backup drive would be to get rid of the copy I'd made of that video.

And the only people who knew I'd made that copy worked for the sheriff's department.

Who from that department was working with those fake agents? Harcroft? Wade? Or both. Maybe someone else who'd been told about the video.

I'd bet it was Harcroft. He'd seemed suspicious of me the moment we met.

What did that video mean? Why was it so important?

Questions and protests spilled from Mom's mouth. I shut her out. I had to *think*.

Two clear points of action lasered through my brain, both of which had to be done now. Call Emily. And hit the nearest bank for the biggest ATM withdrawal I could make.

We wouldn't be going home anytime soon.

Chapter 12

Stone's phone buzzed. Roz's number. He was late. Stone cursed and punched on the line. "*Where* are you?"

"It's done."

"So why aren't you here?"

Roz's breath sputtered.

"What's wrong with you?"

"Nothing."

Stone's eyes narrowed. "What is *wrong* with you?"

"Nothing. Just took . . . longer than I thought. Hurrying . . . back to my car. Be there soon."

The man didn't sound right. "You have her computer?"

"Yeah. And backup drive."

"What'd she tell you?"

"Nothing. She doesn't know . . . anything." Roz's breath came in spurts.

"What do you mean *doesn't*?"

"Didn't. Didn't know."

Stone worked his jaw. "Did you kill her or not, Roz?"

"Yes."

"And her mother?"

"Y-yeah."

"You did."

"Yeah."

Stone sniffed. Was Roz lying? "If you're just leaving her house you should be here in twenty minutes."

"I'll be there."

And he just might be sorry. Stone *would* get out of him what had happened.

"Can't wait, Roz."

Chapter 13

I veered off 280 at Woodside Road and turned left, looking for the nearest bank. There was little traffic at this hour. The digital clock read 3:37.

They'd come for me, wouldn't they. Even if Samuelson was dead, Rutger was still around. And who knew what people they worked with? Or for?

I might have *killed* a man!

Who at the sheriff's department was working with them?

Why? I hit the steering wheel with my fist. Why was this *happening* to us?

"Hannah, don't worry." Mom tried to soothe me, even as her words quavered. "We'll be all right."

She had no clue.

Who did I think I was to run from these people? In my mind, I flicked through movies and TV shows of innocents trying to outrun heartless criminals. Like bunnies fleeing a pride of lions.

I spotted a Wells Fargo down on the left and pulled into its parking lot. Drove right up to the ATM.

"Mom, stay in the car. I'll just be a minute."

She sniffled. "Where are we?"

"The bank."

Hitting an ATM after dark went against one of my own safety rules. I couldn't help glancing around as I slid my card into the slot. The max cash withdrawal was $300. I took it all. I already had another $300 in my purse.

Back in the car I stuffed the money in my purse and headed off Woodside, onto residential roads. I needed a darkened curb where I could pull over and call Emily.

A few blocks down I found what I needed. I rolled to a stop but kept the engine running.

"What are you doing now?" Mom fingered the collar of her shirt.

"Calling Emily."

"Won't she be sleeping?"

"Yes." My fingers trembled as I pulled out my cell phone.

Emily picked up on the first ring. "Mom?" Her tone bordered on panic. I never called at this hour.

"Hi." I tried to lighten my voice, but it came out sideways.

"What's wrong?"

"I don't have long to talk. We had to run from the house."

"*Why?*"

Briefly, I told her.

"Mom!"

"We're driving at night, Emily!" Mom yelled toward the phone. "Your mother got me out of bed!"

"I can't believe this." Emily's words hitched. "You're on your way to the police, right?"

"We can't go to the police."

"Why?"

"Because our 'police' are the sheriff's department. And *they* are the only people who know I put a copy of that video on my laptop."

Shocked silence. I could imagine Emily's mind whirling. "Where *are* you right now?"

"Somewhere off Woodside Road. I hit the bank for some money. I have no idea where I'm going."

"Come here."

"That's the last place I'd go! You think I want to lead those men to you?"

"But you can't just *run*."

"We have to. At least for now. Until I figure something out."

Emily's breathing stuttered over the line. "You're telling me the sheriff's department is trying to *kill* you?"

"Maybe they didn't know that would happen. But one of them told somebody about the video."

"If they didn't want to get you killed, they'll help you now. They'll protect you."

"Most of them, yes. But who told? Who can I *not* trust? And will that person inform someone who'll come after us again?" Bubbles of air knocked around in my lungs. "If it was just me, that would be one thing. But I've got Mom."

"I—" Emily's voice caught. She was crying. "So where are you going?"

"To a hotel somewhere. So I can think this through."

"You can't stay on your cell phone."

"Why?"

"They can track you by it, Mom. If people are after you, they can use your phone."

I pressed back against the seat. I'd never thought of that. "Okay. I'll . . . turn it off and just use it to call you when we get to the hotel."

"No. You can't use it *at all*. You have to turn it off and leave it like that."

"Then how do I talk to you?" I couldn't be cut off from Emily.

"Use the phone in your hotel room."

"Won't that show up on my bill? What if they trace me to the room and see that number? It'll lead them to you."

"Mom, I'll be okay. I'm worried about *you*."

"No, you won't be okay!" My voice rose. "They would have killed your grandmother, Emily! Do you think I want them to get my daughter too?"

"They hurt Emily?" Mom leaned toward me, face stricken. "No!"

"She's okay, Mom, she's okay." I squeezed her arm. For her sake I had to get hold of myself. "Look," I said into the cell, my mind fighting to process, "I'm going to turn off my phone now and drive. I'll call you in an hour or two from a pay phone. Right now I just need to get out of this area."

"Promise you'll call." Emily's words caught.

"I will."

"Mom, I'm so scared."

Me too, I wanted to say. *Me too.* "We'll be okay. I'll figure this out. Gotta go now."

"I'll be praying."

"Thanks. I love you."

"Love *you*."

I ended the call and turned off the phone.

My head flopped back against the seat rest—just for a second. Then I threw my car into gear and took off down the dark street. We had to get *out* of there. Rutger had to be somewhere nearby, trolling the streets for my car. Thank goodness I'd gotten gas in Half Moon Bay, and the tank was still almost full.

Heart pummeling, I turned the corner, headed back toward Woodside Road. From there, it would be a quick hop to the freeway. We wouldn't stop again for a long time.

"Hannah." Mom plucked at my sleeve. "I have to go to the bathroom."

Chapter 14

Emily tossed her cell phone on the bed and dropped her head in her hands. *How* could this be happening to her mom?

"She's crazy for not going to the police," Emily said to her darkened room.

Or was she? Her mother wasn't exactly known for being a conspiracy theorist. And she wasn't all about drama, either.

Emily swung her feet to the floor and stood. What could she do? Not sleep, that was for sure. The minutes would drag like weeks until her mother called back.

What if she never called back?

Emily's breath pooled in her chest.

Hand pressed to her mouth, Emily paced her small bedroom until her head was about to explode. What was on that video anyway? Her mom should've let her see it. Her work days were all *about* videos. Maybe she'd see something that her Mom hadn't—

Online backup.

Emily stopped.

How long had Mom left her computer on after copying that video? Over half an hour? That would be long enough for the auto backup to their shared online account to kick on. Emily had set up the account a few years ago, after her mother's computer crashed with no backup.

Parents and technology.

If that video had been sent to their account, Emily could download it to her computer.

She flipped on her bedroom lamp, blinking in the sudden light. Flung herself into her computer desk chair. She woke up the computer and cruised to the Internet. Logged into the account. Her fingers trembled as she checked the time and date for her mother's last upload.

There was the file: *Morton's Video.*

Real subtle, Mom.

Emily eyed the file name. If she downloaded it, and the man who'd stolen her mom's computer managed to break into this account, he could track the download to her.

Only one way around that.

With a few clicks she sent the video file to her computer. Then she deleted the account.

Back hunched, Emily leaned forward to watch the video.

It was pretty much what her mom had explained. No sound. A machine shaking, then letting off steam until the whole screen went white. The final sequence of another machine near an electrical power plant. Black smoke came from that one.

Emily sat back, frowning. Then watched it again.

Near the end her eye caught something at the bottom right of the picture. What was that? She paused the video. Some kind of pixelation. In technical terms, "noise." Was it just poor quality? The end of the video was more blurry than the beginning. Or was it supposed to be there?

She hit "Play." The noise continued. Then at fifty-nine seconds, it stopped.

Why?

Emily went back to the beginning again and watched a third time. And a fourth. A fifth and sixth. After seven views, she was sure of one thing.

The noise had a pattern.

There was something here, but her laptop didn't have the software she needed to figure it out.

She snatched her cell phone off the bed and checked the time: 4:15 a.m. If she left soon she'd get to the office by 5:00. She'd have three hours before anyone else showed up.

Emily threw on some work clothes and makeup. She grabbed her computer, stuffed it in her laptop bag with wallet and keys, and headed for the door.

Chapter 15

**SPECIAL HOUSE SELECT COMMITTEE
INVESTIGATION INTO FREENOW TERRORIST
ACTIVITY OF FEBRUARY 25, 2013**

SEPTEMBER 16, 2013

TRANSCRIPT

Representative ELKIN MORSE (Chairman, Homeland Security Committee): Sergeant, I'm now going to turn to the early morning hours of February 25, at the address of 738 Powell Street, San Carlos, California. The home of Hannah Shire. How were you informed of the events that occurred there?

Sergeant CHARLES WADE (Sheriff's Department Coastside): Throughout the night I'd been in contact with Deputy Williams, who was running surveillance on the property. Sometime after 3:00 a.m. he stopped responding. At about the same time I was informed by the San Carlos bureau on a possible shots-fired dispatch to that location. I hurried to the address. It took me about half an hour to arrive. There I met San Carlos officer Tim Dunmeyer, who'd checked the house through an unlocked back door and discovered it empty. He reported seeing blood drops in the house, leading out that back door. There seemed to be no sign of forced entry. If the house had been broken into, someone had very efficiently picked the lock. Hannah Shire's car was not in the garage. Williams's unmarked van was still parked on the street. He was behind the wheel, dead, with a single gunshot wound to the head.

MORSE: An unfortunate, sad victim, to be sure. As for Mrs. Shire and her mother, did you think they'd been kidnapped?

WADE: A neighbor reported seeing Mrs. Shire drive away in her car in the middle of the night. There was no doubt she'd left of her own volition.

MORSE: So what was your assessment of the situation?

WADE: I couldn't be sure. But here now, in a matter of hours, I had a third homicide. Plus—where were Hannah Shire and her mother? Were they hurt? Or had Hannah Shire shot the deputy and taken off?

MORSE: That isn't really what you thought, now was it, Sergeant Wade? They were indeed the questions you voiced to the San Carlos bureau, and expected them to act upon. In truth, you knew far more about what had happened that night at the Shire residence, did you not?

Did you not, Sergeant Wade?

WADE: You are mistaken. I did not know the details of what happened.

MORSE: I'm not asking if you knew every detail. I would expect not, since you weren't present. I am asking: why didn't the death of Deputy Williams and the disappearance of Hannah Shire and her mother make you believe her story? She'd said she was in danger. Now she was gone, and there was blood in her house. Didn't you question whether it was her blood?

WADE: Of course. But as I began questioning neighbors, I learned more.

MORSE: And a deputy had been killed. One of your fellow law enforcement officers. How could you not face your own culpability in his death?

WADE: I object to the term *culpability.*

MORSE: Really. Just what would you call it, sir?

Chapter 16

Monday, February 25, 2013

My head swam.

I felt like a refugee—so near to home and yet so far. The night seemed to close in around our car. Mom informed me two more times she had "to go," and I knew that meant now.

I didn't have time for this. But there was no choice. I had to find an all-night grocery store. It would have a bathroom.

At Woodside Road I turned left toward town, away from the freeway. My own hands wanted to fight the turn. If nothing else I could go to the Safeway at Sequoia Station in Redwood City. The one where I shopped. But my car and license plate felt like glowing neon as I drove down the almost empty road. How long before the people who were chasing us discovered I wasn't dead? How long until Harcroft and Wade learned I'd bolted?

I so needed my computer. If I could find a hotel we could hide in for awhile, I'd want to get online, learn more about Morton

Leringer. Who was in Raleigh? Someone who could help me out of this mess?

Without my laptop, I felt more helpless than ever.

My brain churned and churned—until I realized I was already nearing El Camino. Had I passed an open grocery store? Too late. Turning north on El Camino, I headed toward the familiar Safeway.

"I have to *go*." Mom's face pinched.

"I know. We're almost there."

"Why don't we just go *home*?"

"Mom, please—!" I bit down on my frustration, fingers curling into my palms. This was not the time to lose patience with my mother.

Not the time for her to lose it either.

I would have to think of something to tell her. Something to keep her quiet and make her just . . . go along with me.

We reached the store and the near barren, huge parking lot. I pulled into a space and turned off the engine. Mom pulled her hat from the pocket of her coat and put it on.

"Mom, you can't wear that right now." Weren't we easy enough to spot already? The two of us looking disheveled, Mom in mismatched blue and green? What store employee wouldn't remember us if she sported her purple hat?

"Of course I can."

"No, you *can't*."

Her face started to crumble. "Why are you being so mean to me?"

Tears bit my eyes. I couldn't do this. Not with Mom. She'd fight me every minute.

"Listen." I touched her cheek. "We don't want people in the store to remember us, okay? And if you wear your hat, you're always so pretty in it, people will remember."

Her eyebrows knit. "What does it matter?"

"Remember that man in our house? He had a gun. He was going to kill you. If he comes looking for us, we don't want people remembering they've seen us."

"Oh." Confusion twisted my mother's face, then her eyes caught a glimmer. "Was he trying to find out about Morton's daughter in Raleigh?"

"Yes, Mom. He was."

My mother's lips firmed. "Well, we just won't tell him."

"That's right. So we don't want him—and the other men he's working with—to know where we are. Because if they find us, they'll try to pull the information from us."

"They're bad people."

"Very bad."

"But they acted so nice when they came to visit."

So she'd recognized Samuelson. "They were just trying to trick us."

"Oh."

"Do you see why you can't wear your hat?"

"I do." Mouth set, Mom placed her hat on the floor of the car. Chin held high, as if she held back the forces of evil, Mom allowed me to herd her into the store, bare-headed.

After we'd hit the bathroom I thought about food. Mom would be hungry in a few hours. Hustling her around as best I could, I grabbed some donuts—not very nutritious, but Mom loved them—and crackers and cheese. And two large water bottles.

At the counter, we were both silent. Mom refused to even look at the checker, as if the man were a personal spy for the "bad people." Still, there were very few customers in the store. And we didn't look like typical night-shift shoppers. How easy it would be for someone to remember us.

I hustled Mom to the car, placing the food in the backseat. One water bottle remained up front for us to share.

We headed south on El Camino. Back up Woodside to 280, then south. I didn't know where I was going or where I would stop. But we would at least be a little closer to Emily. Not that we could see her, but I couldn't bear to flee in the opposite direction.

"Hannah." Mom's voice quivered. "We're in trouble, aren't we?"

"I'm afraid so."

She pondered my answer. "'Lord, be gracious to us. We wait for You. Be our strength every morning and our salvation in time of trouble.'"

With that, Mom leaned against her door and soon fell asleep, her mouth open.

Around San Jose, I-280 ended. I took Highway 101 south and in time turned east on 152 toward I-5, the long, flat freeway to Southern California. Every car that neared us made me tense. Was it them? Would they try to run me off the road? Before long my back and neck ached.

I tried to sort things out but came up with the same questions. Again and again I searched for the ability to trust the sheriff's department so I could call them for help. I so wanted to believe they hadn't told the "FBI agents" I'd copied that video. But I kept returning to the picture of Samuelson clutching my computer and backup drive even as he staggered out of my house.

I hit I-5 and turned south.

The time neared 6:30 a.m. My scratchy eyes fighting to stay open, I took an exit that led to a chain hotel. No way could I drive any longer. And the sun would rise all too soon, making our car all the easier to spot. I pulled into a parking space and cut the engine. Mom slept on. I aimed a dull gaze at her, biting my lip. Leaving her in the car was risky. If she woke up alone, she'd be frightened and might wander off. If I took her inside she'd be safe, but together she and I would be much more identifiable if anyone came looking for us.

I started the car again and moved to a space I could watch through the hotel door. With any luck, the employee behind the counter couldn't see the car as well as I.

Holding my breath, I opened the car door, purse in hand, and slid out. Then I remembered the large gun in my tote bag, lying on the backseat. Couldn't leave Mom with that.

Couldn't take it inside, either. What if somehow I was caught with it? Plus I had my own gun in my purse. They'd think I was out to rob the place.

The bag could go in the trunk. But closing the trunk might wake Mom.

I hesitated, then leaned over the front seat and picked up the bag. I pulled my body out of the car and eased my door shut. Peered through the window. Mom didn't move.

The few steps to the hotel flamed my body with heat. Was the shape of the gun evident through the tote bag? What if a hotel employee called the police? What if Rutger was following me this very moment? Everything within me wanted to throw wild looks over my shoulder. Was he just waiting until we slipped into a room so he could break down the door? My nerves sizzled and my breaths puffed.

How could I live like this?

A tiny voice in my head hissed that I had it all wrong. I'd fallen down a rabbit hole of pure paranoia. My problem wasn't Bad People chasing me. It was my own delirious brain. Bad People I could run from. My brain, I could not.

Sweat popped out on my forehead as I opened the door.

The small lobby sat empty and foreboding. A young woman behind the counter shot me a penetrating look, as if she saw right through me. The sound of a TV filtered from the employee office behind the counter. I tried to smile. It came out lopsided.

"I need a room for today."

"Today? As in checking out at noon?" Her name badge read *Tina*.

Of course, what was I thinking? My heart sank. Check-in would be around 3 p.m. "I don't know if we'll be out by noon. So maybe I should say for today and tonight." Would that cost me double? My cash would run out so fast.

"So, checking out by noon tomorrow?"

Not that we'd stay here—or anywhere—near that long. "Yes."

The hotel had an available room. Two queen beds. "I'll take it." I slipped a glance out the front door. Mom still seemed to be sleeping.

"Okay, I'll need a credit card."

Credit card. That could be traced. "I'd like to pay in cash. I don't . . . believe in credit cards."

Well, not at the moment, anyway.

"Okaaay. How about a bank debit card?"

I swallowed. A debit card could be traced too.

"It's just to hold funds against your room. If you pay in cash tomorrow, we'll release the hold right away."

But wouldn't that hold show up in my bank account immediately? Even quicker than a credit card charge.

I stood there, vacillating. Feeling my face go hot. "Can I just give you cash to hold against the room?"

"We'd have to take money for three days. Gives us a cushion against incidental charges."

Three days. That would be close to $375.00. "Will I get back what I don't use?"

"Yes." Tina regarded me steadily, but I could almost hear her mind working. What kind of person didn't want to show her credit or debit card? Everything I was doing was making me more memorable.

Then it hit my tired brain. Even with cash, she'd want to see my driver's license. I'd still be traceable. But only if the Bad People managed to trace me to this hotel. If I didn't use a credit or debit card, that would be so much harder.

I nodded. Tried to smile again. "Okay. I'll give you cash for three days." I tilted my purse as I pulled out my wallet so Tina wouldn't see the gun inside. With trembling fingers I handed over the money. Had Tina noticed? "Sorry. I've been driving too long."

Her head dipped. "You do look tired. Let's get you a room so you can rest."

She asked to see my driver's license. With reluctance, I showed it to her.

"Okay, Mrs. Shire."

I winced at the sound of my name.

Tina gave me the plastic room key in a small holder with the unit number written on it. "You can come through here and go down the hall, or you can park down there a ways"—she pointed—"and go through the outside door closer to the room."

"Great. Thanks."

I got out of there as fast as possible without seeming obvious. As I slid behind the car wheel, Mom still slept. How I envied her that ability.

I drove toward the door at the end of the hotel, turned around, and backed into a parking space. Didn't want my license plate blaring out to the world.

Wait. A license plate sat on the front of my car as well.

I closed my eyes, bringing two fingers to my forehead. Such a little thing, yet so big. So indicative that I had no idea what I was doing.

With some difficulty I woke Mom and got her moving. I gave her the bag of groceries to carry. I gathered my purse, her suitcase, our coats, the tote bag. Loaded down, I struggled to find enough fingers to push the key into the slot and open the outside door into the hotel. When we reached our room, I had to manage the feat a second time.

Once inside I locked and bolted the door. Dropped everything but the tote on the floor. The bed looked so inviting it almost made me cry.

Mom looked around, lost. "Is there a bathroom?"

"In here." I walked over and turned on the light for her. She went inside and closed the door.

I hid the tote bag under a pillow on one of the beds. Then sat down hard. Now what? We had so little. I didn't even have a tooth-brush or change of clothes. All I had were two guns, one of them not registered to me. And I had a mother suffering from dementia with needs I wouldn't be able to meet.

I had to call Emily, tell her we were okay. Why hadn't I found a pay phone before checking into a hotel?

And I needed a different car. Couldn't keep driving my own with people looking for it. But I couldn't rent a car without leaving a trail.

Plus I'd soon need more money. But how would I get it without leaving a paper trail?

My head hung. Hot tears stung my eyes. *Lord, please help me. I have no idea what to do.*

Mom shuffled out of the bathroom. Her face drooped with tiredness. I pulled myself together and stood. "We have to call Emily. She's worried about us."

"Okay. I'll tell her we're fine."

"But we have to use a pay phone."

"Oh." Mom frowned. "Why?"

"It's safest."

"Oh."

I should have done this first. How stupid of me. Now we'd have to go back out and search for a phone at a gas station. More driving around—as the sun rose. More danger.

Purse over my arm—with gun still inside—I mobilized the two of us and headed for the parking lot. We both wore our coats against the chilled air. In the car I drove to the gas station across the road, already open for the day, but saw no pay phone.

On the other side of the exit was a second station, also open. Two cars were getting gas. There I spotted a phone—and my heart surged. I pulled up in front of it.

"Stay in here, Mom, I'll just be a minute."

"I want to talk—"

"Next time. Right now I have to hurry."

I got out before she could protest.

Breath on hold, I fingered multiple quarters from my wallet and fed the first into the slot. It had been so long since I'd used a pay phone, I hardly remembered how they worked. Or if I had enough coins.

I dialed Emily's number and was told how much money to put in for the first three minutes. I fed in the quarters, the *ching-ching* rattling my nerves. As her line rang I prayed she'd answer the unfamiliar number.

"Hello?" Emily sounded on edge.

"It's me."

"Oh! Where *are* you?"

"We're at a hotel off I-5. Not far down from Highway 152. I'm using a pay phone."

"No one followed you?"

"Not that I could see."

Emily breathed over the line. "Is Grand okay?"

"Yes. Confused, but okay." I glanced over my shoulder. Mom still sat in the car.

"Mom, listen, this is real bad. I watched the video."

"What?"

"The video. I downloaded it from our online backup account."

No. My chin sank toward my chest. "Emily, I didn't want you to do that! I don't want you involved in this."

"Mom, I *make* videos all day long, remember? Meanwhile, you're out there running and hiding and scaring me to death. What did you expect me to do, just hang around and wait to hear from you? I'd go crazy. And it's a good thing I didn't."

I swallowed hard. My brain was too tired to think of what consequences her action might have. And I didn't like the raw fear in her voice.

"So I watched it over and over—and saw something. At the bottom of the video there's noise. You probably didn't see it. Sort of looks like a blurry picture or static on a TV. I brought my computer into work and used our equipment to study it more. Once I could make out the static, I saw it's a long series of numbers and letters. Looks like an encrypted message."

I blinked. Not once had I noticed any static on the video.

What to ask first? "Can you break the encryption?"

"No. You need the key."

"Oh."

"What if that's what Morton Leringer was trying to tell you? He gave you the flash drive, right? Maybe he was trying to tell you where to find the key."

I took a deep breath. My whole body felt weighted. "Maybe. He did try to say some word that started with *K* or *C*. Maybe the key's in Raleigh?"

"Don't know."

My eyes closed. If I weren't so tired, I could *think*. "So why are these people after me? I have a video that I can't understand, with encrypted data I can't read. What threat am I?"

Two new cars pulled into the gas station. I checked out the drivers, then turned away.

"Because they think Morton told you something. If he was killed for trying to stop people from committing some terrorist act, they'd be scared he told you where to find the key before he died. Maybe that key could stop the event."

Emily's words clawed through me. "Terrorist act?"

"I Googled a machine like the one in the video. It *is* a power generator, just like that deputy said. And then I found another video online that's a lot like this one. Guess what it's about? It was a CNN report from some years ago on how a power generator could be hacked into by terrorists and blown up. I think these guys who are chasing you are going to do that."

Oh. *Oh.* "You mean they want to shut down electricity." My words dropped like stones. "Why would Leringer be involved in such a thing? I researched him and found all the companies he owns. He looks like a successful businessman, not a terrorist."

"I don't think he is a terrorist. I think he found out about this plan—whatever it is—and was killed for it. The words he said to you are about stopping it."

No wonder Morton had been so insistent. So terrified.

"And I told Harcroft and Wade everything Morton said. Now they want to kill me too."

Both of those men must be in on it.

My knees went weak. My mother and I were caught up in some heinous terrorist plot? Those people would as soon kill you as look at you if you got in their way.

Which was exactly what they'd tried to do.

"Mom, something else. I should have told you before, but I was pretty much in shock. No one at the sheriff's department had to tell anyone that you made a copy of the video. Those people could figure that out on their own. All they'd have to do is look at the properties of the file and see the date and time it was created."

What? My mind reeled more. Why hadn't I thought of that?

"So you should go to the police right now. You don't have to be scared of them. You have *a lot* of reasons to be scared of the other guys. Besides, Wade and Harcroft need to know all this. If someone's planning a terrorist act, they have to stop it."

I shook my head. "Emily, they have the same video you have. In fact, they've got the original. If you could figure out it holds an encrypted message, don't you think they could too? They must have shown it to their techs right away."

And if the Half Moon Bay sheriff's substation thought a terrorist act was about to occur, they wouldn't sit on that information. Wouldn't they call the FBI or somebody?

"Yeah," Emily said. "They might know. If they have the software to study it."

I hung on the phone, feeling sick. Split in two. I so wanted to believe I could go to the police right now and entrust myself and Mom into their protection. We wouldn't have to run. They'd put Mom and me somewhere until they caught these guys. But . . .

"Mom?"

"I'm here."

"Go to the police. Now."

I licked my lips. "I'm not sure I can."

"Why?"

How to explain the feeling in my gut? I thought over everything that had happened. How from the very beginning Harcroft had seemed suspicious when I insisted Leringer hadn't said anything to me. How soon the fake FBI agents had shown up my house. How soon Samuelson had returned after I'd told Wade and Harcroft everything.

"Mom, talk to me!"

For the next few minutes, I tried to explain. "And think about it. Those fake FBI agents could have killed me and your grandmother when they first came to the house. But they didn't. They tried to kill me *after* I'd met with Harcroft and Wade. After I'd told those two men everything Morton said."

"Mom, you really think some sheriff's deputy—"

"I don't know, Emily. That's just it. I *don't know*. So—what if I go to the authorities? And what if Wade or Harcroft *are* working with the terrorists? Isn't that what terrorists try to do—recruit insiders? How perfect would that be."

"And what if they're not? And you keep running, with *no* protection, and those guys find you?" Emily's voice bent upward. "You and Grand are both *dead*!"

My heart thrashed. "I don't know. I don't know what to do."

"Go to the police, that's what!"

I squeezed my eyes shut. "Once that's done, there's no going back. I think I should just return to the hotel for now. For an hour or two. Let me think this through."

Behind me a car door opened. I turned to see Mom getting out. I lowered the phone to my shoulder. "Mom, stay there."

She pushed to her feet.

"Please, Mom! I'll just be a minute."

She walked toward me, leaving her door open, the car's inside light shining. Might as well send a message to our pursuers: Here we are!

"Is she okay?" Emily's voice.

"I want to talk to my granddaughter." Mom approached, hand out for the receiver. My pulse beat in my throat. If I fought her, she could have a meltdown. She was tired enough. I could not risk her screams attracting attention from the customers getting gas. I thrust the phone into her hand. "Do it quickly, we have to go."

Mom took the phone in her gnarled fingers. Pressed the black plastic to her white head. "Emily?"

"Hi, Grand." I could just make out Emily's words. "You okay?"

"Awful tired. We're running, you know. From the Bad People. They want to hurt Morton's daughter in Raleigh. We have to get to her first and warn her. But it sure is tiring."

"Oh. Well, you do everything Mom tells you, okay? She knows what she's doing."

Yeah. Right.

I glanced around the station's parking area, then across the street. One car pulled away from a pump; another one pulled in behind. And here we stood, with our lit-up car. Who talked on pay phones anymore? Didn't we look out of place, just using the thing?

"Okay." Mom's voice wavered. "How are you, sweetie? You found a new boyfriend yet?"

I winced.

"No, Grand. I'm gonna take my time on this one."

"Problem is, you're just too good for all the men out there. They can't hold a candle to you."

"Thanks."

Mom sighed. Such exhaustion in that sound. "I need to go now. We'll talk again soon."

"Okay. Love you."

Mom handed the phone back to me, satisfied. I couldn't help but snatch it from her fingers. "Go sit in the car, please. And close the door so the light won't be on."

Amazingly, she obeyed.

The line clicked. An automated voice told me to put in more money. I blew out a breath in frustration, then rummaged for the coins and shoved them in. "Emily, hello?"

"I'm here. Mom! Go to the police!"

"I have to think about this first. If Harcroft or Wade is working with these terrorists, and I ask the police for protection—I'm dead. You understand that? The first thing the police will do is contact those two men. This is their case. I *have* to be sure."

Emily sighed. "Well, think it through in a hurry, okay?"

She still didn't get it. But how could I expect her to? She hadn't seen what I had.

The February chill bit through my coat. My head throbbed, and the unfamiliar phone in my sweaty hand spun a feeling of abandonment through me.

How in the world had I gotten to this place?

"Mom, you hear me?"

"Yes. I'll call you again in a few hours."

"Please be careful. I'm so scared."

"I will. I love you."

I hung up the phone, the sudden break in connection with my daughter slicing through me. As I started the car seconds later I fought the overwhelming terror that I would never speak to her again.

Chapter 17

Five-thirty a.m.—and Roz had still not shown up. And he wasn't answering his cell phone. Stone had spent the last half-hour pacing, swearing, and kicking the furniture. Why had he sent anyone else to that woman's house? He should have done the job himself. Except that he'd needed to be on the phone to other FreeNow members scattered across the country. Now that they were below the twenty-four-hour mark, no one in the organization was sleeping.

His cell rang. Stone snatched it up and saw Tex's ID. Some time ago he'd contacted Tex—"Agent Rutger"—and told him to look for Roz. "Yeah?"

"He's disappeared. No sign of him anywhere. Or his car."

Stone's fingers fisted. Another traitor among them. What if there were more?

"Get's worse," Tex said.

What could be worse at this point? "Yeah?"

"There are no bodies at Hannah Shire's house."

Stone let that sink in. "Maybe he got rid of them."

"No time. Police got a shots-fired call. They were there fast."

"What? Why didn't he use a silencer?"

"I don't know. He has one."

Stone tipped his shaved head toward the ceiling. Shots fired—and no bodies? "Where are the women?"

"Disappeared too. They took off in her car."

Stone's heart jolted. He put a hand to his temple. This could not be happening. "They got *away*?"

"Looks like it."

Stone sat down hard on his couch. Roz had sounded strange when he called. Like he was having trouble breathing. Had Hannah Shire shot him with her own weapon? That would explain the neighbors hearing it.

What kind of woman *was* this?

"Police found blood drops in the house," Tex said. "Good news is, local cops don't have a clue what's going on."

She must have shot Roz. Stone dropped his chin. That was a major loss. Roz and Tex were Stone's own recruits, allowed to work directly beneath him. Those kinds of men were hard to find, needing that certain balance of deep discontent and a thrumming drive to fill their souls with purpose. Roz was older, more mature. But Tex was intelligent as well as burning loyal.

What happened? How had Roz let the two women escape?

Whatever the case, Hannah Shire and her mother were alive.

Stone thought back to Roz's phone call. Talk about lies. The man had to know even then he wasn't coming in. He'd better run like a desert jackrabbit. No place on this earth could hide him now. FreeNow traitors all met the same end.

Stone cursed. "I don't want to think what could happen if those women know too much and go to the wrong people."

Meanwhile the clock ticked.

"Let me go after them," Tex said. "We should have killed them right away. I won't let them get away this time."

Stone grunted. Tex had already killed Nooley for the man's failure to get the video back and silence Leringer in time. Tex had shown no hesitation at the order. But to one hundred percent redeem himself, he needed to fix his own mistake.

"I'm sure you won't let them get away again." Stone kept his voice low. "You got twelve hours to track them down and beat out of them everything they know. Then kill them. And Tex?"

"Yeah?"

"Fail me, and you're dead."

Chapter 18

Emily's coworkers began arriving at the TriPoint Marketing offices around 8:00. She paid little attention. Since her mother's phone call she'd been researching Morton Leringer. Like her mom said, Leringer owned a lot of businesses under his umbrella corporation. But what was his connection to Raleigh? She couldn't find anything on that. And she didn't see anything that made him sound like a terrorist. Why would he want to hurt the country that had made him so rich?

Her muscles were like rocks, and her hand all cramped from holding the mouse too hard. Every minute that passed made her more worried about her mom and Grand. Were they safe at the hotel? Was somebody in the sheriff's department really out to get them?

Emily heard people greeting each other, making coffee.

A big-shot like Leringer would make news if he was murdered. Emily searched CNN.com for the story. A video with a frozen picture of Morton Leringer on a stage caught her eye. It had been posted a few hours ago. She clicked *Play*. Leringer began to move, his audio turned off. Emily stared at the man her mother had tried to help.

"Morton Leringer, owner and CEO of ML Corporation," said the voice-over, "died in the emergency room of a Moss Beach, California hospital yesterday as a result of a stab wound. The coroner has ruled the manner of death as homicide. Police later searched his nearby home in Half Moon Bay, on the Pacific coast below San Francisco, and discovered a second victim—Nathan Eddington, age forty-eight. Eddington was an employee of StarrCom, a Bay-Area-based security company owned by ML Corporation."

Emily leaned forward, mouth open. The video showed a body bag being carried out through a huge front door and down porch steps.

"The homicides are being investigated by the San Mateo County Sheriff's Coastside Patrol Bureau, which serves over sixty percent of the county, including Half Moon Bay. The Moss Beach Substation is the largest law enforcement facility on the coast, staffed with twenty-seven full-time deputy sheriffs, four sergeants, and one lieutenant. So far the substation has not asked for outside help with its investigation. And they are speaking little to the media, saying only that they are following leads."

The video ended. Emily stared at her monitor, thoughts whirling. StarrCom. A security company.

What kind of security?

Hunched over the keyboard, she searched for the company's website and jumped to the home page.

"StarrCom Security," read the header. "Keeping the World Safe." Emily leaned back in her chair, gaze fixed on her desk. Had Nathan Eddington, through the company's own security, discovered a terrorist plot to take out power stations?

Whoever was behind this had killed two people already. And they'd tried to kill two more.

Where were Mom and Grand?

"Hey, Emily!"

She jumped. A long, lean face grinned down at her from above her cubicle wall. Dave Raines, her mentor.

"Whoa." Dave raised his Groucho Marx eyebrows. "Too much coffee already?"

Emily shook her head.

Dave eyed her. "What's up?"

She hesitated. "Can you keep a secret?"

"Depends on how much you pay me."

"I need you to look at a video. Just lasts a minute." She thought she may have seen more pixelation toward the beginning but couldn't be sure.

"Okay."

"But on your computer. You've got better software."

"Let's go." Dave gestured with his head.

"Thanks. Let me copy it to a flash drive first."

"All right." Her mentor disappeared.

Emily copied the file, then snatched up the piece of paper on which she'd written the long sequence of numbers and letters from the video. She hurried into Dave's office.

"There's noise at the end," she told him as he put in the flash drive. "Looks like an encrypted message. I wrote down the sequence."

"What? Who's your client, the CIA?"

"Not a client."

He eyed her.

"But now I'm wondering if there's something at the beginning. Just a little flash. I can't enhance it enough to tell."

"Okay. Let's see what we got." Dave pressed the Play arrow.

Emily leaned over his shoulder and watched with him. "There's no audio."

As it started, Dave stiffened. He leaned closer, watching closely. At the end he gave her a hard look. "You have any idea what this is?"

She looked away. How much to tell him? "Maybe a power generator?"

"It *is* a power generator. A very sick one."

"How do you know?"

"My father worked for a power company."

"Oh." Dave's father had died a year ago. "Didn't know that."

"I've seen these machines up close. This kind of machine controls an entire power station. But something's made this generator go out of control."

Right. Just like she'd seen in that CNN video. "Would that . . . so what would happen?"

"The station goes out. Which means millions of people lose power."

Emily rubbed her arms. "Could it be fixed quickly?"

Dave stared at the monitor. "This doesn't look good. Where'd you get this, Emily?"

She opened her mouth, then closed it.

"If this is real, it wouldn't be like some wire going down. It could cause what my dad called a cascade effect. If a central power station goes dark, it can take another one down nearby. Which takes another one down, and on and on. A whole region could go black."

Emily sucked in her bottom lip.

Dave turned to look her in the eye. "Where'd you get this?"

"I . . . someone gave it to my mom."

"Your mom. Why?"

"I don't know exactly."

Dave's gaze would not waver. "You look scared to death."

No kidding.

"Is this some kind of joke?"

Emily swallowed. Her mom hadn't wanted her pulled into this. Now she understood. She felt the same about Dave. "Please. For now, can you just . . . Did you see the static at the beginning?"

Dave gave her another long look. "Yes. At the left side, bottom, about three seconds in."

Emily's nerves wavered. "I need to know what it says."

Dave nodded. "So do I. Then you're going to tell me what this is all about."

Chapter 19

Back in the hotel I could not sleep. Mom had crawled beneath the covers of her bed, still clothed, and dozed off right away. I lay on top of my bed staring at the ceiling.

What should I do?

The question spun around inside me until I thought I would go mad. The wrong decision could cost us our lives.

And meanwhile terrorists just might be planning to attack the electrical grid somewhere in America. If that was true, how long from now? How could they be stopped?

I might have *killed* a man.

The thought hit me like a rogue wave. What if I did? Me, who worked with a doctor. We *saved* lives.

But that man could have killed my mother. I'd do anything to protect her.

I didn't have to shoot him in the *chest*.

What had I done? He could be somebody's husband. Father. Had I taken away a woman's *husband*?

Tears filled my eyes and ran down my temples. Jeff wouldn't have wanted me to kill someone. Not really. Just protect myself.

Thou shalt not kill. One of the Ten Commandments I'd never expected to break. How did I even ask for forgiveness for something as terrible as that?

I rolled over on my side, sick in my stomach. *God, forgive me. I didn't want to kill him! Please let him live. Let the police find him and take him to jail, away from me and Mom. But let him live.*

How could I have done all this? In one day I'd lied to a sheriff's deputy, then tried—maybe succeeded—to kill a man. How could the honest, peaceful person I'd been all my life cross such a line, just like that?

Guilt poured over me, glazed with fear of the unknown. What would I have to do next? What might I descend to?

I tried to pray again but couldn't do much more than plead for help. And demand answers. *God, why are You doing this to me? Isn't it enough that I lost Jeff?*

What little energy I had drained out with the tears. Despite the grief, after some time I found myself drifting off to sleep . . .

Out of nowhere I thought of Mom's caretaker, Dorothy. My eyes dragged open. I checked the digital clock. Almost 8:00. She would be arriving at the house any minute now. When I didn't answer the door, she'd use her key. What would she think, going through the empty house? Would she call the police to report us missing?

Or would police already be there? The surveillance deputy must have told them I was long gone.

What about my coworker, Sonja, and Dr. Nicholson? What would they think when I didn't show up at the office? I'd *never* failed to be at work on time.

Hard as these questions were, they were better than wondering if I'd killed a man.

Thickness spread through my limbs again, weighing me down.

My body wanted to sleep from sheer exhaustion. But my mind could not rest.

The news. I should turn on the TV and see if I could find anything more about Morton Leringer's death. Or the break-in at my house.

What if there was news about the man I'd shot? And he *was* dead?

I hesitated.

Scraping up bits of courage, I forced myself off the bed to pick up the remote near the TV. I hit the power button and found the channel for ABC's *Good Morning America*. That show would cut to local news numerous times. I kept the volume low while Mom slept.

Hands fisted, I sat on the edge of the bed, watching the screen with bleary eyes.

God, please forgive me if I killed him.

The show dragged on. I had to use the restroom. I headed into the bathroom, leaving the door open, ears still cocked toward the TV. Still my tired mind managed to wander—until I was washing my hands and heard Morton Leringer's name.

I locked eyes with myself in the mirror, then smacked off the water. My feet took me out to the room. The reporter who'd shown up at Morton's accident stood in a field.

". . . happened here yesterday on Tunitas Creek Road in Half Moon Bay." She swept out her arm. "The sheriff's department has confirmed that Leringer died not from injuries sustained in the accident, but from a stab wound in the back. The so-called 'accident' was called into 911 by Hannah Shire, age fifty-five, of San Carlos."

My driver's license picture appeared on the screen. I sank onto the bed.

"When police later searched Leringer's home last night, they found a second victim, Nathan Eddington, an employee of Leringer's security company, StarrCom, in Menlo Park."

A *second* murder?

Wait. Nathan Eddington. Wade had asked if I knew that man.

". . . in this quickly escalating case, a third victim was discovered early this morning—a sheriff's deputy who was surveilling the home of Hannah Shire. His name has not yet been released to the media."

What? The deputy who'd been watching my house was *also* dead?

"Police now view Mrs. Shire as a person of interest in all three murders and seek to question her. Mrs. Shire fled her home in the night, taking along her elderly mother, who suffers from dementia. The sheriff's department is asking your help in locating Hannah Shire. She is driving a dark blue Ford Escort—"

I lunged for the remote and punched off the TV. Couldn't bear to listen any longer. For a moment I stared at the wall, trying to breathe. Three homicides. *Three.* That deputy was dead because he'd been trying to protect *me.* I couldn't bear the thought.

And they thought *I* killed him.

We had to get out of the hotel. Now. How long until Tina, the young woman behind the counter, saw the news?

What if she'd already seen it? The TV in the back office had been on when I checked in.

My head jerked toward Mom. Sleeping so soundly. She'd be almost impossible to move.

I had to check out first. Which was a real gamble, showing my face. Or should we just flee? But I'd be leaving all that deposit money behind. We'd *need* that money.

A minute passed, indecision twisting around my throat.

Next thing I knew, I was on my feet. I grabbed my purse and the door key, and eased out into the hallway. Twice I almost turned around. The minute Tina saw my face, I'd know if she'd heard the news. I reached the front counter, heart slamming in my chest. Tina looked up at me and smiled. My tongue fought to form words. "We need to check out now."

We. I'd said *we.*

"So soon?" She raised her eyebrows. "You couldn't have gotten much sleep."

"I know. But I've got a long way to go yet."

Tina keyed her computer to bring up my account. "Where are you going?"

A natural question anyone may have asked. But the words clawed at me. In an instant I could picture a false FBI badge flashed, demands to know what I'd said, where I might be headed.

"Michigan." The name popped out of my mouth. I didn't even know anyone in Michigan.

"Oh. That is a long way."

She slid me the bill. "I have to charge you for a full day. But I can give you back the cash for the second and third days."

"That's wonderful. Thank you." I slipped the money into my wallet, hoping she wouldn't see my hands shake. "I'll leave the key in the room, okay? I'll be out in just a few minutes."

"Okay."

My knees felt like Jell-O as I walked away.

In the room I threw back the bedcovers and shook Mom hard to wake her. She fought me, arms waving. "No," she slurred, "I don't wanna get up."

"Mom. We have to go. Now."

"I don't *want.* Too tired. And hungry. I want to go *home.*"

I pulled her into a sitting position. Her white hair stood out in all directions, her mouth turned down. Her clothes were wrinkled. "I'll feed you, okay? Let's just get in the car first."

And go where, Hannah? Wouldn't we be more vulnerable in my car, with everyone looking for it?

"No. I . . . ." Mom looked around the room, confounded. "Where are we? Where's my bed?"

"Come on. I'll tell you when we're on our way."

"I'm *not coming*."

"Yes, you *are*!"

Forcefully, I swung her feet toward the floor.

"Stop it, Hannah!" Mom tried to push me away.

"Shhhh." I gripped her hands, forcing them together. Stood over her, breathing hard, my throat closing. Mom in another screaming fit would attract a lot of attention. And she'd take her own time calming down. By then it would be too late.

"Listen, Mom." I felt myself sway, too tired, too overwrought. How would I even drive? "Remember the Bad People? Remember how they're chasing us? That's why we have to go. They could be here any minute."

Mom's head tilted, her confused eyes finding mine. "How do you know?"

"It was on the TV news. Remember that reporter? Now every-one's looking for us."

Three men—dead.

"That reporter knows the Bad People?"

"No. But she's not helping us either."

"I never liked her." Mom listed to one side, her eyelids drooping. "I want to sleep."

"You *can't*." I looked around the room wildly. How to persuade her? "How about if I get you a donut? Remember, I bought some at the store."

Mom scratched her temple. "I want tea."

On the dresser sat a coffee maker. Where were the tea bags? But we had no time for that. We were sitting ducks in this room.

"I'll get you some tea as soon as I can. Promise. But we've got to get moving now. *Please*."

I pulled a glazed donut from its white sack and forced it into Mom's hand. "Here. Eat this while I get our stuff."

Mom blinked at the donut as if she'd never seen one before. "I have to go to the bathroom." She set the donut on her bed.

Now *I* wanted to scream. "Okay. Go. Hurry!"

With both hands I pulled her to her feet.

While she was in the bathroom I gathered our things, including the tote bag with Samuelson's gun. Every sound of footsteps in the hall brought me to a halt. Had someone seen the TV? Was a policeman coming for us?

By the time Mom emerged, I was trembling all over. "Come on, Mom, we have to go now."

"Where's my donut?"

I snatched up the donut and thrust it in her hand. "Let's go."

She frowned at her feet. "Where are my shoes?"

"In the suitcase. You can put them on in the car."

Mom's voice rose to a shriek. "I want my shoes!"

My throat cinched tight. We'd never get out of here. I yanked the shoes out and threw them at her feet. "There!"

Mom leaned over, steadying herself against the nightstand. Her left foot inched out and sought its shoe.

My heart pounded and my mouth went dry. I wanted to shake Mom into action. I wanted to keep her alive. *Come on, come on!*

How far would we get before a cop pulled us over? A *person of interest*!? Harcroft and Wade knew I didn't kill Morton. No question now one of them—or both—was working with the terrorists. This was their way of using all of law enforcement to find me.

Mom's right foot slid into a shoe. She straightened. "I want to eat my donut first."

"In the car, Mom."

"No, now."

I stuck my face in hers. "*Do* you want us caught? Do you want me to go to jail?"

Her face blanched. "They want to put you in jail?"

"They're saying I killed Morton."

She drew back her head. *"You?"*

"Yes."

"The Bad People say that?"

A half-crazed laugh sputtered out of me. Bad People, Good People—they were all the same.

"Mom." I swallowed hard. "If we don't get out of here now, they will take me away. And you will be alone. *Do* you understand?"

Her nostrils flared in fright. She turned and clumped toward the door, back hunched.

The trip down the hallway to the outside exit seemed endless. Twice we passed people. I looked down each time, my chest on fire.

At the door, I struggled to open it with my hands so full. A man stepped out of his room, spotted my predicament, and came over to help. My legs turned to water.

He pushed open the door and held it wide. "There you go, ladies."

"Thank you," I managed, my face averted.

By the time we reached the car I couldn't get enough oxygen. Somehow I managed to unlock the doors and toss our things in the backseat. Mom's purple hat still sat on the floor in the front.

I buckled Mom into her seat belt and threw myself behind the wheel. Started the engine with clumsy fingers. My foot wanted to press to the floor. Just get us away from the hotel, on the road.

As if we'd be any safer there.

As I drove out of the parking lot, an epiphany hit. My one remaining aunt lived somewhere in Fresno, about an hour away. I had little contact with her other than exchanging Christmas letters. Still, we were on good terms. Aunt Margie was a widow, spunky and a bit on the rebellious side, even in her eighties. Maybe she would help us.

On the road I forced myself to drive the speed limit, glancing all directions for a police car.

We hit I-5. I turned north to backtrack a little before we could head east toward Fresno. My back was like steel. I hunched forward, spine not touching the seat.

Mere minutes passed before Mom declared she had to use the bathroom again. She sat with her arms crossed, a beleaguered expression on her face. Confused and scared. An elderly woman who'd been driven from her own home and bed. Rage flew around inside me. It was one thing to do this to me. But to my *mother*.

I patted her arm, forcing my voice to sound even. "I'll stop soon. I promise."

"Why are we in the car?"

"The Bad People. Remember?"

"Oh." She looked around. "Why are they bad?"

"Mom. They tried to kill us."

She blinked at that. "Where are we going?"

"You remember Margie, Dad's brother's wife?"

"She smells like roses."

I almost smiled. "That's the one."

Two exits up I spotted a sign for a McDonalds. A fast-food place would be less likely to have a television. I craned my neck toward the restaurant. How many cars in the parking lot?

Maybe five. No police.

"Mom, I'm going to stop for you in just a minute. But you'll have to move fast, can you do that? It's dangerous."

"Because of the Bad People?"

"Yes."

She pressed her lips together, her head wagging. "I can move fast when I have to."

We pulled into a parking spot toward the back of the restaurant. I hustled Mom inside and back out in under five minutes. Had to be some kind of record.

A short time later we turned off I-5 onto Highway 152. A much smaller road with fewer cars. My lungs expanded a little.

Mom rubbed her belly. "I want another donut."

"They're in the backseat. Can you reach them?"

"No." She sounded petulant. "I need water."

"In the backseat too." Why in the world hadn't I left them up front?

She turned to look at me. Her face looked so worn. "I need them now."

Tears of frustration bit my eyes. I stopped on the side of the road and pulled the donuts and water from the backseat. Crackers and cheese too. "Here." I placed it all at Mom's feet. "Sorry the water won't be real cold."

Mom sighed. "I never got my tea."

"Maybe Aunt Margie will have some for you." *Please, God, let the woman be home.*

"That would be nice." Mom seemed to perk up at the thought. She took a drink from a water bottle. "I had a friend named Margie when I was young. She had bright red hair and three brothers. We used to play jacks."

Amazing, how Mom could remember things from the distant past. "Really? Who won?"

"She did. All the time. That girl had the nimblest fingers you ever saw."

A dark car was gaining behind us. My eyes flicked back and forth from the road to the rearview mirror. Was it a cop?

"Once she won thirteen games in a row. I remember that because it was such an unlucky number. For me, anyway."

The car drew closer. My fingers tightened on the steering wheel.

"Very sad thing. Margie died when we were twelve."

My heart bounced around in my chest. *Was* it a cop? "How terrible. What happened?"

Mom sniffed. "Her pet rat killed her."

"*What?*"

The car loomed closer. I could see lights on top. My pulse hitched.

Oh, God, please . . .

"She took his cage outside to give him some sun. Somehow he escaped. He skedaddled right across the lawn and into the street. Margie chased after him."

The cop stayed behind us. I slowed. He could have passed me. But he *stayed*.

Any minute now he'd pull us over. I'd be done. What would happen to us once we were taken back to the San Mateo County Sheriff's Department? Would one of the Bad People somehow get to my jail cell and kill me? What if they turned me over to the "FBI"? What would happen to Mom?

"Are you listening, Hannah?"

"Yes. Listening." My voice sounded distant to my own ears. The police car behind me may as well have been a fire-breathing monster.

"What did I say?"

Was the cop talking into his radio?

"Hannah!"

I swallowed hard. "Margie. Rat. Ran into the road."

"Yes, he did. And she ran after him. Didn't look for cars. She was hit." Mom sighed deeply. "I lost my good friend."

"I'm so sorry." The words came automatically. My arms shook.

"Me too."

The police car lights flicked on. He was pulling us over.

Chapter 20

Dave focused on his keyboard. Emily stood beside him, all nerves. "Okay," he said. "First we'll enhance the picture and slow everything down."

He brought up a different program on his computer and moved the video into it. Played it again.

"There!" Emily pointed. "I saw something."

"Yeah. But it's still too fast." Dave slowed the video more. And still more. The fourth time, the flash stayed longer, but they couldn't make out what it was.

"Time for the Superman enhance." He hit some keys, and they watched again. When the flash came up, he stopped the frame. Both of them leaned closer to the screen, frowning. "Let's throw in Batman." Dave punched keys, and the flash cleared some more. He leaned right up to the screen, trying to see. Then pulled back, shaking his head. "Maybe your eyes are better than mine."

Emily pushed him out of the way and looked. That close up, she could make out the words on three lines.

Phase 1: 2/25/13 WECC 7 PM RFC 10 PM
Phase 2: 2/26/13 Eastern
Phase 3: 2/27/13 Texas

Her eyes widened. She waved her fingers at Dave. "Get me a pen."

He put one into her hand. She wrote the message on the piece of paper she'd brought with her. Then straightened, her heart hammering.

What did this mean? Something about the electrical grid?

"Let me see." Dave reached for the paper. She tried to pull away, but too late. He snatched it from her hand and read.

His expression flattened. "February 25. That's today."

Emily's throat lumped over. "What's WECC? And RFC?"

"Let's Google it." Dave typed in the search. "Look. WECC. Western Electricity Coordinating Council."

Oh, no.

He typed in *RFC* and got a bunch of hits that didn't have anything to do with power.

"Try RFC electrical grid," Emily said.

Dave keyed it in. After looking at a few sites they had their answer. RFC—Reliability First Corporation. Part of the eastern electrical grid. There were only three main electrical grids in the U.S.: western, eastern, and Texas.

Emily looked at the paper. Phase 2 Eastern. Phase 3 Texas.

This couldn't be real.

The western grid, WECC, covered states as far east as Montana, Wyoming, Colorado, and New Mexico. It even went up into Canada. That was a *lot* of territory. The eastern grid was bigger yet. It was broken up into eight regions. "Why put the RFC with western?" Emily wondered. The RFC included Michigan, Indiana, Ohio, Pennsylvania, and some areas right above Virginia.

As soon as the words left her mouth, Emily knew the answer. She and Dave said it at the same time. "Washington, D.C.'s there."

They wanted to shut down electricity to the *government*?

This had to be a joke, right?

But . . . this video. Fake FBI agents showing up at her mom's door. A break-in at night just to take her mom's computer. And two men dead—Leringer and some guy who worked in his security company. When Emily looked at all that, how could she *not* believe this message was for real?

Leringer had told her mom to "be careful."

Dave looked like a deer in headlights. "Does somebody think the electrical grid's going to be hit here today? And in Washington? Then in the other areas?"

Think it was going to happen? More like they were going to *make* it happen. Starting today. In less than twelve hours. Emily felt her face go white. She had to tell the police. Or the FBI. *Now.* What if the sheriff's department hadn't figured this out?

Dave frowned at the series of numbers and letters she'd written on the paper. "Is this the sequence you saw at the end?"

Emily tried to take the paper from him. He held onto it. "Is it?"

"I—Yes."

Dave studied the numbers and letters some more.

"There's no way you can decode that, is there?" Emily knew the answer.

He shook his head. "Not my line of work. Who gave this video to your mom? And why?"

The western states and D.C. today. Tomorrow, the east. Then Texas. In two and a half days, the *whole country* would be dark.

"Emily. Talk to me."

What if Harcroft and Wade *were* working with the terrorists, like her mom said? And they found out that now she—Emily—knew all this? They'd send people after her too. All three of them would be dead.

"Dave." Emily looked down at him, her knees weak. "I have to go home."

He gazed at her. "Why won't you tell me what's going on?"

She shook her head. "I'm sorry. I can't." She had to get out of there. Had to do . . . *something*. "I need my flash drive."

Dave pulled it out and gave it to her. He didn't look too happy about it.

"And erase the copy in your program," she said. "Please."

He spread his hands—*why?*

"Just do it."

Dave's mouth firmed. "I don't think so."

Emily hung there, willing him to listen. Knowing he wouldn't. "At least don't tell anyone you've seen this." Tears pricked her eyes. "I mean it. *Nobody.*"

Dave shook his head. "*What* is going on, Emily? Is this for real?"

She reached for the piece of paper again. He let it go.

Clutching the flash drive and paper, she turned toward his office door. "I'll tell you when it's all over."

If she lived that long.

Chapter 21

The police car lights whirled.

My world seemed to narrow. So many horrible pictures flashed through my head—me in jail, Emily crying, Mom alone. The last was the worst. I *couldn't* let something happen to me, because Mom needed me. I'd fight to the death for her.

A siren whooped. With a leaden heart, I signaled and pulled over.

Mom looked at me. "What was that?"

I couldn't reply.

My eyes flicked back to the rearview mirror. The police car wasn't behind me.

What—?

In my peripheral vision, I saw him speed by.

I gawked at the car, disappearing down the road. Was he chasing someone else?

"Hannah, what are we doing?"

Thick relief weakened me, the relief of waking from a horrible nightmare. I dropped my chin toward my chest.

"Hannah?"

I tried to breathe.

"Are you sick?"

"No, Mom. I'm . . . fine."

"You don't look fine."

I raised my head. "I just needed to let the police car pass. He was after somebody."

Mom pulled in the sides of her mouth. "At least it wasn't you."

A sick little laugh pushed up my throat. "Yeah."

"Well, good then." She raised her shoulders and let them fall. "Let's go. I want my tea."

I pulled back onto the road, my body numb. Within a minute I realized something. That policeman must not have heard the notification about me and my car. Yet. But he could at any time. When he did, would he remember seeing us?

Muscles wooden, I drove. The exit for Highway 99, leading to Fresno, seemed to take forever to reach. I turned south on it, watching my car eat up the road. I longed for it to gobble faster. Sheer willpower—and the fear of attracting another policeman's attention—kept me from flooring the accelerator.

We reached the outskirts of town. Here we were in the most danger, with police cars liable to come along at any time. My heart beat harder, and my throat felt parched.

"Are we there?" Mom plucked at her pants, a sign of uneasiness.

"Almost."

"Can I have my tea?"

"I hope so, Mom."

"And a nap?"

"That would be great, wouldn't it."

I had no idea where my aunt lived. It had been years since I visited her.

Slipping down a busy street, I looked for a 7-Eleven or gas station. Something with a pay phone. I could swear my car pulsed with light and sound. Everyone who saw it would be reaching for a phone to call the police.

What if my aunt had seen the news? Would she turn me in the moment I called?

Maybe I shouldn't do this.

But what, then?

Blocks went by before I spotted a phone at a Quik Stop. I turned into the parking lot and cut the engine. "Mom." I looked her in the eye. "It's very important you stay in the car. I'm going to try to call Aunt Margie."

"Who?"

"Aunt Margie. Remember?"

"Oh. Roses."

"You'll stay in the car?"

She shrugged. "Okay."

Praying she wouldn't change her mind, I hurried to the pay phone and looked up Aunt Margie's number—and found it listed.

Thank You, God.

I punched in the number and turned around, watching Mom and the street as the phone rang. One ring. Two. My eyes closed. *Please.*

The third ring cut off. "Hello?" My aunt's rich alto voice.

"Aunt Margie. It's Hannah."

"Why, Hannah, how nice to hear from you."

Her unsuspecting tone thumped me in the chest. She hadn't seen the news. Maybe she'd let us stay for a while and rest.

But what if she got into trouble for helping me?

"Aunt Margie, I'm in Fresno, and I need to come see you." I couldn't keep the tension from my voice.

"Of course, dear. Is your mother with you?"

"Yes. She's fine. Can you give me directions to your house? It's been so long since I've been there."

"All right. Where are you?"

I told her. With no pen and paper, I repeated her directions twice. She lived about two miles away. "Thank you. Do you have room in your garage for my car? I'd like to pull into it."

"All right. Less walking for Carol."

"Great. See you soon."

I crashed down the phone and got back in the car.

"Where are we going?" Mom asked. She had donut sugar on her lips. I wiped it off for her.

"Aunt Margie's. Remember her?"

"I had a friend named Margie once."

"Yes. You told me." I started the car.

"Oh." She lay back against the head rest and closed her eyes.

Two miles, and we'd be home free. For the moment. My eyes flicked again and again to the rearview mirror, searching for a police car. By the time we reached the house I'd swear we'd gone ten miles.

The garage door stood open. I pulled inside and saw Aunt Margie waiting for us, hands clasped at her waist. She was a large, no-nonsense woman, round and soft-skinned, her hair pepper-gray. As I stepped from the car, she hit a button to slide down the door.

"Well, my dear." She put her hands on her ample hips. "According to the news, I'd say you're in a bit of trouble."

Chapter 22

Tex checked his watch for the tenth time. Nine o'clock. Three and a half hours since he'd been given his do-or-die assignment.

Eight hours and thirty minutes left.

Fear and determination burned in his soul.

Before he'd found Stone's organization four years ago, never in the nineteen years of his wretched life had he thrilled to such purpose. People in America just didn't get it. Did not understand. The country's government was evil, bent on its citizens' destruction. Just like his own abusive father and worthless, runaway mother. Two of his older brothers went off to war for their country and came back in boxes. The third and oldest returned alive from Afghanistan in body only. At night when he slept, he screamed of death. During the day he spewed hopelessness. He'd fought for his government—for what? To tell people in some faraway country how to live?

Now the American government wanted to tell its own people how to live. It wanted to run Americans' lives in every way. This country had been founded on freedom, but the expanding government was taking that away, piece by piece. Just this year had come news of the IRS targeting certain groups for no reason—as if taxing everyone in the first place wasn't enough. Then there was NSA, spying on millions of people. Their phone calls and emails. *No one* was safe from the government anymore. The only way to keep the country strong at this point was to start over. As the famed anarchist Edward Abbey said, "Anarchism is not a romantic fable, but the hardheaded realization, based on five thousand years of experience, that we cannot entrust the management of our lives to kings, priests, politicians, generals, and county commissioners."

Tex had printed out that quote and framed it. His girlfriend, Bo, had hung it above their bed.

Problem with most anarchists was they didn't push for what they wanted. Freedom from ruthless government would never happen unless it was made to happen. That's what FreeNow was all about. Tex would do anything to see its goals reached. And they would do it. Stone's organization remained underground and secretive yet was run with tight precision. Its top-notch engineer and tech members had created the perfect solution. And today was D-day.

FreeNow had planned for this event for two years—starting long before news of the IRS and NSA scandals hit. Showed how right-on the organization was. They'd *known*. Now everything and everyone stood in place. No way would Tex not complete his task.

Tex had no doubt if he failed to find the two women, Stone would have him killed. Just as he'd called on Tex to kill Nooley for his failure to get the flash drive that could stop everything. Tex made a disgusted sound in his throat. Killing Nooley hadn't been difficult, given all the wounds the man had already suffered in his botched mission. The traitor Eddington must have fought back hard. Nooley shouldn't have been allowed to join the group in the first place. Man was an idiot.

In searching for Hannah Shire, Tex first needed to learn where she worked. Armed with that knowledge he'd tracked down the home of the physician she served and banged on the man's door before sunrise. A flash of his FBI badge had gotten the perturbed doctor talking. He hadn't spoken to Hannah Shire since the previous Friday, the doctor said, and had no idea where she was. But Hannah had worked for him for years, and he knew quite a bit about her and her family. "She lost her husband, Jeff, two years ago," the doctor said. "That's been very hard on her."

He refused to believe she would have any involvement in a murder. "Not possible." He shook his head. "Hurting another person isn't a part of Hannah Shire's makeup."

Tex changed tactics. "Then she may be in danger. We need to find her at once. Who would she turn to in a crisis?"

The good physician had told Tex everything he needed to know.

Chapter 23

At Aunt Margie's words, my face froze. I would have jumped back in the car and raced away if it weren't for the closing garage door. Had she lured me here just to turn me in?

My aunt raised her hand. "Don't worry, I've not called the police. I learned a long time ago you can't believe everything you hear on television."

I nodded, my heart beating sideways.

"Well, come on, get your mother out of the car. You both look like something the cat dragged in."

Mom was already fumbling with her seat belt. I unfastened it for her and helped her out.

"Margie!" Mom spread her hands for a hug. "How nice to see you!"

The two women hugged. Aunt Margie engulfed my mother's small frame.

"You still smell like roses." Mom turned to me, waving her fingers at Aunt Margie. "She still does."

"Same toilet water. Keep thinking it might sweeten me up some." Aunt Margie walked over to hug me too. "Come on in the kitchen. We'll have something to eat, and you can tell me your story. I imagine it's a whopping one." She took Mom's arm and began ushering her out of the garage. I followed on hollow legs.

"Do you have tea?" Mom asked.

"Of course I do."

"Oh, good. You know, I had a friend named Margie once."

"Well, you'll just have to tell me about her sometime. But for now, let's get you some tea."

They stepped through the kitchen door. I grabbed my purse from the car and trailed behind.

My aunt sat us down at the table, then bustled about making tea, toast, and scrambled eggs. For a few moments I watched her, my body graceless and my mind on hold. Aunt Margie was smart enough to give Mom her tea as soon as possible. My mother gave a soft crow of delight and lifted the cup to her lips. "Ah. *So* good!"

I wanted the moment to last forever. Mom satisfied. The two of us safe. After the night we'd had, everything seemed so surreal.

Emily.

"Oh!" I pushed back from the table. "I have to call my daughter."

"Of course." Aunt Margie whisked eggs in a bowl. "You can go down the hall to the guest bedroom, if you like. There's a phone in there."

"Thanks." I rose. "Stay here, Mom. Okay?"

She nodded and sipped her tea. As I left the kitchen, I heard her say, "Did you know the Bad People are after us?"

I hurried into the bedroom and dialed Emily's work number. And was informed she'd gone home sick.

"You mean she was there and left?" I sank down on the bed. This was not good. Emily was much safer at work than in her apartment alone. And she hadn't seemed sick the last time we talked.

"Yes, she just walked out the door a minute ago."

I checked my watch. It was now 9:45. "All right, thanks. I'll try her cell phone."

Emily answered on the first ring. "Hello?"

"Em, it's me. Are you sick?"

"Mom, thank God! Where are you?" Emily's breath came in puffs, her voice with an echo.

"At your Great Aunt Margie's in Fresno. Are you sick?"

"No. I have stuff to tell you. How are you and Grand?"

"Not good. Did you see me on the news?"

"What? No!"

"The sheriff's department says I'm a 'person of interest' in Leringer's death, and that I've fled to escape. And that I also likely killed two other men—a man who worked for Leringer, *and* the deputy who was watching my house. *Three men*, Emily. Everyone's looking for me. Everyone. They showed my picture and even gave out my make of car and license plate."

"That's . . . " Emily exhaled over the line. "This is *insane*."

"Yeah. I know."

"I saw national news about Leringer's and the other guy's murder—what's his name, Eddington?—but nothing about you."

"This was local news, the latest update. It was the same reporter who showed up at the scene."

"And they think *you* killed all those people."

"They can't really think that. I told you Harcroft and Wade couldn't be trusted. This is their way of getting everyone to help bring me in."

"This is just crazy." Emily's voice rose. "They really are after you."

"I told you."

A beat passed. I could still hear Emily breathing hard. "Where are you?"

"I'm going down the back stairs to my car. I needed to get out of the office an hour ago, but I got pulled into this meeting. So frustrating! Now we've lost time."

At Emily's last sentence the echo in her voice stopped. I could hear wind over the line. "Time?"

"I'm at my car now, but I have to tell you." Emily rattled off the news about finding a stunning message on the video. *A terrorist attack—for real?* I listened, unable to utter a word. "That's today, Mom, get it? Tonight at seven o'clock the West Coast goes dark. And Washington, D.C.—that means the government. Tomorrow it's the East, and next day it's Texas. The *whole* country. Who knows for how long. I don't even know if we'll be able to call each other. I mean, how do cell phone towers work without electricity?"

My lungs felt like lead, and my brain chugged. This couldn't be happening. I couldn't take it all in. The West Coast *and* Washington, D.C? After that, the rest of the country? Our nation would be crippled.

This couldn't be true.

"So I'm taking the video and the encryption code to the FBI office in Los Angeles. I Google-mapped the address. It's an hour and forty-five minutes away. I gotta get going."

I shook my head hard. "Emily, you can't get any more involved in this! All I did was stop to help a man at an accident, and look what's happened to me. Your grandmother and I were almost killed. I told you before—I don't want them after you too."

"Even if someone did come after me, they wouldn't be fast enough. Once I get to the FBI, *they* can worry about this."

"You really believe you're safe? Then why did you tell your office you're going home sick? Apparently you're worried about telling anyone else about this."

Emily had no response to that.

"And how do you know you'll get a real FBI agent? He could be fake, like the ones who tried to kill me."

"Those men showed up at your door with fake badges, Mom. Anybody can get a fake badge. I'm going to their big office in L.A. Where they work every day. That's different."

A stunning new thought sped through my brain. "Emily, what if Rutger and Samuelson *are* real FBI agents? If people in the FBI are involved in this, we *really* don't know who to trust."

"Why should they be real agents? One of them tried to kill you."

"That's just the point."

"Deputy Harcroft told you they weren't real agents."

"Yeah, and look how much we trust him."

Emily fell silent for a moment. "It doesn't make sense. If those men had been real agents, and working with the terrorists just like Harcroft and Wade are, Harcroft wouldn't have brought you to the station so fast. He wouldn't have put surveillance on your house to protect you."

I closed my eyes, trying to logic through it. "But they all *are* working together, whether those FBI agents are fake or real. Looks like that whole thing of 'protecting us' was nothing but a set-up."

"Still, even if those fake agents were real ones, it doesn't mean *all* of them are bad."

"Emily. The sheriff's department already has that video. Let them handle this."

"No, not the whole sheriff's department. The two men who interviewed you have it. And if they're bad guys, you know they're not showing it around."

"But maybe someone else at the department has seen it. Someone who'll try to stop this."

"Even if that's true, what if they haven't seen that message I found? You want to chance having the entire West Coast and

Washington, D.C. go black tonight? Think of the chaos. And that's just for starters."

"This can't be true." I got up and paced the room. "It just can't be."

"I know. I kept trying to tell myself that. But we have to believe it. I mean, this country's known about homegrown terrorists for years. Remember the blown-up building in Oklahoma City?"

Emily had been nine. She'd watched the news at some friend's house, including the covered bodies of children being carried out. She'd come home sobbing.

Still, I didn't want to believe this. Even after everything that had happened. I just wanted to go back to my peaceful life, where the hardest thing was putting up with Mom's music. That life never had to face down the reality that Americans like this existed.

"At least let me drive down and go with you. Maybe Aunt Margie will lend me her car."

"That'll take too long. And you're much safer where you are."

Tears scratched my eyes. If something happened to my daughter, I would never forgive myself. "Emily, please don't do this. You don't have to save the world."

"Well, Mom, apparently I do. Whether we like it or not."

My thoughts tripped over themselves. "No, don't. I'll go. I'll turn myself in to the police here. I'll tell them about the message on the video. They can download a copy from our online account, just like you did. They can call the FBI."

"And first thing, you'll be turned over to Harcroft and Wade. Who might just put you in a jail cell with the wrong person. Besides, I deleted our account."

"You what? Why?"

"So they couldn't trace a download of that video back to me."

Oh. Of course.

I shivered. "Well, anyway, once the information is in the hands of authorities who can stop this from happening, there's no reason for the terrorists to still want me dead. It'll be too late."

"Really? What if you're wrong? And what happens to Grand while you're in jail for murder until all this gets figured out?"

I don't know, I don't know! Tears dropped onto my lap. Why were they chasing me in the first place? As if I could stop any of this.

"They won't do that," I said. "I'll tell the FBI that Harcroft and Wade are lying."

"Oh, like they're just going to believe you over their own buddies."

Now it was my turn to be silent.

"Look, Mom, if I go, maybe I can clear up these lies about you. I won't tell them where you are. And while you're safe, once the FBI starts investigating Harcroft and Wade, they'll find some dirt on 'em."

Maybe. And maybe she was just being naïve.

Emily sighed. "Thing is, no one, not even the real FBI, can stop the attack from happening tonight—unless we find out what *Raleigh* means. *If* that word is the key to the encrypted message in the first place."

What if that encrypted message had nothing to do with stopping the attack? It could be nonsense, for all we knew.

But Raleigh had to mean something. Even now I could picture Morton's stricken face as he mouthed the word.

"I gotta go, Mom."

"Emily, no. Please let *me* go."

"Mom. *Stay where you are.* You're safe at Aunt Margie's."

I quit pacing, unable to move. Emily and I hung on the phone, breathing. Argued out.

If this was all true, if the electricity was being taken down tonight, what would happen to us? To our country?

"Hannah!" Mom's distant voice trailed into the bedroom. "Your breakfast is ready!"

"Mom," Emily said in my ear, "I'm losing time. I *have* to go."

I knew she had to. Millions of people, maybe even lives, depended on the attack being stopped. But why *my* daughter? "No, Emily. Please. I'll do it."

"No way. Not. If you call the police, they'll arrest you. Then I won't be able to call you and tell you what happened. *Don't* do that."

I hung my head, spent and sick to the core.

"Okay," I said. "But watch out for a young, lanky guy with a buzz cut and a Southern drawl. He's no FBI agent you can trust."

"Got it."

"The other one was older. And muscular. But I don't think you have to worry about him. I shot him so many times—" I pressed my hand against my forehead. "I think I killed him."

"Mom." Emily's voice turned quiet. "You had to."

"I know."

"He would have killed you. And Grand."

"I know." But I didn't. I didn't know much of anything anymore. The phone clicked in my ear. I stiffened. "Emily?"

"Oh, great," Emily mumbled. "Work's calling me on the other line. Gotta go, Mom. I'll call you soon, promise. Love you."

The line went dead.

Chapter 24

SPECIAL HOUSE SELECT COMMITTEE INVESTIGATION INTO FREENOW TERRORIST ACTIVITY OF FEBRUARY 25, 2013

SEPTEMBER 16, 2013

TRANSCRIPT

Representative ELKIN MORSE (Chairman, Homeland Security Committee): Sergeant, I think we need to back up here. Because I still do not understand parts of your testimony. You are claiming that on that fateful day of February 25, even as you and your department maintained possession of the video, instead of focusing on it, you saw fit to spend the day pursuing fifty-five-year-old Hannah Shire and her eighty-two-year-old mother. Who was struggling with dementia, I might add.

Sergeant CHARLES WADE (Sheriff's Department Coastside):

Hindsight is twenty-twenty, Chairman Morse. As I've been telling you all day, at the time it seemed the best course of action.

MORSE: As I understand it, you were also trying to track Hannah Shire by her cell phone?

WADE: We weren't tracking it at that time. I had put in a request to do so. But gaining permission to track her, and setting up the plan with the cell phone provider, took time. Not until later in the day did an attempt to track become possible.

MORSE: All right. We will return to that. Regarding Deputy Harcroft, did you have any knowledge of what he was doing on the day of February 25?

WADE: Certainly. He was assisting me in the investigation of the two homicides—Morton Leringer and Nathan Eddington. Plus we were assisting the San Carlos police regarding the homicide of Deputy Williams.

MORSE: As a sergeant in the Moss Beach sheriff's substation, did you oversee all the deputies beneath you in rank?

WADE: There are four sergeants at our substation. On that day I was intensely focused on the cases at hand. Deputy Harcroft was assisting in those cases, as were other deputies. I oversaw those deputies, but I wasn't aware moment to moment what every deputy in the substation was doing.

MORSE: Yes, quite. That was the problem, Sergeant Wade.

Regarding Mrs. Shire, you told your superior that you and Harcroft now viewed her as a strong person of interest in the murders of Morton Leringer, Nathan Eddington, and Deputy Williams. Correct?

WADE: I did.

MORSE: And this was your stated reason for releasing her picture and information about her to the media?

WADE: It wasn't just a "stated" reason. It *was* the reason.

MORSE: And meanwhile, again, you did nothing with the video.

WADE: That's not true. On the morning of the 25th, I turned the flash drive over to a tech in our department and asked him to view it. I'd also planned to show it to our lieutenant. But by then Deputy Williams had been killed, and Mrs. Shire and her mother had fled the scene. That situation required my immediate attention. The imminent importance of the flash drive was not apparent at the time.

MORSE: It would have been "apparent," Sergeant Wade, if you'd looked more carefully at the video.

WADE: Chairman Morse, you are failing to understand. I had three homicide victims on my hands that day. And Hannah Shire had fled. My thinking was, if she was innocent, why would she flee? If someone had tried to harm her, why wouldn't she call me? She had my number. And Harcroft's.

MORSE: So you maintain to this day that your actions at the time were justified?

WADE: I do.

MORSE: And that you had no hidden agenda in failing to pursue further knowledge about the video.

WADE: As I told you, I turned the video over to a technician.

MORSE: How could you not put a priority on that video, Sergeant? Three men had already died because of it.

WADE: I could not be certain of that at the time! I couldn't even be certain of Mrs. Shire's claim that Leringer gave her the video. Or that two men posing as FBI agents had threatened her in her home. If she was responsible for Leringer's death, and for Eddington's and Williams's death, everything she told us could be a lie. In fact, remember, when she first talked to Deputy Harcroft she did lie. She admitted as much to us.

MORSE: And so you ignored the video.

WADE: I *did not* ignore it. I placed my priority on finding the woman who had given it to me, perhaps as a way to cover up for killing three people.

MORSE: I'm just shaking my head, Sergeant, hearing your testimony. Seems to me you've used the last seven months to conjure up an explanation for your actions on that day.

WADE: On the contrary, Mr. Chairman, my testimony is true.

MORSE: Let me tell you what is true, Sergeant Wade. On that day of February 25, when our nation faced one of its greatest potential traumas of all time, you *ignored* a vital piece of information. And while you and your department ignored this information, a twenty-seven-year-old *marketing video producer* deciphered the hidden message on that video and took it upon herself to do something about it.

WADE: Hindsight again, Chairman Morse. I. Couldn't. Have. Known.

MORSE: Neither could Emily Shire have known. But unlike you— and your entire department—*she* paid attention to the video.

Do you have a response to that, Sergeant?

WADE: No other response than what I've already told you again and again.

MORSE: And so, I assume, you refuse to take responsibility for the highly unfortunate events—and that's putting it mildly—that occurred during the remainder of that day?

Chapter 25

Monday, February 25, 2013

Emily made a face at the incoming call on her cell. The laptop bag was getting heavy, hanging off her shoulder. And why wouldn't work stop bugging her? She *had* to get going.

She ignored the call. Started to unlock her car.

At the last minute she relented and punched the icon to answer. "Hi." If she sounded impatient, she didn't care.

"Sorry to bother you. It's Ronnie." The receptionist at the front desk. "We just had an FBI agent here asking for you. Just wanted to warn you before he gets to you."

Emily froze. "What?"

"He said he wanted to talk to you right away. Wouldn't say about what."

Emily's head jerked up, her gaze fixed on the building's back entrance. "Did he have a badge?"

"Yeah. And he had a picture of you. Showed it to me to make sure you were the right person."

A picture of her? For one crazy second Emily hoped the man was for real. Maybe the San Mateo Sheriff's Department had called them about the video. But how——? "What did he look like?"

"Young guy with a buzz cut. Sounds like my cousins from Texas."

All air sucked out of Emily's lungs.

She dropped her laptop bag onto the hood of the car. Scrabbled around inside for her keys. "What'd you tell him?"

"That you just left. And if he didn't see your car, you're already on the way home."

"He knows what kind of car I'm driving?"

"Well, yeah, I told him what to look for."

No.

Emily snatched up the computer bag and backed away from the Kia, shooting wild looks right and left. "Front parking lot or back?"

"Front, I guess. Oh, you're in the back?"

Emily's heart kicked at her ribs. "Ronnie. Tell me you didn't give him my home address."

Silence.

"Ronnie!"

"I . . . I did. Sorry. I mean, he's the FBI——"

Emily threw the cell in her bag and ran.

Chapter 26

"Sit down, dear." Aunt Margie indicated the plate of scrambled eggs, bacon, and toast at the table. Mom was already eating and looking very happy about it.

I couldn't sit. My body couldn't relax. And my pulse wouldn't stop spinning. "Oh. It looks lovely. Can I . . . can we eat in front of the television?" I picked up my plate and fork. "I need to see the news."

Aunt Margie glanced at Mom, then gave me a meaningful look. "Why don't you go ahead in there?" She pointed to her small living room. "I'll stay here with Carol."

"Thanks." She was right. I was so overwrought I hadn't thought how the news might upset Mom. I swiveled and headed for the TV, around the corner.

I put my food on the coffee table and yanked up the remote. "Where's CNN?" I called.

"Channel 20. There's a guide sitting on the TV."

With trembling fingers I poked in the numbers. Nothing about the case on CNN. Or FOX. I surfed local channels, muttering,

"Come on, come on." I had to know . . . something. My daughter was out there. I just needed some piece of knowledge to make me think she'd be all right.

I returned to CNN—and spotted the front yard of *my house*, surrounded by yellow crime scene tape.

My legs sank me onto the couch.

". . . the home of Hannah Shire in San Carlos, California . . ."

I watched, nerves fraying, as the female reporter intoned about blood drops of an unidentified person leading out my back door. "Police are concerned for the safety of Hannah Shire's mother, who lives with her. Carol Shire is eighty-two and suffering from dementia . . ."

My mother? The police wanted people to think I'd hurt my *mother*?

A picture of Mom filled the screen. Someone had taken it at the night club where she used to go. She wore her purple hat. Her eyes were closed, one hand to her chest, and the other arm held wide in her form of dancing. Without context the photo made her look absolutely mindless. Rage flashed through me. I gripped the cushions of the couch.

Dorothy, Mom's caregiver, appeared on the screen next. She was standing on the sidewalk in front of our house, looking shell-shocked. "I just came to take care of Carol." She gazed at the yellow crime scene tape. "Now . . . this."

"Do you think Hannah Shire had anything to do with the murder of Morton Leringer?" a reporter asked.

"No. Absolutely not." Dorothy shook her head. "I just want her and Carol to be okay. They're nice people."

The screen switched to another reporter interviewing Sergeant Wade and Deputy Harcroft. "Sergeant, are you convinced Hannah Shire is responsible for the deaths of Morton Leringer and Nathan

Eddington? As well as Deputy Williams, who was conducting sur-veillance on her house?"

Wade shook his head. "All I can tell you is we have three homi-cide victims on our hands. And Hannah Shire and her mother are missing. I don't know the complete truth of what has happened. I do know that we need to talk to Mrs. Shire as soon as possible."

"Deputy Harcroft, in case she's watching what would you like to say to her right now?"

Harcroft looked into the camera. "Mrs. Shire, we need you to come forward. We just need to talk to you. Wherever you are, please report to the nearest police station."

Right, they just wanted to "talk" to me. What about the flash drive and the video? The real story? No one was even mentioning it, including these two.

The scene morphed to an interview with a coiffured blonde woman—maybe midforties?—identified as Cheryl Stein, Morton Leringer's daughter. Good thing Mom wasn't watching. It would remind her of her quest to find Leringer's daughter.

"We are devastated." Cheryl lifted tear-filled eyes to the cam-era. "Whoever is responsible for my father's murder will never know how much has been taken from us. How much has been taken from the world. Just two years ago we lost our mother to a stroke. Now this." She swallowed hard. "One thing I can assure you," her voice stiffened, "his entire family will use every resource we have to bring whoever's responsible for his and Nathan Eddington's deaths to jus-tice—male or female. And we still not stop—*I* will not stop—until that's done."

Male or female. My body went cold. She thought I'd killed her father and his employee. She really believed that. No telling what Sergeant Wade had filled her ears with.

The camera moved from Cheryl Stein to a younger woman standing next to her. The reporter identified the second woman as

Ashley Eddington, wife of Nathan. Ashley's face looked hard and sun-browned, dark straight hair hanging past her shoulders. She clutched the hand of a little girl, about five. "I want answers too." She looked into the camera, her eyes red-rimmed and defiant. "And I think that woman everyone's looking for—Hannah Shire—has them."

Her voice held such hatred. My heart folded in on itself.

"Like Cheryl said, we won't stop until justice is done. If anyone out there has seen Hannah Shire, please, please call the police." Sudden tears spilled onto her cheeks. "I've lost a husband. My daughter has lost her father." Her face twisted. "That woman doesn't deserve to live."

Oh, dear God, help me.

The camera panned down to Ashley Eddington's little girl. Her expression looked lost, her large eyes sad. She clutched a brown stuffed dog to her chest, his neck encircled with a red-and-white-checkered scarf. Across the back of the scarf I noticed black stitched lettering in all capitals. My gaze bounced away, then tore back to those letters.

What did they say?

Heat flushed my veins. I leaned forward, eyes lasering the TV. The camera pulled in for a closer picture of the girl. I gasped.

The letters spelled RAWLY.

Chapter 27

Emily sprinted toward the back of the parking lot as fast as she could in heels. At the end was a knee-high wall she could climb over. Beyond it lay the parking area for the building facing the opposite side of the block. If she could just get there, maybe hide in the building . . .

Her laptop bag bounced against her hip. She threw a hand over the thing to steady it.

Behind her she heard a car coming down the drive on the side of her work building.

Emily swerved to duck behind a car. She turned too close, hit the bumper, and went down hard. The laptop bag flew off her shoulder. She skidded against the pavement and ripped her pants at the right knee. The skin peeled away. She gasped in pain and gripped her knee. That hurt worse. She pulled her hand away. Her palm was bloody.

Emily tried to breathe.

She grabbed the laptop bag and slid its long handle over her shoulder and head so it wouldn't fall off again. No way could she lose it—the video and encryption message were inside. She huddled behind the car, listening. Her knee throbbed.

The car she'd heard came closer, then stopped. Turned. Stopped again.

A door opened and shut. She heard footsteps. Was it just someone coming to work late? Or was it him?

Silence. Emily's muscles were like stone, pulse whooshing in her ears.

Still no sound. She leaned down to look underneath the car. All she could see was the pavement around the cars in the next few rows. She straightened and listened some more. What was he *doing*?

Fingers against the car's back bumper for support, she rose up halfway and leaned to her right to see around the vehicle. Nothing. She pulled up a little higher, craning her neck.

There. In profile. In an instant she took in the lanky body, the buzzed hair cut. He was standing by her Kia, looking around.

Emily dropped to the ground, panting. Now what? He had to know she was still nearby and would wait for her to come back.

The footsteps started up again. Coming closer.

Was he checking rows to see if she was hiding?

Sweat dripped down Emily's forehead, even in the chilly February air. She hung there, trembling, her knee aching.

She looked around the car again.

No sight of him. And no footsteps.

Her heart beat like crazy. What if he'd seen her? He could jump out any minute. Then he'd drag her to his car—

The footfalls sounded again. He was coming toward her.

Emily leaned down to look under the back of the car—and spotted his feet at the front. She froze.

He walked to the right, then disappeared. He must be checking between all cars in that row. If he came down one more row, he'd see her.

She huddled against the bumper for a minute. Then crab-walked around to the left side of the car. All the way up toward the front. She peeked around the edge.

No sign of him.

She stilled. Was he walking down to the next row?

Emily rose up more, peering over the hood. The man was at the end of the row, headed down to the next one—where she'd been hiding. She counted to three, then moved around to the front of the car.

The footsteps neared until she knew he was behind the car, right where she'd been hiding. Then they faded again.

There were two more rows he'd check. Then he'd come back.

She leaned her head just above the pavement and watched for his legs.

A forever minute ticked by. Two. Emily's wrists burned, and her neck cramped. Where *was* he?

Maybe he'd circled back. Would come at her from behind.

When she couldn't stay that way any longer, she heard him again. Coming toward her on her right. Close.

If he came up right by this car, it was over. But she couldn't risk rising up to look again.

She crept around to the right side of the car. Flattened herself to the pavement again and saw his legs two cars over. Headed back up.

Emily didn't dare make a sound. She slipped around to the back, where she'd started.

The footsteps soon stopped again. A curse word floated to her ears.

Then another noise. A kind of punch, and a hiss of air. Seconds later the sounds came again.

He was slashing her tires. Emily dropped her chin to her chest.

Two more times she heard the sounds. Then nothing—until the click of the building's rear metal door opening.

He'd gone back to look for her in the building? This was her chance.

She rose up to peer over the car, making sure he was gone. Then straightened all the way up and tried to run. But her hurt knee made her limp. Sucking in big breaths, left hand clamped against her laptop bag, she headed for the rear of the parking lot. When she reached the barrier she flung one leg over it. In that split second she glanced back at the building—and saw the man through the large stairwell window on the second floor.

He was looking straight at her.

Emily cried out and brought her other leg over the barrier. She took off limp-running toward the nearest office building. Where she would go, she had no clue. With her bad leg, no way she'd be able to outrun the guy.

Behind her she heard the building's door crash open and slam shut. Hard steps pounded toward her.

Emily ran faster, heels smacking the pavement and tears squeezing out of her eyes. The footsteps drew closer—no time to look back.

God, just get me to some people.

An eternity passed before she reached the building. She slammed into its back door, wrenched to open it.

Locked.

Emily swerved away to run around the building. In her side vision she saw the man leap over the barrier. As she neared the corner of the building she heard the back door open behind her. Emily pivoted, saw a man exit. "Call the police!" she flung out her right arm toward the fake agent. "He's chasing me!"

"Wh—"

She kept running.

"Hey!" She heard the man call to her pursuer. "What are you doing?"

The fake agent's footsteps sounded nearer. He veered at a diagonal to run straight for her. "FBI!" The words pumped from his mouth. Emily saw him flash his badge toward the other man.

He was going to catch her. And no one would stop him.

She rounded the corner, running as hard as her bad knee would allow. As she passed the front corner, she knew the "agent" was close. She burst onto the parking lot and wove through rows of cars. At the street about 100 feet away was a bus stop, a large black man, and a mother and small boy waiting. Emily careened toward them, screaming.

The man's head jerked around.

"Help!" She had little breath. "He's trying to kidnap me!"

The man took one look at the "agent" in pursuit and started jogging toward her. She met him halfway and almost fell into him. "Please. Get me . . . out of here."

"Stop!" The "agent" was a mere thirty feet away. "I'm FBI!"

"He's not!" Emily hung on to her protector's arm. "His badge is fake!"

The man looked down and saw her torn pants, the bloody knee. "Come on." He headed her toward the street. Then called toward the woman waiting at the bus stop, "You got a cell phone?" She and her child were watching them, mouths open. "Call 911!"

Her hand disappeared into her purse.

The "agent" caught up and grabbed Emily's arm. She gasped.

"Stop." The "agent" wasn't even winded. His face was like granite, showing no fear in the presence of the other man, who was much taller. "This woman's wanted for murder." He stuck out his badge and FBI name tag with his picture on it. "Agent Rutger."

Emily cringed. The badge and picture tag looked so real. *Were* they? What if the FBI *was* part of this?

She tried to break free. "I'm not, he's lying! He tried to kill my mother!"

The man's gaze jumped from Emily to Rutger.

"I'm telling you, back off." Rutger pointed at the man. He gripped Emily's arm harder. "Or I'll have to bring you in too."

Emily yanked away. "He *can't* bring you in. He's a fake!"

Rutger caught her arm again and clamped down.

The bus was coming. One block up the street.

The black man's expression hardened. "She's not going anywhere with you."

"The police are coming!" called the woman at the bus stop. She held up her cell phone.

Something flashed across Rutger's face.

"What, you don't like that?" The man sneered at Rutger. "I thought the police and FBI were pals."

Rutger pulled at her, hard. Emily stumbled sideways.

"Let her go." The man shoved Rutger. "Now."

Brakes squealed. The bus was pulling up to its stop.

"I said *now*." The man smacked his hand over Rutger's and pried the "agent's" fingers off Emily's arm. "Go get on the bus." He jerked his head from Emily toward the street.

She hesitated. What would happen to this man when she left?

"Go!"

She spun around and ran. "Wait, wait!" She waved her arm at the bus.

Scuffling sounded behind her. Emily didn't turn around. She reached the bus and threw herself up the steps.

Heart jamming, her legs like water, Emily threw two dollar bills at the driver and skidded into a seat up front. Across the aisle the mother and son looked at her, wide-eyed. The driver stared at her through the rearview mirror.

The bus door closed.

Emily bent forward, trying to breathe. Her knee pulsed with pain. As they drove away she glanced toward the parking lot. The man who'd saved her was staring after Rutger, who was running back toward her office building.

Air backed up in Emily's throat. The agent—real or fake?—was headed for his car. And she knew what he would do.

Rutger would come after the bus.

Chapter 28

RAWLY.

I stared at the TV screen, mouth open. Could a stuffed dog be our "Raleigh"?

"Hannah!" My mother's voice trailed from the kitchen. "Isn't your breakfast wonderful?"

I pressed my hands to my cheeks. The TV switched from the news to commercials. The sudden loudness made my ears hurt. I punched the *mute* button.

"Hannah!"

"Yes, Mom." I felt my mouth move. "It's great." My eyes lowered to my plate. I hadn't eaten a bite.

What was I supposed to do now?

I started to rise from the couch—and dizziness hit. I sat back down.

Somehow I had to figure this out. Was that dog what we were looking for?

I'd never know. Because no way could I ever get close to it. Clutched in the hand of a little girl who believed I'd killed her father? Her mother wanting me dead?

My gaze landed again on the plate of food. I hadn't eaten in a long time. Or slept. I couldn't go on much longer without fuel.

I picked up the plate and shoved eggs into my mouth. Chewed automatically. Commercials continued to run on the screen. When they ended, the news show turned to another story. I turned off the TV.

Where was Emily? How long until she got to the FBI? When she called, she could help me think this through . . .

Like a robot, I kept eating until all my food was gone. I got up slowly, carrying my plate, and returned to the kitchen.

"There she is." Mom had cleaned her plate as well. "Wasn't it wonderful? Best breakfast I ever had."

I managed a nod. Aunt Margie patted Mom's arm, but her eyes were on me.

"I've been telling Margie all about my new friend Morton," Mom said. "But it's so sad—he died. So now we have to go to Raleigh. If we can just get away from the Bad People. Do you have Bad People here, Margie?"

"Well, I certainly hope not." My aunt threw me a sad smile.

Mom tilted her head. "'The fear of the LORD is this: wisdom. And to turn from evil is understanding.'"

My aunt surveyed Mom. "Is that from the Bible?"

"Yes." Mom frowned. "But I can't remember where . . ."

She took a slow drink of tea, as if trying to recall.

Her face cleared. "Margie, did I tell you about my other new friend? She didn't die. Her name is . . ." Mom's eyes grew cloudy. "What was her name, Hannah? She has six sisters. Can you believe that? *Six*."

"Nance." I walked to the sink to set down my plate.

"Oh, yes, Nance! Can you believe she had *six* sisters?"

"That is amazing." Aunt Margie carried the rest of the dishes to the sink, then looked at me and lowered her voice. "See anything on the news?"

"It's bad." I felt my throat close. "Real bad. They think I killed three people. And they're calling for me to turn myself in. Even the families of the men who were killed think I'm guilty."

She sighed. "I don't know how long before they show up here. Somebody's bound to find out I'm your closest family member and come around asking questions."

I began rinsing the dishes, my movements automatic. "I know."

We should leave right now. But where would we go? In a car everyone was looking for. Besides, I hadn't the energy.

"Here, let me do that." My aunt nudged me aside and took over. I stood by helplessly, my mind unable to hold a logical thought.

"You need to rest, and I don't want no for an answer," Aunt Margie said. "Carol says you've been up all night."

"How can I? What if they knock on your door?"

"I don't have to let anyone in."

"They're *police*."

"Good for them."

"I'm tired." Mom pushed back from the table. The animation on her face just a moment ago had faded, replaced by blank helplessness.

"Little wonder." My aunt dried her hands on a dishtowel. "Come on, let me take you to the guestroom, where you can lie down."

"Thank you so much, Aunt Margie," I said. "For taking care of us."

"Yes, well. You should sleep too." With gentle hands she helped my mother up and led her across the kitchen.

RAWLY. I stared at the whiteness of the sink. "Aunt Margie. Do you have a computer?"

"Yes. At the little desk in my bedroom. Be my guest; it's already on. But I still think you should rest."

I followed her and Mom down the hall. Aunt Margie veered Mom into the room where I'd talked to Emily. "It's on down at the end," she said to me.

My aunt's room was pink and gray. Roses and steel. The bed called to me. A block of exhaustion sat in my chest.

I passed the bed and sat down at the computer. For a moment my brain wouldn't process what to do next. Amazing that twenty-four hours ago Mom and I had been eating breakfast at the Ritz Carlton. Watching the ocean. Leading normal lives.

Just hours later I would be lying to a sheriff's deputy. And that night I would try to kill a man. I may have succeeded.

That wave of grief and guilt crashed over me again. Chilled me to the bone. My head sank to my chest. I gripped the desk and closed my eyes. "Dear God, I just don't understand what's happening to me. Please . . . help."

For some time I stayed in that pose, frozen by the cold weight of my emotions. Yet—shouldn't I be feeling even more? My exhaustion cloaked even my regret. Someday, if I survived all this, I would have to deal—*really* deal—with what I had done. What I'd become. Had I so little trust in God that I would lie to a deputy rather than rely on Him to get me through the consequences of telling the truth? So what if my mother had melted into a screaming fit?

As for shooting Samuelson, I'd *had* to do that. It was either him or us. But why had God allowed me to be in such a horrible position in the first place?

Oh, to be like my mother. Even in her simple-mindedness, she clung to God's promises.

Help me be more like her, Lord.

My eyes scratched open. Time to move onward. I had work to do.

I raised my head and tried to focus on the computer screen. A desktop saver ball slow-bounced. My fingers felt like lead as I placed them on the keyboard.

At the Internet I searched for "Ashley Eddington" + Nathan. Multiple news stories about Nathan's and Morton Leringer's deaths came up. I clicked on the one for ABC local news. It told me what I needed to know. Leringer's security company, StarrCom, was in Menlo Park, as the news had said. Ashley Eddington and her late husband, Nathan, were residents of San Carlos.

San Carlos. I slumped in the chair. My home town, the one I'd just fled. No way could I go back there.

But why should I even try? This Rawly was a stuffed dog, for goodness' sake. The name had to be nothing but coincidence.

I stared at the monitor, trying to focus. It took awhile for my mind to register the name of Leringer's daughter—Cheryl Stein of Menlo Park, California.

Maybe she could help. On TV she'd appeared at least a little more reasonable than Ashley Eddington. If I could just talk to her, tell her everything her father said before he died . . .

But why should she listen, when she believed everything Wade had told her? And how could I get to her anyway?

I put my head in my hands and tried to *think*. To reason. There had to be a plan that would fix this. But my thoughts would not gel. They sloshed, then seeped away, pale liquid.

My body longed for sleep. If I didn't get it, I would be good for nothing. I had to have the strength to watch out for Emily and take care of Mom.

In defeat I pushed back from the computer. Stumbled to Aunt Margie's bed and fell upon it.

Tired as I was, it still took some time for sleep to draw its blanket over me.

As I sank into a fitful doze, I sent up silent prayers for my daughter. And for the man I may have killed.

Chapter 29

For hours Stone had been on his cell phone. He'd checked up on all his major people in the western and RFC regions—targeted to be hit that evening. He'd spent extra time grilling his men in D.C. Did they have everything in place? Was every member beneath them accounted for and ready?

When the lights went out on these two areas, FreeNow members would hit the pavement, breaking store windows, whipping up people to join in the chaos. Truckloads of men were set to barrel down the streets, shouting violence. Goading scared citizens to arm themselves, make hasty decisions.

Tomorrow at the same time, Phase 2 would blacken the entire eastern portion of the U.S. And in Phase 3, Texas would go dark. Power in the whole country—gone.

Sure, some businesses and homes would have generators for a backup power supply. Particularly government and commercial buildings. But generators were built for temporary use, and the damage FreeNow's virus did to the power grid's computer systems would take much longer to fix. Before long the generators, too, would stop working.

Stone had first gotten the idea from watching the spreading havoc in New Orleans after Hurricane Katrina. Widespread tragedy led to fear. Fear led to chaos. Chaos led to violence. Violence would lead to government upheaval.

But even he couldn't control the weather.

Then, through research, he began hearing dire warnings about the U.S. electrical grid. How it was suffering from aging infrastructures with little built-in security measures. One specialist even said a "sixty-dollar piece of software" could bypass current security. And the shutdown of a local electrical grid could cause a cascade effect that would blacken an entire region.

Now *that,* Stone could do. With the right recruits in the needed fields, FreeNow could create that "sixty-dollar piece of software."

The best, smartest recruit of all had been Nathan Eddington. Skilled in security measures for power companies, he knew how to bypass them. But something happened to Eddington when he learned Stone planned to take the whole country dark. How could Eddington not have suspected that was the plan? FreeNow didn't do anything halfway.

Stone looked out his dirty window. No matter about Eddington now. Stone's other members remained ready to play their parts toward a new America. They were proud, brave men, willing to fight for what they believed in. But most of them didn't know their worlds would be dark. The only people who knew of the plan to hit the electrical grid were Stone and his chosen few, which included the top man at each membership location. Too many people in the know meant too many potential talkers. Some idiot would have bragged to a neighbor.

The darkness would help his men. Hide them. Stone wished he could tell them all that.

They'd learn soon enough.

And in the blackness, it wouldn't take long for outsiders to join in the violence. It would grow and grow until police were far outnumbered.

But he *had* to tie up this loose end of the video.

Stone had not yet heard from Tex. He knew the kid had flown to Santa Barbara to hunt down Hannah Shire's daughter, Emily. Tex would not fail FreeNow.

He dialed Tex's number. No answer after six rings. He smacked off the line and dialed again.

"Tex here." The man was breathing hard.

"What's going on?"

"I'm in pursuit."

"On *foot*?"

"In my car now." More huffing. "I've found her. Call you back?"

"Make it quick. And make it good news."

Stone hung up.

Chapter 30

How long 'til the next stop?" Emily leaned toward the bus driver.

"Six blocks."

Six blocks. If they hit stoplights, Rutger would have time to run to his car and catch up with the bus.

"I need to get off now."

"Can't stop."

"But I *have* to."

"Lady, I can't stop where there's no bus stop."

"That guy is chasing me. He could catch up."

The driver shook his head. "Call the police."

"I called 911," the woman in the opposite seat said. "They said they were on their way."

"Thanks." Emily gave her and her son a grim smile. But it didn't matter if she'd called. Some officer would show up back at the bus stop, see nothing, and leave.

She peered through her window back down the street. No sign of Rutger yet, but she couldn't see very far. And she didn't know what kind of car he was driving.

What if he *was* a real agent? And she'd been headed to the Los Angeles FBI office. What if others there were part of this?

Emily counted the blocks. One. Two. At the third, they stopped for a red light. *Come on, come on.* She sat on the edge of her seat, ready to move the minute the bus pulled over. How long had it been since she saw Rutger running? Two minutes? Three?

The light turned green. They rolled again. Block four. Five. Emily looked out her window. Nothing suspicious yet.

The bus began to slow. Emily gathered her energy and leapt up. Pain shot through her knee. She looked down to see it still oozing blood.

Terrific.

They stopped. The doors whooshed open. Emily jumped onto the sidewalk, hurting her knee even more. Her head swiveled to check the street. None of the drivers in the first few cars behind the bus were Rutger. Beyond that, who knew?

She stood in front of a gas station. Next to it, a strip mall. She limped toward the strip mall and veered into the first business—a small Mexican restaurant open for breakfast and lunch. Emily spotted the restroom sign and followed it toward the back, into the women's bathroom. With shaky hands she pulled out her cell phone and dialed information for the L.A. FBI office. The automated service read off the number and connected her.

"FBI, Agent O'Malley."

Emily's head came up. "I . . . need to talk to Agent Rutger, please."

"Rutger."

"Do you have an Agent Rutger?"

"Not here. But there is an agent by that name in the San Francisco field office. Do—"

Emily punched off the call and stared at the phone. Of course

Rutger was from the San Francisco office, near her mother's home. He'd come down here after her.

Rutger was *real*.

Now what was she supposed to do?

Could she trust the L.A. FBI office? How would she know?

She leaned against the wall and closed her eyes. *God, I really need Your help. I'm going crazy here.*

Footsteps sounded outside the bathroom. She pushed off from the wall and listened.

The steps faded.

Emily stayed still for a moment longer. Then dialed her friend Dave's private line at work.

Please, please answer.

"Emily?" Dave's voice came on the line, sounding worried.

"Hi. I'm in trouble."

"Ronnie said an FBI agent was looking for you."

"He's trying to kill me. They already tried to kill my mom and grandmother."

"What?"

"It's the video. And now you have a copy. See why I didn't want you to keep it?"

"Who wants to kill you?"

"The terrorists who are going to hit the grid tonight."

"But this is FBI."

"Some of them are part of it, Dave!"

Shocked silence.

Emily's throat was closing. Any minute now she was going to totally lose it. "I need to get out of town. Now. Can you help?"

"Where do you want to go?"

"Fresno."

"Fresno?"

"I can't stay anywhere near here. And I sure can't go home. Ronnie gave that guy my address."

"I don't—"

"She also told him what kind of car I drive, so guess what—he slashed all my tires." Tears bit her eyes.

Dave made a sound in his throat. "You call the police?"

"Yes. I mean—no. It's a long story. I need to get to Fresno."

"What's there?"

"A place to stay. Can you come get me now? I'm hiding, and that guy's looking for me. I had to hop a bus, and my pants are torn, and my knee's bleeding. And I really. Have. To get. *Out* of here!"

The last words exploded from her. She leaned against the wall, gasping air.

"Okay, okay. Tell me where you are."

She managed to tell him. "Dave, you wouldn't happen to have a black wig lying around, would you?"

Chapter 31

SPECIAL HOUSE SELECT COMMITTEE
INVESTIGATION INTO FREENOW TERRORIST
ACTIVITY OF FEBRUARY 25, 2013

SEPTEMBER 16, 2013

TRANSCRIPT

Representative ELKIN MORSE (Chairman, Homeland Security Committee): We come now to the fourth homicide, correct?

Sergeant CHARLES WADE (Sheriff's Department Coastside): Yes. About ten o'clock on the morning of February 25, a policeman discovered a body in a vehicle at the rest stop off Freeway 280, south of Highway 92. Slumped in the front seat was a man who looked to be in his thirties. He'd been shot four times. In his pocket was an FBI badge and a tag with his picture and signature, reading "Samuelson." In the passenger seat was a laptop computer and small backup drive. Subsequent investigation of both items found them to belong to Hannah Shire.

MORSE: And how did this information tie into your current investigation?

WADE: A body discovered on an I-280 rest stop would normally fall under the jurisdiction of California Highway Patrol. But when it was discovered the victim had items from Mrs. Shire's house, we became part of the investigation. Further, this victim looked very much like one of the forensic sketches we'd done the previous evening with Hannah Shire. And she had told us one of the supposed FBI agents who'd shown up at her house had the name of Samuelson. I contacted the FBI to find out about this apparent agent. There was an agent Ted Samuelson at the Sacramento field office, but he was very much alive. It became clear this victim had been impersonating an agent, using the real agent's name.

Months later we would verify that the blood drops in the Shire residence matched the blood of this latest victim. But at the time we could only surmise this man had been in the Shire home and taken the items. This now left *four* dead men connected to Hannah Shire.

MORSE: What about the real identity of this victim?

WADE: His driver's license read Arthur Rozland, age 34, of San Bruno, California. He was divorced, a father of two. No criminal record.

MORSE: Yet you couldn't possibly believe this man was as innocent as the other three victims. He'd posed as an FBI agent and stolen two items from the Shire residence. And he looked like one of the two men who'd threatened Hannah Shire the previous afternoon.

WADE. He could have been one of those men—assuming Mrs. Shire's story was true.

MORSE: Did you not make the connection between the video Hannah Shire gave you and the theft of her computer and backup drive?

WADE: She'd copied the video onto her own computer, but we told her to erase it. Talk about connections—at that point I had *four* homicides, and every one of the victims was connected to Mrs. Shire. Who had fled. And was refusing to turn herself in, despite public pleas that she do so.

MORSE: This man broke into her house and stole her computer!

WADE: As I told you before, there was no sign of forced entry. We surmised he'd been in her house, and maybe she'd shot him. But she could have let him in, and then some kind of argument ensued. Hannah Shire knew about the surveillance, and even which car our deputy was in. Maybe she told Rozland to come to her back door. Maybe she told him to shoot the deputy first.

MORSE: Did it not occur to you that this FBI poseur shot Deputy Williams on his own? And then expertly jimmied a lock to break into the Shire house?

WADE: That was a possibility. But without a tip from Hannah Shire, how could this man have known about the surveillance?

MORSE: Indeed, Sergeant Wade. How *could* he have known?

Chapter 32

Monday, February 25, 2013

The minutes seemed like hours. Emily huddled in the Mexican restaurant's bathroom, clutching her cell phone. Any moment Rutger could show up. By now he could have followed the bus to its next stop and seen she wasn't on board. He'd backtrack to this stop. Search the strip mall, asking if people had seen her. It didn't help that three women had come in and out of the restroom, all eyeing her torn pants and wild expression with curiosity.

Five minutes passed. Six. Dave should be there by now.

Emily's cell phone rang. Dave's number. She jammed the *Talk* button. "Hi."

"I'm in back of the building. There's a rear entrance."

"Be right there."

She stuck her head out of the restroom, then eased out into the hallway. At the corner, she leaned around, peering across the tables of the small restaurant. No Rutger. No back door, either.

A waitress came by. Emily tapped her on the shoulder. "Where's your back entrance?"

The young woman frowned. "Oh. You must mean the one through the kitchen." She pointed. Emily limped toward the kitchen door. "Hey, that's just for employees!"

Emily flung back the door and hurried through the bustling kitchen as fast as she could. Smells of eggs, cilantro, and sizzling tortillas swirled in the air. Heads turned to gaze at her, eyes taking in her limp, her frightened face. She kept going.

If Rutger came looking for her, she would be remembered.

The back door drew near. Emily ran outside, ignoring the pain in her knee. Dave sat waiting, his passenger door open. She threw herself into the car, sliding far down in the seat. "Go, go!"

Dave took off.

Emily unlooped the laptop bag's handle off her head and shoulder. Pulled her cell phone out of her bag and turned it off. "Lock the doors." She replaced her cell and tossed the bag in the backseat.

Safety. At least for the moment. Emily tried to breathe.

"Thank you. For saving my life."

"What kind of car is he in?"

"Don't know." If only she did. How were they supposed to watch every car on the road?

"Baseball cap's back there." Dave pointed backward with his thumb. "Sorry I didn't have a black wig handy."

Emily reached into the backseat and snatched up the cap. She put it on her head and tried to shove her thick shoulder-length hair underneath. Her hair wouldn't stay. She needed bobby pins. Something.

"Doesn't work?" Dave glanced at her.

"No." She gave up and slipped further down in the seat. Unless Rutger was up high in a truck, he wouldn't be able to see her.

"That knee doesn't look very good." Dave gestured toward it with his chin.

"Doesn't feel very good either."

"How'd you get it?"

"I fell. I was hiding in the parking lot . . ." Words clogged in Emily's throat. How had she ever gotten away?

God. Nothing but God.

"Sorry I don't have tissues or anything in the car," Dave said.

"Doesn't matter. Blood's drying now anyway."

Dave tapped the steering wheel. "I suppose you won't be surprised to hear I kept looking at that video after you left."

"Yeah. I figured."

"I saw something else at the end. Just before the encryption. I had to enlarge it just like the message at the beginning."

"And?"

"One word. 'Abort.'"

Emily gasped. "Abort?" She rolled the word around in her mind. "That has to mean the encryption that follows tells how to stop the plan."

"Guess so."

Emily's eyes fixed on the dashboard as she checked her logic. She could see no other reason for the word to be there. "So I was right. There is a way to stop this." Excitement and hope shot through her. "We just have to find the key."

"Big 'just.'"

Emily ran a hand through her hair. So much of this made sense now. It was one thing to possess a video that depicted a terrorist plan. But to possess the means to stop it . . .

"Dave, I need your cell phone."

He handed it to her.

Wait. She'd captured her mom's last incoming call from her aunt's number on her own phone. Emily hit the seat with her fist in frustration. She'd have to turn her phone on again.

What might that cost her?

"What's the matter?" Dave glanced at her.

"I want to make a call *now*."

"So make it."

"I'm afraid to turn my phone on in case they're tracking it. Better wait at least half an hour, until we're out of this area."

For thirty interminable minutes Emily scrunched down in the seat. Her muscles went numb, and her knee hurt, but she tried to ignore the pain. Meanwhile her mind raced. All her conjecture was proving true. Morton Leringer *had* told her mom how to stop the terrorist attack.

Raleigh.

This was way too much for her and Mom to handle.

Emily rubbed her forehead. "You might as well know it all, Dave." Hidden down in the seat, she told him about Morton Leringer's accident. His message to her mother.

He frowned. "What's Raleigh mean?"

"That's what we have to find out. Mom and me, that is. Not you. I just want you to drop me off and head home. Erase that video on your computer. If we fail, you'll at least have time to get home before the electricity goes off."

Dave's mouth thinned. "Part of me can't believe this is happening."

"Nobody in America wants to believe it. And look what happened on 9/11." Bitterness tinged Emily's voice. "Total surprise and shock. Terrorists like this—they want us to think our safe little lives will go on forever."

She cradled her head in her hands. "But why us? Why me and Mom?"

"Wrong place, wrong time."

Too pat an answer. Emily couldn't bear the randomness of it. Who was she to stop this? Or her mom? They were just normal people.

She swallowed hard. "Where are we?" They'd head north on the freeway for about eighty miles, then go east toward Fresno.

"Just turned onto 101."

Time to make the call.

Emily twisted around to fumble her phone out of her bag. She turned it on, found her aunt's number and dialed it on Dave's phone, then turned her own cell off.

Her phone had been on less than a minute. She prayed it wouldn't matter.

"Hello." Her aunt's voice sounded cautious.

"Aunt Margie. It's Emily."

"Emily, dear, how nice to hear from you." The edge in her tone remained. "Your mother and grandmother are both napping. Well, maybe they're awake now, with the phone ringing."

"I need to talk to Mom right away."

"I'll get her."

Emily heard footsteps, then low voices. The click of a second receiver being picked up.

"Emily, hi." Her mother's greeting sounded thick with sleep and fear. "Where are you?"

"In a car on the way to Fresno."

"What?"

Keeping her voice as factual as possible, Emily told her mom what had happened. She didn't mention her hurt knee or how close she'd come to being caught. Her mom was already worried enough. "We've been driving a half hour. So we'll be there around"—she calculated—"2:30. I'll need directions."

A long silence followed. No doubt her mother was trying to take it all in. "That young man with the Southern accent is with the real FBI?"

"Looks like it. But I've got something else." Emily related what Dave had found on the video. "So apparently the encryption is about how to stop the attack."

"Oh." Her mother spoke almost under her breath. "And now . . . This is . . ."

"Mom, *what?*"

"I think I know what 'Raleigh' is. It's R-A-W-L-Y."

Emily listened to her mother's tale of the news story. When the words ran out—where to begin?

"A stuffed dog? A favorite toy of a little girl who just lost her dad. Oh, that's just terrific."

Her mother sighed. "I thought maybe something's sewn inside it? A piece of paper with the key on it for the encrypted message."

"But we don't know that. It sounds so crazy. May be just coincidence."

"It's all we've got."

Emily closed her eyes. She was so tired. Half an hour ago she'd have been thrilled to learn what Raleigh may mean. But *this.* "What are we supposed to do? We can't get anywhere near that family. They've got to be in constant contact with Wade and Harcroft."

"I know. And even if we could, I'm not taking that poor little thing's toy away. You should have seen the way she clutched it."

Emily blinked back tears. Man, she was on edge. Or maybe it was because she'd lost her own father not that long ago. "Mom, we have to call somebody. I mean, not everybody in law enforcement is in on this. We can't do this! We don't have the slightest idea what we're doing."

"I know." Her mother sounded even more exhausted than Emily. "But my brain can't think right now."

"Homeland Security," Dave said.

Emily stared at him. Of course. Clearly she wasn't thinking all that well herself. "How about Homeland Security, Mom? This is what they're for."

"Oh. Right. I'll call them." Her mom didn't sound convinced. Little wonder, after so much had gone wrong. Would they even listen? The story sounded so bizarre. But it had to work. It had to. Already the weight on Emily's shoulders was too much to bear. "Okay. Let me know what happens. Call me back on this number. My cell phone's off."

She punched off the line and laid her head against the seat, struggling to understand the inexplicable. Why would people do this to anyone? Much less their own country.

Emily heaved a sigh. She'd been crunched down long enough. With effort, she sat up in the seat, stretching her muscles.

"Recline the back of the seat if you want," Dave said. "Take a rest."

She touched his arm. "Thank you so much. I don't know what I would have done without you. What did your wife say, by the way?"

"She doesn't know yet."

Terrific. She'd think they'd run off together or something. "You'd better call her."

Dave hesitated. "I don't know how much to say. I don't want her in danger."

The comment punched Emily in the stomach. That's what she and her mother had become, wasn't it. A danger to anyone who tried to help. Her grandmother was already caught up in it. Now her aunt was involved. And Dave. Maybe his wife. "I'm so sorry," Emily whispered.

"It's okay."

But it wasn't okay. Not at all. Either they'd be caught today and killed, or tonight their world would go black. Then who knew what kind of chaos would follow?

Chapter 33

SPECIAL HOUSE SELECT COMMITTEE
INVESTIGATION INTO FREENOW TERRORIST
ACTIVITY OF FEBRUARY 25, 2013

SEPTEMBER 16, 2013

TRANSCRIPT

Representative ELKIN MORSE (Chairman, Homeland Security Committee): Now, regarding Hannah Shire's daughter, Emily—was it around this time you began to look for her?

Sergeant CHARLES WADE (Sheriff's Department Coastside): Yes. I thought it would be likely that Hannah Shire would contact her. I asked local police to go to her Santa Barbara apartment, but she wasn't there. At that point they needed to find out where she worked and send an officer to talk to her. They informed me they would let me know when this task had been completed.

MORSE: So in this escalating situation, wouldn't you agree the time had come to call the FBI for help? You had *four* murders, *two* missing women, a victim posing as an FBI agent, and a video that showed the destruction of a power generator.

WADE: Looking back, I could say yes. And I wish I had. At the time, I was working with my colleagues at the Moss Beach substation, including Deputy Harcroft, as well as the San Carlos police and California Highway Patrol. We had a lot of men on this. As for the FBI, I did call them regarding the badge victim number four was carrying.

MORSE: But you did not tell them about the video.

WADE: At the time I didn't believe it necessary.

MORSE: Some members of this committee see that as a rather convenient belief.

WADE: Nothing about that day was convenient, Mr. Chairman.

MORSE: Well, while you were busy chasing Mrs. Shire and her mother, and focusing on these murders instead of the video, the zero hour of 7:00 p.m. Pacific Time was fast approaching, was it not? And despite the working together of you and your colleagues at the substation, and the San Carlos police, and the California Highway Patrol—not *one thing* was being done to stop it.

Chapter 34

Monday, February 25, 2013

Stone stood in front of his TV, legs apart and arms crossed, watching the news. More pleas for Hannah Shire to turn herself in. More posturing by Sergeant Wade.

No mention of the video. Stone narrowed his eyes at the screen. Couldn't be better.

His cell phone rang—Tex. Relief shot through him. "You get her?"

"She got away." Tex sounded enraged.

"You let her *get away*?"

"I didn't 'let' her. She hid in a restaurant and escaped. She had help. But I talked to people who saw her go. She's with a white male in his fifties. Driving a black Nissan."

"Terrific, but you have no idea where they went."

"I'll find her."

"You let her get away once."

"I'll *find* her."

"You don't have much time."

Traffic noises sounded over the line. "Stone. I'll die before I fail to come through for you."

Stone knew he meant it. Tex and his girlfriend, Bo—both of them lived for FreeNow.

He eyed the TV. That video of Eddington's little girl and her stuffed dog was playing again. Too bad for that family. Eddington should have thought of them before he turned traitor.

Stone was tired of men not coming through for him.

"Let's just see that doesn't happen, Tex." He punched off the line.

Stone checked his watch. Eleven o'clock. In eight hours the cyber worm they'd released into the targeted power generators would go into action. Nothing would stop it except the code he'd instructed Eddington to encrypt on that video. The video was their backup plan, a way to halt the worm's destruction if something went wrong. Stone had instructed Eddington to hide the code's encryption key in a place no one would find it. When he turned traitor and gave the video to Leringer, Eddington must have also told the man where to find the encryption key. Had Leringer told Hannah Shire? Even if he had, now that Wade had ensured Shire and her mother were pariahs in hiding, their finding the key wasn't likely.

Still, *not likely* wasn't good enough.

Stone jabbed in the private number to one of his badges—a number known only by him and a few members of FreeNow. The first ring cut off. "Hi."

"You take care of it?"

"It's done."

The TV had turned to commercials. Stone pressed the *mute* button.

"Something else," the badge said. "Roz was found dead in his car. Shot four times. He had Shire's computer and backup drive."

The information jagged through Stone's veins. "Who killed him?"

"Can't be sure, but it looks like Hannah Shire."

Roz's voice, sputtering, breathy, when he'd called. Stone's theory had proven right. The man had already been shot. "Where's the computer and extra drive?"

A second's pause. "Also taken care of."

Why did that sound like a lie? "You sure?"

"It's done."

Stone nodded, a smile on his face. About time these loose ends of potential evidence were sewn up. No thanks to Roz. Now just one danger remained.

"Stone, I have one more thing. Not sure if it'll help, but . . . Shire's got an aunt in Fresno. Margaret Dexter. And a policeman not far from that area thinks he may have seen Shire's car heading that direction."

Why hadn't Tex discovered this aunt? Stone had a gut feeling Emily Shire would be headed to the same place. He smiled. "Good."

He hung up, more than satisfied.

His next call was to Tex. "Get back here," he growled, then punched off the line.

Humming to himself, Stone searched his cell's address book for the number of Mack, his main man in Fresno.

Chapter 35

buffed my face with both hands. The short sleep had made me feel worse. My body may as well have been drugged and wrapped in chains.

Aunt Margie stuck her head in the bedroom door. "Emily all right?"

"For the moment. She's on her way here. She's being chased too."

My aunt's eyes widened.

"I have to use your computer again."

She waved a hand. "Go ahead."

I sat down at my aunt's small desk and searched for Homeland Security. The organization had to be our saving grace. They'd know what to do. If I'd had my head on straight—and more sleep—I'd have called them hours ago.

The website popped up: www.dhs.gov. I searched the home page for a phone number. Not too far down in the middle was a

How Do I? box. The top link read "Report Suspicious Activity." *Yes.* I clicked on it and read.

Report Suspicious Activity
What You Need To Know
Prompt and detailed reporting of suspicious activities can help prevent violent crimes or terrorist attacks. If you see suspicious activity, please report it to your local police department. Local law enforcement officers can respond quickly. Once they assess the situation, they can obtain additional support.
Start Here
Citizens should always call local law enforcement. If you see something suspicious, please call local law enforcement.

I leaned back in the chair, head shaking. *Three* times they said call local police? I *couldn't* call local police.

Back to the site's home page. Under the *How Do I?* box near the bottom was a link to *Report Cyber Incidents.* That had to be it. I followed the link. The next page was full of information about cyber incidents but had no phone number. Near the end was another *Report Cyber Incident* link. I clicked it—and ended up on a form.

They wanted me to fill in a form and submit it? There was no time!

I searched the links at the top of the page. Clicked *About Us.* At the bottom of that page I found a phone number.

With a quick prayer, I picked up the phone and dialed.

"Computer Emergency Readiness Team, Agent Johnson."

My heart picked up speed. "Hi. I'm . . . I need to report an incident."

"Did you fill out the form on our website?"

"No time for that. You have to do something now. In the next eight hours. At 7:00 tonight Pacific Time the western electrical grid plus the area that includes Washington, D.C. will be hit."

A long pause. "Would you give me your name, please?"

I cringed. "I don't want to give it."

"Okay. Tell me more about what you know."

I told him, my words tripping over each other. How I'd met Morton Leringer. The flash drive. The men chasing me.

"And this is supposed to happen tonight?"

"Yes. And tomorrow it happens to the rest of the eastern grid. And the next day, Texas. The video says so."

"You gave this video to your local sheriff's department?"

"Yes, but—"

"Your department will be in contact with Homeland Security."

"I thought *you* were Homeland Security."

"We're a team within the department."

"Then give me the main number."

"If you have seen suspicious activity, you need to report it to your local law enforcement. You've done that. Rest assured that law enforcement will be in contact with DHS."

"But they won't because the sergeant there is one of the terrorists!" My hands were shaking. Why wouldn't he listen to me?

"Ma'am, that is a very serious charge you're making."

Oh, tell *me* it's serious. "Look, I think I know where the key to the encrypted message is. If you'd just listen to me and get to it—"

"What sergeant in which sheriff's department?"

"Sergeant Wade. Moss Beach substation, part of San Mateo County, California. And he's got a deputy working with him. Harcroft."

"All right. I'll contact the substation. If you'll give me your phone number I'll get back to you."

With a phone number they could find me here.

What if they'd traced the number already? Or captured it through ID?

I smacked the *Off* button. Then put down the phone. I stared at it, at the computer. What had I done?

Mom and I couldn't stay here any longer. They could come for me anytime. But if I woke her up now, she'd be too tired. She'd fight me hard. Likely go into one of her meltdowns.

I pushed to my feet. If I could sneak out now, maybe Aunt Margie would let me leave Mom here. She wasn't the one the police were looking for anyway.

My gaze swung back to the computer. What if I could find a main number for Homeland Security? Not their cyber branch.

I sat down again and searched the DHS home page. At the top was a "Contact Us" link. Should have gone there the first time. I followed the link, and after a couple clicks, found the number for the Operator.

Here we go again. I dialed the number.

"Department of Homeland Security."

"I need to talk to someone about a terrorist attack that's going to happen tonight."

"Just a moment, please." The operator sounded so calm, as if she heard such words every day. My heart was already beating double time. This was my last chance for help.

"Hello, I'm Greg Branson. You say you have news of a terrorist threat?"

Relief trickled through me. "Yes." I launched once again into my story. "The video says 7:00 p.m. tonight for the western electrical grid, and 10:00 for the area that includes Washington, D.C. Tomorrow and the next night, it's the rest of the country."

"And you say this video has been given to the sheriff's department in Moss Beach."

"Yes, but that doesn't matter. Sergeant Wade is part of the

terrorist group. And I think Deputy Harcroft is too. I don't think they're doing anything with the video."

"Why do you think this sergeant is part of the group?"

"He sent two men to kill me. At my house. Now he's hunting me down on TV, telling everyone I'm a suspect in the death of Morton Leringer and two other men. I didn't kill them! I just stopped to help at an accident."

"If your local law enforcement are asking you to come in and talk to them about some homicides, it's important that you do that."

"But who knows what will happen to me if I'm put in Wade's custody? And meanwhile, no one's doing anything about this video!"

"You don't know that. They may well be working on it."

"Really? Have they contacted you about it?"

Silence.

"Don't you think this is something Homeland Security should know?"

"Certainly. Here's what we need to do. You should go to the nearest police station so you can talk to the sheriff's department about the homicides. They'll want to question you. I will contact the Moss Beach substation to see what they know about the video. We'll take it from there."

If he called the substation, they'd just put him in touch with Wade. Or Harcroft.

"There's not much time for talk. You need to get the key to the encrypted message, which tells how to stop the attack."

"I will speak to the sergeant about that."

"He won't tell you the truth! Look, I think the key may be sewn into—"

Aunt Margie's doorbell rang. I froze.

"Hello?" Branson's voice filtered through the phone. "You there?"

Had that cyber team already discovered where I was?

I crept over to the window and eased back the curtain.

A police car sat at the curb.

Chapter 36

**SPECIAL HOUSE SELECT COMMITTEE
INVESTIGATION INTO FREENOW TERRORIST
ACTIVITY OF FEBRUARY 25, 2013**

SEPTEMBER 16, 2013

TRANSCRIPT

Representative ELKIN MORSE (Chairman, Homeland Security Committee): So we are now up to around 11:15 a.m. on February 25, 2012. What were you doing at this time?

Sergeant CHARLES WADE (Sheriff's Department Coastside): I was going door-to-door in the area where Morton Leringer lived, asking if anyone had seen anything that might have been related to the homicides. This procedure took time. I was also in regular contact with the San Carlos police regarding the homicide of Arthur Rozland. And, of course, I was in contact with many people in the field who were trying to locate Hannah Shire. We had deputies and police officers talking to her neighbors, her friends at work, friends at the church she attended.

MORSE: And you learned some information about Hannah Shire, correct?

WADE: By that time we'd heard from Tina Crylon, the employee at the motel at which Mrs. Shire and her mother stayed briefly. Miss Crylon had seen Mrs. Shire on the news and called our department, but that was a couple hours after the two women had checked out. We then discovered that Hannah Shire had an aunt about an hour away in Fresno—Margaret Dexter. And a policeman in the area thought he may have spotted Mrs. Shire's car headed in that direction. I called Fresno police and asked them to send someone to Mrs. Dexter's house.

MORSE: Okay we will come back to that. So what time did you return to the Moss Beach substation?

WADE: About 11:50 a.m.

MORSE: This was after you received the calls from Homeland Security?

WADE: Yes. The first call came into my office line around 11:20. The second came in right after. The substation alerted me on my cell phone. I immediately called the first number—the Computer Emergency Readiness Team of DHS—and spoke with Agent Johnson. He told me about a call from a woman who must be Hannah Shire. In the second call I spoke with Greg Branson of DHS, who told me a similar story.

According to them, Hannah Shire claimed the video she'd given me contained information on a "Phase 1" terrorist attack. I had no knowledge of such information being on that video—and I'd watched it numerous times. Neither had I received any such information from the technician I'd given it to. So it was imperative that I report to the substation right away and look again at that video.

MORSE: But you were not able to look at it. Were you?

WADE: Not immediately, no.

MORSE: Please tell this committee why.

We're waiting, Sergeant Wade.

WADE: When I returned to the substation and spoke to our tech, Deputy Morris Landow . . . he couldn't find the video.

MORSE: Couldn't "find" it.

WADE: That's correct. He agreed I'd given it to him that morning. He knew where he'd placed it in his office. But it was no longer there. We conducted a thorough search throughout the substation, but it could not be found.

MORSE: So you lost this crucial video. And, as I understand it, there was no backup. Correct?

WADE: There was no backup done by our department. Deputy Landow had not done that yet. He should have, but he didn't. Needless to say, I was not happy about that.

MORSE: Had he even *looked* at the video?

WADE: He had looked at it numerous times, but had not had time to do an in-depth analysis on it. As it turned out, we didn't have that capacity at our substation and would have needed to turn it over to the San Mateo County Sheriff's Department.

MORSE: Why didn't you do that right away?

WADE: As I've told this committee over and over, I could not have known at the time how critical the flash drive was, nor that it contained an encrypted message. And I was working on multiple homicides.

MORSE: But this is the crux of the matter. Because you've also told us when you first viewed the video along with Deputy Harcroft, you both knew the equipment in the scene was a power generator.

WADE: Yes. But a short clip of a generator falling apart in and of itself did not signal a planned terrorist attack. That would have been a big jump in logic at the time.

MORSE: It would have been the right jump, wouldn't it, Sergeant Wade?

Chapter 37

Monday, February 25, 2013

I jerked back from the window, nerves searing.

"Hello?" A distant voice from the telephone reached my ear.

I punched off the line and threw the receiver on Aunt Margie's bed.

The doorbell rang again. Followed by hard knocks.

I ran to the doorway of the bedroom and listened. My aunt's footsteps sounded in the front hallway. The door opened.

"Margaret Dexter?" A man's voice.

"Yes."

"I'm Officer Turney. I'd like to talk to you about your niece, Hannah Shire."

"Hannah? Is she all right?"

I could picture my aunt's raised, innocent eyebrows.

"I don't know. She's missing."

"Missing!"

"She left her house last night along with her mother. No one has seen her since."

"They must be on a trip. It's not like Hannah to just disappear. She's far too reliable for that."

"I'm sure. But the sheriff's department in her area would like her to come in and talk to them about a couple of homicides. It's been all over the news."

My aunt *hmph*ed. "I don't watch much TV. And what in the world would Hannah have to do with a homicide?"

"That's what the sheriff's department needs to find out."

"She certainly wouldn't be responsible, if that's what you're thinking."

"If she talks to the sheriff's department she can tell them that."

"Of course." My aunt paused. "Who's dead? Someone she knows?"

Vaguely, I heard the policeman's answer. My eyes had strayed to the closed bedroom door where Mom slept. If she happened to walk through it right now, it was over.

"Tell you the truth," my aunt said, "I don't see Hannah very often. We call once in awhile. And send letters at Christmas. But she doesn't get down here much. Today's a work day for her. Have you checked there?"

"Yes, I'm sure they have. Let me give you my card. Please call if you hear anything."

"All right."

"Before I leave, mind if I check around?"

I grabbed the doorway.

"In my house?"

"Yes."

"Whatever for?"

"I'd just like to look around, if I may."

My knuckles went white.

"You seem like a nice young man, but really, I see no need to let you snoop around my house. I'm just a widow, living here by myself."

"I see." The policeman's voice edged. "We can come back with a warrant, you understand. Then you'll have no choice but to let us in."

"Is that so." My aunt put on her most imperious tone. "And on what grounds would you convince a judge to give you a warrant?"

"This is a serious situation, ma'am."

"Serious or not, I thought the Fresno Police Department had better things to do than threaten old ladies."

"No threats here. I'm just telling you—"

"Fine then. You just go get a warrant. And when you come back and poke in my closets, I'll hand you a dust rag so you can clean the shelves!"

The door slammed shut.

I couldn't move. Trembling, I cocked an ear toward the window. Was the cop leaving?

Seconds ticked by. A car door shut. An engine started.

Aunt Margie's footsteps approached from the entryway.

She rounded the corner, steps firm and cheeks red. But anxiety shone in her eyes. "You heard?"

I nodded.

"They'll be back if they can finagle that warrant. On what grounds, I can't imagine."

She was right. They probably had no grounds. But what law enforcement had proven trustworthy to this point? "We can't stay here. We can't chance it."

My aunt sighed.

"I'll have to get Mom up. That won't be easy."

"You should leave her here. It's safer."

"No, it's not, if they're likely to find her. They'll haul her to Wade. He'll try to get out of her what she knows. He already sent a man to kill us!"

My aunt gazed at the floor. "You can at least take my car. They'll be looking for yours. But where will you go?"

There was just one place we could go. Back to the Bay Area, to the heart of danger. Somehow, some way I had to find Ashley Eddington and convince her to listen to me. Because no one else would.

"I have a job to do. We've tried to go for help. The police. The FBI. Even Homeland Security. Nothing has worked. Now it's up to me."

Even as I spoke the words, I knew they were ridiculous. I was no savior of the world. I was just a widow trying to take care of her failing mother. Trying to protect her daughter.

My aunt raised her chin. "What do you need to do?"

I filled my lungs with air. Someday I would sleep again. "Aunt Margie, if I fail, the electricity will go off at seven o'clock tonight. And will stay off for who knows how long. The terrorists have to be doing it to cause chaos. Violence will follow. Looting, murder. Stay in the house. Keep the doors locked."

Aunt Margie's eyes had gone wide. "I thought this was about some homicides."

I managed a grim smile. "That's what they want you to think."

Chapter 38

Get back here." Stone's terse command echoed in Tex's head as the plane's wheels left the runway.

He was returning to the Bay Area, all right. Furious and frustrated, and more determined than ever. *How* could he have failed to bring in Emily Shire? She'd make him look stupid and worthless to Stone. That was unforgivable.

She would pay. One way or another, he would get Emily Shire.

And he'd make it up to Stone, whatever it took. The man wouldn't kill him, even if his twelve hours ended. He was too valuable to FreeNow. Too loyal. Stone had trusted Tex as part of his inner circle.

Tex watched the world fall away. Tonight it would all begin.

He and Bo were ready. They had a generator for the house, had stocked up on food and portable lanterns. While the rest of the city suffered, they would not. He wanted her comfortable, alone at night in the surrounding blackness. He would be on the streets.

She'd wanted to hit the streets with him. He'd told her no. They'd fought about it. She was just as valuable, she said. Just as well trained, maybe more.

At some point their generator and batteries and candles would run out. They were prepared for that as well. They and all FreeNow members could live off the land if they had to. Whatever it took, and however long, as they worked from within to topple the corrupt government. Return America to her once powerful state, where the people ruled and were truly free.

Underneath him, Tex could feel the plane wheels tuck themselves into its underbelly. This short flight would be the last he'd take for a very long time. Maybe forever. He leaned back in his seat and closed his eyes. Tried to shove his anger aside. He'd fix this, oh yes, he would.

He would *get* Emily Shire.

Chapter 39

A twangy country song jarred Emily awake. Her eyes popped open, tried to focus. How in the world could she have fallen asleep?

The awful music was coming from Dave's cell phone.

He picked it up and glanced at the ID. "Must be for you."

Emily sat up, blinking hard. The number was from her aunt's house. "Mom?"

"*Don't* come here. The police have been here looking for us and will be back with a warrant. We have to leave."

Air kicked out of Emily's mouth. "Where will you go?"

Her mother told her, the words thin and tight.

"Mom, you can't do that!"

"What choice do I have?"

The question slammed around in Emily's head. "I don't know. But—"

"If I can convince Ashley Eddington to listen, and we find something in that stuffed dog, she and Leringer's daughter will speak out. They can get to law enforcement who's not involved in the plot. *I* can't do that. Neither can you. Since right now it's all about arresting me."

"And if she doesn't listen, she'll turn you right over to Wade. There has to be another way."

"Tell it to me. Please." Her mother had never sounded so old.

Emily gripped the phone. "You can't go in your car. Everyone's looking for it."

"Aunt Margie said I can use hers."

"Oh, great. So if you're caught, Aunt Margie will be in trouble too—for helping you escape. Besides, if the police look through her house, they'll find *your* car."

Her mother hesitated. "That's what I told her. But if I stay and they come back, she's in trouble anyway."

Emily pressed a hand to her forehead. This was so . . . "Where does Ashley Eddington live?"

"In San Carlos, of all places."

"San Carlos!"

"I don't know the street address."

"So how do you—"

"Aunt Margie's trying to find out on the computer. If we can't find it right away, I'll just have to start driving and trust she *will* find it by the time we get there. Right now I have to get Mom up. Without her having a complete meltdown."

"You're taking her with you? No way."

"I can't leave her! They'll find her here for sure. Can you imagine your grandmother being taken away all by herself for questioning? She'd be petrified."

"But they won't hurt her. She doesn't know anything."

"Emily. An armed man broke into our house in the middle of the night and kicked down her bedroom door."

Emily's eyes searched the road. Had the whole world gone crazy?

She saw a sign to turn east for Fresno. Good. Still time to change direction.

"Okay, Mom. I'll meet you in San Carlos."

"What? No you won't!"

"I can help. *I'll* talk to Ashley. She takes one look at you, with your picture plastered everywhere, and you're done for. You won't get one word out."

"Emily, no."

"Okay then, what would you like me to do, Mom? I can't go home. And cops are all over your house."

"Go home with your friend. The one who's driving you."

And take the danger to Dave's family? Plus leave her mother and Grand in danger on their own? No way.

"Does Aunt Margie have a cell phone?" Emily asked.

"Yes. She's letting me take it."

"Give me the number."

For once her mom didn't protest. Emily entered the number into Dave's phone. "Okay. Call me when you're about there."

"Emily, I don't want you to do this."

"And I don't want *you* to do this, so we're even."

Her mother breathed over the line. "This is insane."

Yes, it was. But her mother was right—it was also their one chance. And time was ticking. It was already noon. Even if they could find the key to stop the terrorist attack, how long would it take computer geeks to *do* that?

"Listen, Mom, when you find out where Ashley Eddington lives, give me a call."

"And if I don't?"

"I've got my computer with built-in Wi-Fi, I'll find out myself."

Dave threw her a look.

"Emily, you are too hard-headed."

"Well, wonder where I got that from."

"It's atavistic. You got it from your grandmother."

"Sure, whatever you say. I'm hanging up now. *Call* me."

Emily hit the *Off* button and turned to Dave. "Would you mind driving a little bit farther?"

Chapter 40

I opened the door to the room where Mom was sleeping. Even as I entered, I argued with myself. Maybe I should leave her. Maybe she was safer here than with me.

But if I left her, what would happen when the police came? To Mom and to Aunt Margie?

Mom was snoring softly, her mouth open. I inhaled a long breath. This wouldn't be easy.

I shook her shoulder.

She snored on.

I shook her again, harder. She swallowed a snort and opened unfocused eyes. "Hunh?"

"Mom, it's me. You need to get up now."

"Why?" The question swam up from half-sleep.

"We have to go now. The Bad People will find us here if we stay."

Her eyes blinked. She turned toward me, one hand finding her chest. "Can't get up. Too tired."

"I know. I'm sorry. But you have to."

"No. Later." Her eyes closed.

I leaned against the bed and gathered myself, then shook her again.

"Leave me alone!"

"Mom, you *have* to get up."

"I don't wanna."

"I'm sorry. Just move to the car, that's all I ask. You can sleep there."

"No. Here."

How long had the police been gone? How long until they ran down a judge and got a warrant? Given the attention the media was giving this case, probably not long.

"Here. Let me help you up." I slid an arm beneath her shoulders and pushed her to sit up. She rose like a puppet, her face blank. Then her arms came up, offended and waving. "No." She grabbed my arm in her weak hand, trying to pull me away. "I don't want to!"

"Shh, Mom, it's okay."

"I don't want to get up!"

"I'm so sorry."

"You can't treat me like a child. I want to sleep!"

"I'll get you some tea before we go, how about that?"

"I don't want tea, I want you to leave me alone."

Anger chewed at me. This was so unfair to my mother. Who *were* these men, that they could do this to us?

"Mom, come on now, stand up. You're almost there." I nudged her feet toward the floor.

Her jaw locked and her face flushed. Her arms waved more wildly, hands hitting at me. "I'm not getting up!" Her voice rose, panic-hollowed and old. "I'm *not*."

"Stop it." I chased her jerking hands, caught them by the wrists. "You have to calm down. Look at me, look at me."

"Nnno!" She squeezed her eyes shut and fought harder.

"Mom, pl—"

"*No!*"

She opened her mouth wide and screamed. A second time, and a third. I let go of her wrists and stepped back, palms up. She shrieked a fourth time, and fifth, and sixth, until I lost count and my head vibrated. The sound bounced off the walls and slashed my ears, my heart.

What if the neighbors heard?

Tears trickled down my cheeks. Why did she do this to me?

My mother's eyes opened. She glared at me, fists clutched to her neck and chest heaving.

Aunt Margie scurried into the room. "What—?"

"She won't let me sleep!" Mom thrust a forefinger toward me. "Tell her to leave me alone!"

"Yes, dear." Aunt Margie bustled over to the bed. "It's all right now."

"Tell her to go away!"

"I'm going, I'm going." I backed up more. In fact, I considered going all the way to the front door. Walking outside and down the street, letting the policeman find me. I couldn't do this anymore.

Mom's face scrunched up, and she started to cry. "Why does she treat me like this?"

I leaned against the doorway, soul-sick.

Aunt Margie sat down beside Mom and put an arm around her. "Shh, now, she's only trying to help you."

"She's *not* helping!"

My aunt patted Mom's shoulder as she locked eyes with me.

"Did you find it?" I mouthed.

She shook her head. "You can see where I was on the screen."

I took her cue and left the room, hoping Aunt Margie could calm Mom down. She couldn't fail any worse than I'd done.

"Listen, Carol, you remember you told me about the Bad People?" Aunt Margie's voice filtered to my ears as I walked down the hall. In the bedroom I stopped and prayed. "Lord, help me do this. I'm terrible on my own."

The memory of Mom's screams still zinged my nerves.

How much time did we have before the policemen showed up? I checked my watch. A new sense of urgency filled me.

With a deep breath, I headed to the desk and sat down. The monitor showed hits from a search for *nathan eddington + san carlos*. The top links were for newspaper articles about his death. I searched for a few pages, then got a better idea. In California, the tax evaluation on homes was public information. I typed in *nathan eddington san carlos tax*. Up came a link for the San Mateo County property evaluation for the Eddington house.

Address: 1287 Sloat Street.

For a moment I stared at it, wishing it hadn't been this easy. Now I really had to go there.

I grabbed a piece of paper and wrote down the address.

Back in the hall I could still hear Aunt Margie's soothing voice. Mom was quiet. I went to the bathroom. Then to the kitchen, where I guzzled a glass of water. I put the address in my purse. After that I found myself in the TV room, trying to think what needed to be moved from my car to Aunt Margie's vehicle. Probably everything.

Except Samuelson's gun. That still lay in the tote bag. If the lights went out tonight and stayed that way, would Aunt Margie need it for protection?

But if the police searched her house and found it, she could be arrested.

She may be arrested anyway, as soon as police spotted my car in her house.

I dropped my face in my hands. I couldn't even make this simple decision. How was I supposed to drive over three hours back to

San Carlos? I'd fall asleep at the wheel. And that would be just the beginning of what I faced.

Footsteps sounded in the hall. I walked that direction—and saw Mom headed for the bathroom.

Aunt Margie approached me, her cheeks pale. "I'm so sorry you had to go through that." She kept her voice low. "Don't know how I managed to calm her down. For some reason the logic worked."

"I know why." My throat tightened. "Because you're not me."

"Oh, Hannah, don't say that."

"It's true. I'm her caregiver. And she takes it out on me."

"She doesn't know any better."

"I realize that. Still, it's . . ." I looked at the floor.

Aunt Margie squeezed my shoulder. "You're wonderful with her. It wouldn't be easy for anyone."

I managed a nod.

Down the hall the bathroom door closed.

My aunt turned toward the kitchen. "I'll get you my car key and cell phone."

"And I need to move our things over to your car." I walked out to the garage and transferred the items over. When I picked up the tote bag, I hesitated, then took it into the kitchen. "Aunt Margie, there's a gun in here. A big one with a silencer. Do you want it?"

Her eyes rounded. "Whatever would I do with that?"

"Protect yourself."

She considered the bag. "I'd just shoot myself in the leg. You keep it." She shuddered.

I returned to the garage and put it in the trunk of her car.

As I stepped back through the kitchen door, I found Mom standing at the sink next to my aunt, drinking water. "Margie has some water bottles for us," she told me. "And some cookies. Isn't that nice?"

Did she even remember her outburst?

"Yes, Mom, that's nice."

She set down her glass. "We're going to find the daughter now, aren't we. In Raleigh."

I gave her a sad smile. She wasn't too far off. "Yes."

"So we can keep our promise to Morton."

"That's right."

"He was such a nice man."

"He was."

"How he must have suffered." Her chin trembled.

"I know. That's why we have to fix this."

Mom cocked her head. "Hannah, you can't fix everything. Sometimes you just have to let God do it."

Her words struck the core of me.

"Like the Bible verse says, 'He guards the steps of His faithful ones, for a man does not prevail by his own strength.'" Mom's gaze drifted out the window. "I can't remember what book it's in . . ."

My aunt and I exchanged a glance. What was that in her expression? Agreement? Surprise? Sadness?

Maybe all three.

I aimed another smile at my mother. "You're a very wise woman, Mom."

She beamed at me.

A few minutes later the three of us were in the garage, hugging each other. "Aunt Margie," I had to warn her one last time, "you know you're going to be in trouble if the police come and find my car here."

She shrugged. "Don't you worry about me. I'll handle it."

But what if she got into the hands of the wrong police officer? Someone who was working with Wade and Harcroft? "Maybe you should go with us."

That was insane. She'd be in even more danger with me.

Aunt Margie chuckled. "You want to be responsible for *two* old women?"

I opened my mouth, but no answer came.

She patted my arm. "Don't you worry about me. Just go and do what you have to do. Someday you're going to tell me the whole story."

My throat tightened. I gave her another hard hug. Then turned to help Mom into the car. I buckled her seatbelt for her.

Aunt Margie moved to open the garage door. "I'll be praying. Call me when you can."

"I will."

The garage door opened, and we backed out into the unknown.

Chapter 41

Stone picked up his cell the second it started to ring. The ID was from Fresno.

"Yeah, Mack."

"I've spotted 'em. They're driving away from the house in a blue car."

Stone smacked a fist against his thigh. "Why weren't you there sooner? Two minutes, and you'd have had them in the house."

"Got here fast as I could."

Stone seethed.

"At least we found 'em. I'll follow the car. When they stop I'll get 'em."

"*Don't* let them out of your sight."

"Won't happen."

Stone checked his watch. Twelve thirty. As long as the women remained in a car the police weren't looking for, law enforcement had less chance of finding them. Which gave his man some time.

"Check in with me every half hour, let me know where they are. If we're lucky, they'll lead us someplace important."

"Will do."

Stone ended the call and punched in Tex's number to leave a message. "We've found the women in Fresno. Call me as soon as you land."

Chapter 42

Mom was fumbling with the side of her seat. I glanced at her. "What are you trying to do?"

"See if the seat will go back. Oh. There." Her arm moved—and the seat reclined. "Hah!" Mom eased herself back and settled in.

In five minutes she was asleep.

I drove out of Fresno and turned north on Highway 99. My back was ramrod straight, arms tense. Every thirty seconds my eyes flicked to the rearview mirror, looking for police cars. I saw none.

A half-hour later I turned west onto Highway 152.

Once again I warred with myself. To call my daughter or not? If I didn't, she'd worry. Plus I had no doubt she'd end up at the Eddington's house anyway. As long as we were both headed there, we should coordinate our efforts.

Talking on a cell phone while driving was illegal in California. I checked for police once more, then picked up Aunt Margie's phone and keyed in the number. Emily answered immediately. "Mom! You okay?"

"We're fine. In the car."

"I was worried. It took you a long time to call back."

"I had to get Mom up. And I wanted to get off 99. Not as many cars now."

"How far away from San Carlos are you?"

"Maybe two and a half hours. How about you?"

"About three. You get the address?"

I told her the address already branded into my mind. "You know where the street is?"

"Yeah. Don't do anything until I get there."

"Okay."

"What are you planning?" Emily asked.

"I have no idea."

"Well, do you think you're just going to ring the doorbell?"

"Maybe, who knows?"

"Mom, what if cops are there?"

"Emily, I *don't know*. Besides, I doubt if they are. If anything, family has gathered." Family who would be ultra protective of Ashley Eddington and just as suspicious of me. "We won't know how to do this until we get there."

"Kinda like flying blind."

Yeah. Kinda like that.

My eyes flicked again to the rearview mirror. One car behind us in the distance. "Look, I better go. I'll call you when we arrive."

"Okay. Love you."

"Love you too." I ended the call and set down the phone.

For the next two and a half hours I drove. Part of the time I was numb. Then my brain would fly around in circles, no place to land. Other times I fought to keep my eyes open. And still others I begged God to help me. Help our nation. And keep Mom and Emily safe. Because of me they'd been dragged into this. Whatever it took, I had to protect them both.

And, please, Lord, help me trust in You like Mom does. Like I should.

Mom slept the entire trip. No having to stop for bathroom breaks. In the silence, questions crowded my mind. What condition would Mom be in when we reached San Carlos? Rested and willing to do what I told her—or volatile?

And what about Aunt Margie? Had the police been to her home by now? Twice I started to call, then stopped myself. What if they were there when the phone rang? What if they saw the ID with my aunt's own name? They'd know I had her cell phone.

What about that man I shot? Could he possibly be alive in some hospital? I'd seen nothing on the news about him. If he was dead, was a wife mourning for him? Maybe children. How could I ever face them, tell them how sorry I was? It wasn't their fault, what their loved one had done.

We drew closer to San Carlos. With every mile I felt more like a refugee. I'd be in my town but couldn't go to my home. Couldn't show my face to friends or coworkers. To anyone.

What would it be like tonight if the electricity went out—and stayed that way? Then more blackouts in the next two days—until the whole country was hit? How would we live?

For the first time, I took a serious look at that dismal scenario. How to make a cup of coffee? Fry an egg? Think of the cold, especially in Washington, D.C. People would die from no heat. No computers, televisions, ovens, microwaves. So many jobs could not be done without electricity. What about the transportation systems? Food and other goods would fail to reach their destinations. With higher unemployment, lack of food and heat, even law-abiding citizens in the blacked-out areas could rise up in anger. What kind of lawlessness would ensue?

What would I do in such a world? How would I take care of my mother? I'd still be sought by police.

I turned onto I-280. And before long I passed the Woodside and Farmhill exits. The Edgewood exit—mine—was next. What to do when I reached it?

With a final glance around for police, I picked up the phone to call Emily.

Chapter 43

While Stone was on his cell phone, a beep sounded in his ear. He checked the ID and cut the first call to switch over. It was the fourth call in two hours from his man in Fresno. "Yeah, Mack."

"She's almost to San Carlos."

Stone planted a fist on his hip. What was she doing *there*? She couldn't be going home. Nothing but danger for her in the area. Unless some friend had offered to shelter her.

Or maybe she was on to something.

Stone ran through the options in his mind. He wanted Hannah Shire before the police got to her. Police would just make things more complicated. But he also wanted to know where she was headed.

"All right. Stick with her. If she stops somewhere, call me."

He smacked off the line and called Tex. "You set to go?"

"Anytime."

"Good. Got a job for you."

Chapter 44

**SPECIAL HOUSE SELECT COMMITTEE
INVESTIGATION INTO FREENOW TERRORIST
ACTIVITY OF FEBRUARY 25, 2013**

SEPTEMBER 16, 2013

TRANSCRIPT

Representative ELKIN MORSE (Chairman, Homeland Security Committee): When you failed to find the flash drive anywhere in the substation, what did you think had happened to it?

Sergeant CHARLES WADE (Sheriff's Department Coastside): I had no idea. It was an absolute mystery to me. But not one I could think about for long. There was too much to do.

MORSE: It never occurred to you that someone in the substation had taken that flash drive?

WADE: I had no reason to suspect such a thing.

MORSE: And, just to press the point—the disappearance of this crucial flash drive was a surprise to you.

WADE: A complete surprise.

MORSE: Again, you must understand how convenient this appears. First you ignore the video. Then, when you *have* to look at it due to the calls from Homeland Security, the flash drive is gone.

WADE: I cannot control how the truth *appears* to you, Chairman Morse.

MORSE. Well. I could hammer the point, but we will move on. What did you do upon learning that the flash drive was missing?

WADE: Turns out we did have a backup. Remember, when Arthur Rozland's body was discovered in his car, Hannah Shire's computer was also found. That computer was logged into evidence by the California Highway Patrol. What if Mrs. Shire hadn't erased the copy of the video she'd made? It was our one hope at that point. So I contacted Highway Patrol and asked if someone there could check the computer for that file. They did—and found the video.

MORSE: You had not asked to see the contents of Mrs. Shire's computer before this time?

WADE: No. I'd been busy investigating multiple homicides. I knew California Highway Patrol would be looking at it.

MORSE: And I'll ask again—did it not occur to you that Arthur Rozland had stolen Mrs. Shire's computer *because* of that video?

WADE: I may have entertained that thought briefly. But it didn't seem likely at the time.

MORSE: Once again, I am amazed at your answer, Sergeant Wade. Hannah Shire had reported being harassed by two men posing as FBI agents, demanding to know what Morton Leringer had told her before his death. She gave them a copy of the video. Why wouldn't these same men return to her house for her computer if they thought that computer might contain the video as well? They were clearly trying to recover any and all copies.

WADE: We know all these details now. A lot of the dots have been connected, and hindsight makes everything seem obvious. It's this way in many cases, Chairman Morse. I've investigated a lot of homicides, and often it takes weeks, months, even years to solve a case. When it's all done, how easy it is for someone outside the investigation to armchair quarterback. "Why didn't you do this? Why didn't you see that sooner?" But I have to keep reminding you how complex the events of that day were, and how fast one twist came upon another. Do you realize how few hours had gone by since I'd first even heard Hannah Shire's name? So let me state this clearly: at the time I didn't know the men posing as FBI agents were aware Mrs. Shire had retained a copy of the video. And let me also remind you—when Harcroft and I heard she'd made that copy, we told her to erase it.

MORSE: Erasing that copy would certainly be in the best interest of FreeNow, wouldn't it?

WADE: I resent any insinuation that I would share in FreeNow's "best interest." As for Mrs. Shire's computer—if you'd like to get back to that topic—upon hearing it contained the video, I asked that a copy be made at once and hand-delivered to me at the San Mateo

County Sheriff's station, where we could use better technology to look at it.

MORSE: Why not send it electronically? Hand-delivery took more time. Another delay.

WADE: I wanted to keep that video secure. Sending it through cyberspace did not meet that standard.

MORSE: Were you informing Homeland Security as these events occurred?

WADE: Yes.

MORSE: And what did you discover when you finally watched the video?

WADE: As it turned out, the technology available at the San Mateo County Sheriff's station was not advanced enough. We were able to see something at the beginning and end of the video, but we couldn't distinguish any letters. Remember that up to this point I had serious doubts that Hannah Shire was telling the truth. Now that it was clear the video did indeed contain some sort of message, I couldn't take any chances. I took the flash drive to the FBI's San Francisco Joint Terrorism Task Force. It took time for me to reach that destination. After some work at that office I and a number of agents were able to watch the video frame by frame. We discovered the "Phase" text at the beginning. And we saw the encrypted message at the end, proceeded by the word "Abort."

MORSE: In other words, Sergeant Wade—Hannah Shire was right.

Chapter 45

Monday, February 25, 2013

The car ride seemed to take forever. Emily longed for her computer in the backseat. With her built-in Wi-Fi, she could be looking up information, checking the news, learning more about cyber terrorism—as if that would do them any good at this point. But what if the cops could somehow track her computer like they could a cell phone? She asked Dave if that was possible.

He shrugged. "I don't know. Never heard of it." He picked up his phone. "I'm going to check the office again."

Dave had called once already and talked to Ronnie. Had the FBI agent been back? Was anyone else asking about Emily? Or Dave?

No and no, Ronnie told him. She pestered him to tell her what was going on.

"If that agent shows up again," Dave had said, "*don't* tell him anything."

Now Dave's second call found nothing new. No one else had come around looking for Emily. Dave set down the phone, his shoulders sagging in relief.

"I keep thinking about my computer, sitting there at the office," he said. "With that video on it."

"I told you to erase it."

He threw her a hard glance. "You want me to turn around and take you back home?"

"No. Sorry. I'm just . . . nervous. And scared."

"That makes two of us."

Emily fidgeted in her seat, every nerve itching to *do* something. Finally she couldn't stand it any more. "Okay, here goes." She twisted around in her seat to get her computer.

On the Internet she first went to Bay Area news and watched the segment of Cheryl Stein and Ashley Eddington that her mother had seen. Those two women looked so angry at her mother. How in the world would she and her mom get past that?

The sadness on the little girl's face was heartbreaking. Emily found herself tearing up again. Then at the end was the stuffed dog. RAWLY.

Dave's cell rang. He picked it up and winced at the ID. He showed it to Emily: his wife. "Hello."

"Where *are* you?"

Emily could hear Tania's voice through the phone. "I called the office and they said you hurried out hours ago."

Dave glanced at Emily. "I had to take a sudden road trip."

"Road trip. Where?"

"I'll tell you all about it when I get home."

"Why not now? What's going on?"

"Tania, are you at work?"

"Of course, where else would I be?"

"Look, after work, don't go home. Go to your parents' and wait 'til I get there. I won't be home until about 9:30 or 10."

"*What?* What are you doing?"

"Just tell me you'll go."

"I . . . okay. But you need to—"

"And make sure you have candles and flashlights."

"Dave. You're starting to scare me."

"Yeah, I know."

Emily shut her eyes. She should never have gotten Dave into this. But if she hadn't, Rutger would have caught her for sure.

"Look, Tania, I need to go now. Don't want to stay on the phone for long."

"Tell me you're all right."

"I am. I'm fine. Just helping out a friend. Talk to you again when I can." Dave ended the call.

Emily shook her head. "That went well."

"Could have gone a lot worse."

True.

They drove in silence.

The familiar roads and landmarks whipped by, Emily giving Dave directions. Soon they were in San Jose. Then merging onto 280. Seeing the exits close to the area in which she'd grown up had always raised a lump in Emily's throat. Those streets stood for good memories, a happy childhood. Now they just looked menacing and dark, even in the daylight.

Dave's cell phone rang again, Aunt Margie's number in the ID. Emily snatched it up. "Mom?"

"I'm here. Almost to Edgewood exit."

"We're not far behind. Must have driven faster than you."

"Where are we?" Grand's distant voice trickled over the line. "Isn't this close to home?"

"Just a minute, Mom," Emily's mother told her.

"I want to go home!"

"Just . . . I'm trying to talk to Emily."

Emily winced. Her grandmother sounded so confused. "So what—"

"Hannah, I have to go to the bathroom." Grand's voice again.

"Okay, in a minute. Let me talk to Emily."

"I have to go now!"

"All ri—"

"Right now!"

"Mom," Emily said, "you'd better take her."

"I know, but where? I can't go into *any* store in this area."

"Hannah!" Grand was downright wailing.

Emily gritted her teeth. This was never going to work with Grand along. She should have stayed with Aunt Margie. "Let's meet up somewhere. I can take her inside."

"Okay." Emily's mother sounded so tired. Like she'd never be able to make decisions. "Where can we go?"

"How about Sequoia Hospital?" No one would take a second look at a confused, elderly woman there.

"Okay."

"Hannah!" Grand yelled.

"I know, I know." Mom's voice shook. "We're going to take care of you right away."

The tension between them flowed over the phone. Just hearing it pulled Emily's muscles into knots. They still had much to get through, and Grand could be so . . . crazy.

"Okay," Emily said, "here's where we meet." She chose an area in the hospital parking lot. "What kind of car are you in?"

"A light blue Camry."

"We're in a black Nissan. See you soon."

They ended the call.

Emily let her head fall back against the seat. This would never work.

"Where are we going?" Dave asked.

She told him the way. "Just drop me off and leave. Get home to Tania. Some day I'll make this up to you, Dave. Some day."

When would she even see him again? What if she and her mother failed, and the electricity went off for a long time? Did their building even have a backup generator? If so, how long would it last? And meanwhile they still wouldn't have Internet, right? So what would be the point of going to work?

Dave shot her a look. "Will you be okay?"

No. "Sure."

A few minutes later they pulled into Sequoia Hospital parking. Mom and Grand were already there. Emily's throat tightened when she saw them. She grabbed her laptop bag, gave Dave a hug and final thank-you, and jumped out of his car.

Ow. That hurt her knee.

Emily flung open the backseat of the Camry and threw her bag inside. Her mom slid out of the car. She looked terrible, old makeup smeared and clothes a mess, her hair uncombed and fear in her eyes. She looked down at Emily's knee and gasped. "What happened to you?"

"That fake FBI agent, that's what."

Her mom's mouth opened, but nothing came out. Emily could see the guilt on her face. "Mom, I'm fine. It's not your fault."

Her mother's eyes teared up. Emily hugged her hard. For a moment they just stood there, feeling each other shake.

"Emily!" Grand called.

"Coming." Emily broke away from her mom and helped Grand out of the car. Her grandmother's hair was smashed on one side, the lines in her face deeper. She wore crazy clothes, mismatched blue and green, all wrinkled.

"Oh, it's so good to see you!" Grand reached out her arms.

"Good to see you too." Emily hugged her, feeling the boney back, the slight frame. Had her grandmother ever felt so frail? "Let's take you inside to a bathroom." She clasped Grand's fingers and pulled her toward the building.

"I need to go too," Emily's mom said. "I'll follow at a distance and keep my head down."

Too dangerous to be seen together. How many times had her mother's and grandmother's faces been shown on the news?

Grand allowed herself to be led. "Did you know Bad People are following us?" She fluttered her hand in the air. "We have to get to Raleigh. It's very tiring."

"Yes, Grand. I know."

Emily's gaze cut left and right as they crossed the parking lot. Was anyone following? Was her mom all right? Everything within Emily pulled to look over her shoulder, check on her mother. But she didn't dare.

As they entered the hospital, her pulse skipped.

She asked for directions to the nearest bathroom, then hustled her grandmother along. Once they entered the restroom, panic clawed at Emily's throat. What was her mom doing? Had anyone recognized her?

"Hurry, okay?" she whispered to Grand.

As they left the restroom, from her side vision Emily spotted her mom ready to go inside. Grand saw her too. "Hannah, what—?"

"Shh!" Emily squeezed her fingers.

"Ow!"

In the hallway, heads turned.

"Come on, Grand, let's go." Emily pulled her grandmother away, heartbeat in her throat. If anyone had heard the name *Hannah* . . .

They crossed the parking lot as fast as Grand could go, Emily praying for her mother. At the car she noticed it unlocked, keys still in the ignition. Her mom's purse sat in the backseat. Woman wasn't thinking very straight. Emily helped Grand into the front passenger seat, then slipped behind the wheel. She started the car.

"Where's Hannah?" Grand sounded so scared. How had she made it through all this?

"She's coming. We'll go up and get her."

"We can't leave Hannah!"

"It's okay, Grand. It's okay."

She drove toward the entrance and put the car in Park. *Come on, where are you?* Long seconds stretched by.

Her mother came out of the building. Emily could have cried. Her mom reached the car, opened the back door—

From nowhere a gray van surged in front of them and jerked to a stop. Its side door gaped open. A man jumped out, gun in hand. Emily gasped. The man grabbed her mother and dragged her toward the truck.

"No!" Emily leapt from the car.

A second man appeared in the van and pulled her mother inside. The first man flung open the Camry's front passenger door and yanked out Grand.

"Ahhhh!"

He clamped a hand over her mouth. In no time she disappeared into the van. Emily ran toward her. "Nno—!"

An arm gripped around her neck. Then shoved her—hard. Other strong arms caught her at the van's door and pulled her inside to dimness, a hard floor. A man climbed in after her.

Her knee *hurt.*

Was she dreaming? It happened so fast.

Someone slammed the door, plunging them into darkness.

The van took off.

Chapter 46

**SPECIAL HOUSE SELECT COMMITTEE
INVESTIGATION INTO FREENOW TERRORIST
ACTIVITY OF FEBRUARY 25, 2013**

SEPTEMBER 16, 2013

TRANSCRIPT

Representative ELKIN MORSE (Chairman, Homeland Security Committee): Am I correct in assuming that, once you saw the messages on the video, you finally believed Hannah Shire?

Sergeant CHARLES WADE (Sheriff's Department Coastside): I believed her words about the video. I still had four homicides to investigate, and her role in those deaths remained unclear.

MORSE: Did you not rethink your theories at this point? Those homicides could be linked to the video. Hannah Shire and her mother could be on the run from the people responsible, who were now trying to kill her.

WADE: All of that went through my mind. We still had many pieces of the puzzle to fit together. At that point things were happening so fast my theories could change from one minute to the next. However, if Hannah Shire believed she was in serious danger, why didn't she call law enforcement? As I've mentioned before, she had my direct number. And even if she didn't trust me, at any time she could have gone to the nearest police station. She could have called the FBI. Her refusal to reach out to any law enforcement did not fit with the theory that she was a mere victim.

MORSE: She clearly did *not* trust you.

WADE: So she claimed. Which was pure insanity. She'd made a very serious accusation against me to Homeland Security—that I, a veteran of law enforcement for twenty-eight years, was a terrorist plotting against the government. You say she didn't trust me, Chairman Morse. At the time, I could not trust *her*.

MORSE: So once you saw the messages on the video, what did you do?

WADE: The FBI was now involved, as well as Homeland Security. We all needed to work together. First everyone needed to be brought up to speed on what had transpired. Homeland Security needed to tell the FBI task force what Hannah Shire had said on the phone. I needed to brief both parties regarding Mrs. Shire's interview and the homicides.

MORSE: You had taped that interview. Did the task force view it?

WADE: There was no time. If that video was accurate, the power grid would be hit within hours. So I briefed them to the best of my ability.

MORSE: I understand you were interrupted during that briefing with another piece of information.

WADE: Actually, two. The first involved the tracking of Hannah Shire's cell phone. That tracking was now in place. But it soon became clear that Mrs. Shire's phone had been turned off. The second involved Emily Shire. A Santa Barbara police officer had just gone to her place of business. There he had an "odd" encounter with the office receptionist, who seemed terrified to talk to him. The woman claimed a "fake FBI agent" had already been there looking for Emily.

MORSE: So Miss Shire had also disappeared?

WADE: Yes. Apparently aided by a man in the office, Dave Raines, who'd left in a hurry soon after she did and had not returned. And it took some amount of questioning on the officer's part to persuade the receptionist to say that much. The officer found Miss Shire's vehicle in the back parking lot of the building, all four tires slashed. He obtained the plate number for Mr. Raines's car and put out a BOLO—a Be On The Lookout.

MORSE: Did this disturbing news about Emily Shire lead you to now believe Hannah Shire's story?

WADE: Yes, it did. Further, the receptionist was able to identify the man as matching the sketch we had drawn the previous night, after Mrs. Shire's interview. The supposed FBI agent calling himself

'Rutger.' We already knew one of those men was dead, and now the other was after Emily Shire.

MORSE: Did you think that mother and daughter were together?

WADE: We didn't know. We had to look for both of them. At the same time we had to put priority on the video. In her calls to Homeland Security, Hannah Shire had been insistent that the word "Raleigh" was crucial in finding the encryption key. We had to act on that theory—it was all we had.

MORSE: Did it occur to you that perhaps Hannah Shire had been attempting to track down this "Raleigh" on her own? That this is at least one of the reasons she'd been on the run? That in fact she had nothing but the best of intentions in trying to save her country?

WADE: On her own? While taking care of a mother suffering from dementia? And without the help of any law enforcement. In fact, while *running* from law enforcement. No. Frankly, Chairman Morse, it did not occur to me that any private citizen would attempt such a feat.

Chapter 47

Monday, February 25, 2013

What happened?

I lay in the dark, stunned, my head throbbing from having hit a hard floor. Somewhere nearby my mother moaned.

"Mom?" I leaned toward the sound.

"Shut up." A man's voice, cold as ice.

"Haannnah." Mom croaked out my name.

Panic rushed me. "I'm here—"

"I *said* shut-up." A hand cracked across my face. My head reeled to one side, pain shooting through my cheekbone.

Someone gasped. "Mom!" Emily's voice, calling for me.

"Emily?" I spoke her name weakly, my hand to my face. Was she here too? Last I remembered she'd been in the car with her Grand. I was getting in . . .

Rational thought surged through my mind. They'd found us. The Bad People. The terrorists. Thrown us into the back of a van.

Where were they taking us? How would I save my mother and daughter?

Somewhere on a different plane my heart managed to beat. I tried to pull in air, but so little found my lungs.

Beneath my body, an engine rumbled.

Time swayed. One moment terror squeezed my throat. The next I . . . what? Faded away? Then came to. And the cycle began again. I didn't know how many minutes passed. Five? Thirty?

No one spoke. In time my eyes became accustomed to the darkness. I made out the forms of two men across from me. Emily, hunched in a corner. My mother, lying on the floor. Unmoving.

Fear for her pushed me to sit up. "Mom?" I slid toward her.

"Stop moving." The man who'd hit me raised his hand again.

I jerked around to face him. "What a big man you are. Kidnapping an eighty-two-year-old woman."

He hit me again.

"Stop it!" Emily choked.

The pain shook me, but I was beyond caring. My mother needed me. I began moving toward her again—and the van stopped.

Somewhere up front, a car door slammed. Behind us, a vague grinding sound.

The van's side door slid back, powered by a short, muscular man with a shaved head, hard-edged goatee. He held a gun. Daylight filtered inside the vehicle. I turned toward Mom—but hands grabbed my arms and forced me out of the van. I spun around, seeking my daughter, my mother, seeing two other men pull them out. Emily first. She fell into my arms, and we hugged hard. I heard Mom's cries, and let go of Emily to catch her as she was pushed from the van.

The two men inside the vehicle jumped out. One was Rutger, the young FBI agent with the Southern accent. Was he a real agent—or not? Emily saw his face, and her cheeks paled. He looked at her with shimmering, satisfied hatred. "Welcome to my house, Emily."

The other man, older, dark-haired, I hadn't seen before.

We stood in a garage. Its automatic door had shut.

"Inside." Shaved Head pushed me toward a door at the back.

"Ohhhh," my mother groaned. I looked back to see her stumble, her expression sheer confusion. I listed toward her.

"Go." The man pushed me again.

"I have to hel—"

"Go." He flung open the door and shoved me inside. I went down on my knees. He grasped my elbow and yanked me to my feet, his gun pointed at my head. Pulled me across a small kitchen into a half-furnished living room with a worn wooden floor. He sent me flying into a tattered brown couch. I hit it head first—spinning renewed pain across my face. I flipped around. He flattened a huge palm against my chest and pushed me to sit.

Rutger dragged Mom to the couch and shoved her down. She fell against me, crying.

"Whaaat is happening?"

I put my arm around her shoulders and tried to soothe her. What would this trauma do to her? Send her deeper into dementia?

Hatred for these men stiffened my limbs.

Emily hit the sofa next, on the other end. Her knee was bleeding. She leaned toward her grandmother, cheeks red with rage. "We're here, Grand. It'll be okay."

"Where are we?" Tears ran down my mother's face.

The three big, courageous heroes faced us, lined up in a row. Shaved Head put his gun on a nearby table. Then stood with legs wide and arms crossed, focused on me. He had to be the leader. The other two stood on his either side, mirroring his stance.

"You kept a copy of the video." Shaved Head's voice stuck to me like wet fingers on ice.

My insides trembled. I looked him in the eye, unblinking.

He stared back. "What do you know about a key to the encryption code?"

Mom lifted her head from my shoulder. Her chin trembled. I eased her head back down. "Code?"

"*Don't* play dumb."

"I don't know anything about a code."

My mind tripped over itself, hunting for logic. Hadn't Harcroft or Wade told these men Morton Leringer's words to me? Why did Shaved Head act like he didn't know anything about Rawly?

"Is that so. Then why have you been on the run?"

I glared at him. "Maybe because *you* sent someone to kill me?"

He worked his jaw. "You shot my man?"

No words came to my lips.

"You killed him, you know."

The words knifed me. "No," I whispered. "I didn't."

I could feel the anger rolling off Emily. Her eyes shot darts at Rutger. He shot them right back. *Please, God, make my daughter hold her tongue.*

Shaved Head's searing gaze moved from me to my mother. My pulse stilled. He looked back at me, and I read the thought on that evil face. He could get to me through her.

He stepped forward and poked Mom hard in the shoulder. She cried out and raised her head. Her cheeks were puffy and her eyes clouded. She took shallow, rapid breaths. I tightened my arm around her.

"Leave her *alone!*" Emily spat.

Shaved Head ignored her.

"*Don't!*" Emily smacked his arm away from her grandmother.

Quick as lightning he backhanded her across the face. The sharp *crack* ripped at my stomach. Emily jerked to the arm of the couch and hung there, gasping.

"Ahhhhh!" Mom sat up. "Emily!" She reached for her granddaughter.

I could not do this. Not at the expense of my mother and daughter. Who was I to save the world? "Please." The word snagged in my throat. "Stop. Let them go. Keep me. I'll tell you whatever you want."

Shaved Head loomed over me, sneering. "Do I look like someone who needs to bargain?" He leaned closer. "*Do* I?"

I lowered my chin. A single tear fell and darkened my pants.

"Emily." Mom's voice shook.

"I'm okay, Grand, I'm okay." With effort my daughter straightened and took her grandmother's hand. She turned a defiant expression on the man who'd hit her.

Rutger laughed. He pointed at Emily and mouthed, *Knew I'd get you.*

Shaved Head turned on him. "What was that, Tex?"

Rutger/Tex shook his head. "Nothin'."

"So shut up. She's not here because *you* found her."

Tex clamped his jaw shut.

Mom *whoosh*ed out a breath and faced the man above her. Her eyes cleared. "Who are you? What do you want?"

Mom, no.

Emily laid a hand on her arm.

Shaved Head glared at my mother, then placed a hand of mock gallantry on his chest. "Forgive me for not introducing myself. I'm Stone."

"Stone? That's your name?"

"Remember that car accident? Morton Leringer?"

Mom blinked, as if trying to catch up to Stone's turn of subject. "He was my friend."

"What did he tell you?"

Something flicked across my mother's face. "You're the Bad People, aren't you?"

Tex and the third man chuckled. An evil sound.

Stone smirked. "Yeah, we're bad, all right. Which is why you better listen to us, old lady."

Mom gazed at him, puzzlement creasing her forehead. She swallowed hard. "Don't hurt my girls."

"He's not, Grand," Emily whispered. "I'm fine."

My head throbbed and my face burned.

The man looked at his watch. Mumbled to himself, "Four thirty."

I didn't react. Didn't want to show them I knew what that meant. Two and a half hours. It didn't matter what we did now. It was too late.

So why were we here?

Sudden clarity washed through me, leaving me cold and quivery. Even if it was too late to stop tonight's blackout, that was only Phase 1. These men needed to make sure I hadn't given someone the key. Someone who'd have the time to stop tomorrow night's attack. And the one after that.

Stone would not stop until he got that information from me.

We were dead, all three of us. These men had shown us their faces. Once they learned what we knew . . .

They would not let us get out of here alive.

Chapter 48

SPECIAL HOUSE SELECT COMMITTEE
INVESTIGATION INTO FREENOW TERRORIST
ACTIVITY OF FEBRUARY 25, 2013

SEPTEMBER 16, 2013

TRANSCRIPT

Representative ELKIN MORSE (Chairman, Homeland Security Committee): After you learned that you needed to look for Emily Shire as well as her mother, what were your next steps?

WADE: I knew the FBI task force and Homeland Security had begun checking computers that powered the western electrical grid generators. If these computers had been infected with a virus that was set to wreak its havoc at 7 p.m. Pacific Time, I hoped they would find it and be able to stop it.

MORSE: But there would be no stopping the virus without the key to unlock that encryption, correct? And you did not have that key.

WADE: Yes. Still, I hoped there was another way to stop the attack. The task force had informed me that, even if we were to locate the key within the next few hours, it would prove difficult to insert the code into infected computers in time.

MORSE: How convenient for the terrorists. So now in your recounting, we are up to what time?

WADE: Around 3:45. I had numerous deputies, including Deputy Harcroft, researching what connection "Raleigh" might have to Morton Leringer or Nathan Eddington. We weren't sure which one of those men had hidden the key, so we needed to look at both of them. Leringer's home was about to be searched a second time, as was Eddington's office at StarrCom. Then at 4:15 I received two calls back-to-back.

The first was from the Fresno Police Department. Hours earlier I'd requested that an officer stop by the residence of Margaret Dexter, Hannah Shire's aunt. An officer had done so, but had been refused entrance. A neighbor told the officer she'd seen two women matching the description of Hannah Shire and Carol Ballard drive into Ms. Dexter's garage in a Ford Escort. On that basis the Fresno department pursued a warrant to search the premises. In the house they found no sign of Hannah Shire and her mother but did discover her car. She must have been there and left again in Mrs. Dexter's car. I was in the process of requesting they put out a BOLO for the vehicle when the second call came in. This was the call about the kidnapping.

MORSE: From San Mateo police.

WADE: Yes. An eyewitness had seen a kidnapping in the Sequoia Hospital parking lot in Redwood City. According to the witness, two men had pulled three women from a car and shoved them into a gray van. A third man was driving. The car had been left still running. It was the vehicle belonging to Mrs. Dexter. Inside, San Mateo police found numerous items, including a purse belonging to Hannah Shire, as well as a laptop bag containing a computer and wallet belonging to Emily Shire. In that bag was also a flash drive, and a piece of paper with a long string of numbers and letters written on it, plus the "Phase" text. All of this was the same information we'd extracted from the video.

MORSE: Some guns were also in the car, I understand?

WADE: Hannah Shire's purse contained a Chief's Special handgun. A second, much larger weapon was found wrapped in a plastic bag and stuffed in a tote bag, which had been placed in the trunk.

MORSE: Any leads on the gray van?

WADE: The eyewitness had been able to record the van's license plate. We ran the plate, hoping this would take us straight to the kidnappers. Armed with all the information we'd learned in the last few hours, we now feared these women were in great danger. Time was of the essence. We had to find them immediately.

MORSE: But you couldn't.

WADE: No.

MORSE: You need to speak louder for the recorder, sir.

WADE: No. The van had been stolen. Our lead went nowhere.

Chapter 49

Monday, February 25, 2013

God, just let me save my mother and daughter.

I sat on the ratty couch with Mom and Emily, my brain awhirl. How *could* I save them? I didn't dare tell these men where the encryption key was hidden. How could I send these killers to yet another family, another mother and daughter.

To a *child*?

The very thought made my stomach turn. I'd already killed a man. I could *not* be responsible for the death of a mother and little girl.

"You have to let us go now." Mom blinked, as if surprised she'd spoken.

Stone shot her a sarcastic smile. "Tell us what we need to know first. Then you can go."

Emily stiffened, as if ready to hit him again.

Mom eyed him. "What?"

"What did Morton Leringer tell you?"

Confusion limned Mom's face. Was she faking it? "I can't remember."

"I think you do."

My mind cleared—and I saw what I had to do.

"Mom." I patted her leg. "We need to tell him. It doesn't matter now."

She turned to me, indignant. "But Morton *told* us not to tell."

"Yes. But it doesn't matter any more."

"Why?"

"Stone will hurt Emily. Do you want him to do that?"

Mom's eyes widened. *"No."*

Emily shot me a look over her Grand's head. Her hurt cheek was flaring red.

Stay quiet, please.

My mother faced our captor, anger straightening her spine. "*Don't* you hurt my granddaughter."

Dark amusement pulled at Stone's mouth. With slow precision he turned and walked to the table where his gun lay. Picked it up.

My lungs clogged.

Mom drew a sharp breath.

Stone returned and placed the trigger against my daughter's temple.

Words gushed from me. "No-don't-he-said-Raleigh!"

Stone's eyebrows raised. "Ah. We seem to be getting somewhere."

Emily sat very still.

"Yes, Raleigh." Mom's voice cracked. "North Carolina. We were going there. To see his daughter."

Stone frowned. "Leringer has a daughter in Raleigh?"

"Take that gun away from her head." My throat ran dry. "You *don't* need it."

The man tipped the gun toward the ceiling. Stepped back. Then pointed the weapon at my mother. "You. Tell me."

"Th-that's all we know." Mom fingered her blouse. "He wanted us to see his daughter in Raleigh. He hadn't seen her in years."

Stone focused on me. "Why didn't you just call her?"

Mom had done what I needed her to do. It was clear to Stone she was telling the truth. As she knew it. "Please, put that gun down."

He moved it to point at me. "Talk."

"I would have called her. But then you sent someone to kill us, and we had to run."

"I see. How inconvenient. Why didn't you head east toward North Carolina?"

"In my car? Everyone was looking for it. I needed my aunt's car."

"Why did Leringer want you to see his daughter?"

"I don't know. He couldn't say much except that it was important, and not to tell anyone. He didn't say anything about the video, even though I found out later he'd slipped it in my pocket. He didn't say anything about an encrypted message—" My mouth snapped shut. Too late, I realized my mistake.

Stone narrowed his eyes. For the longest moment we locked gazes. My heart turned over.

"So. He didn't tell you anything about our plan."

"No."

"Then how do you know about it?"

I glanced at Mom. She stared at Stone, her expression empty and eyes glazed. She'd checked out, the trauma too much for her.

"I watched the video. Saw the power generator falling apart. At some point, I figured it out."

The gun remained pointed at me. Emily still held her grandmother's hand.

"Smart woman you are." Stone's mouth twisted. "How do you know it's going to happen tonight?"

My mind spun. I couldn't turn his attention on Emily. But this was a trick question, right? Stone couldn't be sure I knew the timing.

Of course he could. I'd told Homeland Security. They'd called Sergeant Wade.

I licked my lips.

"I'm waiting, Mrs. Shire."

"*I* told her." Emily bit off the words.

No.

Tex laughed low in his throat.

"Oh." Sarcasm coated Stone's response. "It's the daughter, is it." The gun barrel moved toward her chest. My breath stopped. "How did you do that?"

Emily kept her chin high. "I make videos for a living. I knew how to slow it down. I saw the words at the beginning."

"And the encrypted message at the end, I'll bet." Stone sneered at me. "Since apparently Leringer didn't mention that."

"Yes." Emily's jaw was tight.

Stone's voice hardened. "Where's the key?"

"It must be in Raleigh," I said. "He phoned it to his daughter."

Stone lasered me with his eyes. Then did a slow turn toward his two men. "Tex." His voice sounded casual.

"I'm here." Tex took a step forward, eager to please.

"Didn't I tell you if you didn't bring the girl to me in twelve hours, you'd be dead?"

Before Tex could reply, Stone swung the gun around and shot him in the chest. Mom jerked. Emily and I screamed.

The hole in Tex's shirt bloomed blood. He fell with a sickening thud.

The third man turned horrified eyes on Stone.

"Don't worry." Stone shrugged. "You did your job."

He turned back to us. I couldn't move. How could anyone kill another person so easily? Someone who was supposed to be his friend?

"Now. You." He pointed the gun at me. "Get up."

"Mom," Emily wailed.

"Get up *now*."

Somehow I pushed off the couch. Would my legs hold me?

"Don't hurt her." My mother's voice, plaintive and weak.

"I don't like people who lie to me." Stone's expression blackened.

"I haven't—"

"Shut up." He half-turned toward his remaining man. "Mack. Take her to the other side of the room."

Mack grabbed my arm and pulled me across the floor.

"Please," Emily said. "Don't. We'll tell you everything."

"Yes, you will. When I'm done with you."

I reached the far wall. Mack spun me around to face the couch. Stone stood in the middle of the room, halfway between me and the two loves of my life. They clung to each other.

God help us! I could not send this killing machine to Ashley Eddington and her little girl.

Stone turned his back on me, the gun aimed at the couch.

"No! Stop!" This could not be real. My knees started to fold. Mack yanked me up.

"You choose." Stone's chilling voice filtered over his shoulder.

"What?" My vision was blackening. I couldn't get air.

"One of 'em dies for your lies."

"*No!*"

"You don't choose one, they both go."

"*Please . . .*"

"You got ten seconds." Stone's arm moved, and I knew he'd grasped his weapon with both hands. "So, Mrs. Shire. Tell me. Which one gets to live?"

Chapter 50

SPECIAL HOUSE SELECT COMMITTEE INVESTIGATION INTO FREENOW TERRORIST ACTIVITY OF FEBRUARY 25, 2013

SEPTEMBER 16, 2013

TRANSCRIPT

Representative ELKIN MORSE (Chairman, Homeland Security Committee): Again I must note the sudden change in your actions, Sergeant Wade—now that you were at a point where you knew the blackout could not be stopped. Suddenly you were doing everything you could to save the woman you'd hunted before. When the van's license plate failed to provide the lead you needed, what did you do?

WADE: I called Cheryl Stein, Leringer's daughter. I asked her again if she knew why her father would have kept repeating the word "Raleigh" before he died.

MORSE: "Again." So you'd had this conversation with her before?

WADE: Yes, on Sunday night. But she'd just lost her father and had been on site when a second body—that of Nathan Eddington—was found. Perhaps she hadn't been thinking all that clearly. And, of course, now we had a better sense of how important it was to discover what "Raleigh" meant.

MORSE: And what did Cheryl Stein tell you?

WADE: She had no idea what her father had been referring to.

MORSE: So it was at this point you called Ashley Eddington with the same question?

WADE: Yes.

MORSE: And you had not had this conversation with her previously?

WADE: I was not able to question Ashley Eddington to the extent I would have liked. Ashley had to deal with the loss of her husband while caring for a young daughter. She'd been overwrought and unable to continue answering questions. We'd had to stop.

MORSE: So. Once again it just so happened that more time was lost.

WADE: Chairman Morse, you *were not with me* on the days of February 24 and 25. You can insinuate all you want, but you weren't there as I worked around the clock, without sleep. You weren't there as I made minute-by-minute decisions while one body after another piled up. You weren't there when I discovered three women had been kidnapped. You have *no idea* what it's like to bear the pressure I face every day on the job—and that day in particular.

MORSE: Now that you've made your speech, Sergeant, tell this committee the answer you received when you asked Ashley Eddington about "Raleigh."

WADE: At first she made no connection. After all, the word had come from the mouth of Morton Leringer, not her husband. Then she paused and said, "It couldn't be my daughter's stuffed dog. R-A-W-L-Y?"

Chapter 51

Monday, February 25, 2013

Was time moving? The world had screeched to a halt, even as my heart rattled out of my chest. Blood pounded in my head, a faint grating sound somewhere in the distance.

"Nine seconds." Stone's voice. Matter-of-fact, as if he discussed the weather.

I tried to speak. No words came.

"Which one, Hannah? Seven. Six."

A mewling sound came from my mother's throat.

"Four. Three."

Behind me a door opened and slammed. The sudden noise bounced across the room.

Stone whirled around. Mack's hold on me loosened. Footsteps sounded in the kitchen. "Tex?"

Stone jerked his chin toward Mack. "Stop her."

Mack let me go. In peripheral vision I saw a woman appear at the door. Clad in jeans and a blue shirt. She gasped at the sight of the body on the floor, then screamed.

Mack reached her. Caught her arms. She fought him. "Tex! What have you done? *Tex!*"

"Shut up, Bo!" Stone stomped toward her.

Emily launched herself off the couch. In that split, forever second I saw her run. Lower her head. With a primal cry she rammed Stone in the back.

"Ungh!" He stumbled forward.

She skidded to a halt and kicked his hand holding the gun. It flew from his fingers and flipped across the floor.

Adrenaline surged through me. I jumped for the gun, snatched it up. Spun to face Stone.

He twisted toward Emily, hands stretched for her throat. He didn't need a gun to kill her.

Bo pummeled Mack with her fists. He saw me with the weapon and let her go. Reached into his pocket.

She jerked up her pant leg and brought up a gun. Her cheeks were red, raw. "You're dead, Mack!"

A gun appeared in Mack's hand.

Stone grabbed my daughter's throat.

I aimed and pulled the trigger. The kickback punched my arms, a thunderous sound in my ears.

A bullet tore into Stone's shoulder. He grunted and fell back. Emily veered toward the couch and threw her body over her grandmother.

I pulled the trigger again. And again. My finger wouldn't stop. It pulled and pulled, my body jerking, the sounds echoing, and my insides screaming and screaming—*I'm killing another man!*—and someone else yelling, and the world falling away—until nothing but clicks sounded.

My mother yelled once more, hands over her eyes.

Stone crumpled to the floor, blood all around. Then so did Mack, a hole in his forehead.

Did I do that too?

Bo stood over him, horror on her face, hand like a claw around her gun. And for the first time I looked at her, really *looked* at her.

She ran toward me, shoved me away. Fell to kneel beside Tex, calling his name, touching his face, tears streaking her cheeks.

I stood unmoving. No breath.

I shot Stone. Killed him.

She shot Mack.

My ears roared. From some great distance I heard my mother wail. Emily slid off of her. "Grand, Grand, you okay?"

Still I couldn't move. Could only stare at Stone. Riddled with bullets. Dead. Then at the woman they called Bo.

She reared up from Tex's body and swiveled toward me, hate flattening her expression. "This happened because of *you*." She raised her gun.

My mother uncovered her eyes. "*Oh.*" Wrenching relief smoothed her face. "It's my friend, Nance." Her voice cracked. "You came to save us!"

Chapter 52

For a moment nobody moved.

"Nance." Mom was still smiling. Had she forgotten what just happened? Could she not see the three dead bodies on the floor? She scooted forward, ready to rise from the couch. Emily held her back.

"Grand. She's not your friend."

"Yes, she is! She has *six* sisters." Mom struggled against Emily. My daughter held firm.

Nancy Bolliver still pointed her gun at me. My fingers loosened, and Stone's spent gun clattered to the floor. Mom jumped.

Somehow my throat uncurled. "He killed Tex." I pointed to Stone.

"You started all this." Nance's words twisted. "Running off. Making us chase you."

I shook my head. "You? *Why?*"

She looked at Tex, and I could see the loss in her eyes. He'd entered her life—and changed her.

Nance gazed at the three dead men. Her cohorts. She straightened her back, pulled herself up as if to say, *It's up to me now*.

She shot me a dark look, then turned her gun on my mother. My insides fell away.

"No!" Emily pushed her Grand back and leaned across her once more.

"Makes no difference to me." Nance's voice sounded dead. "One of these bullets will pass through both of you."

I stepped toward her. "What do you w——"

"*Don't* you move."

My feet carved to a halt.

Nance swallowed hard. Tears glistened in her eyes. "Hannah. *Do* you know where the encryption key is?"

In that split second the last twenty-eight hours flashed before me. Morton's accident, my house break-in, running for our lives, the TV reports, the lies, the panic, the near loss of my daughter and mother. Killing two people.

I was done.

I'd tried and failed. Was no hero. Could put my family in danger no more.

"Yes." The word fell from my mouth so easily.

"Where?"

Mom was struggling against Emily. "What is happening? Why does she have a gun?"

"Please, Nance," I said. "They've done nothing to you."

She jerked her chin toward Tex. "That's not enough?"

"It's in a stuffed dog. Nathan Eddington's little girl has it."

Surprise rippled her face. "How do you know?"

"Morton told me the name. Rawly."

"Rawly." She repeated the word as if she'd never heard it. Hadn't Wade and Harcroft told her? Or had they left her—the female—out of their inner circle?

"Hannah, you weren't supposed to tell anybody about Raleigh." Mom sounded indignant.

"Does anyone else know it's there?" Nance asked.

"No. It doesn't matter now anyway. It's almost five."

But I knew it did matter. This was no longer about tonight. It was about protecting Phase 2 and 3.

"Where does she live?" Nance asked.

What had I done? I could not have a gun turned on a five-year-old. "You can't hurt her."

"That'll be up to you. Where does she live?"

I couldn't tell her.

"*Where?*" She shook her gun.

"San Carlos."

Calculations played across Nance's face. For the first time it occurred to me I didn't even know what town we were in.

"You know the address?"

"Yes."

"We'll go in my car. You." She spoke to Emily. "Get up. And your grandmother."

Emily didn't move.

"You think you're going to pull another stunt on *me*? Get up!"

Emily rose. "Come on, Grand." She pulled my mother up. Mom swayed on her feet, blinking at Nance's weapon. A slow stain of horror spread across her face. "Are you a Bad Person?"

Nance drew a shaky breath and turned her eyes once more on Tex. She swallowed hard. Then her jaw set. "Okay, let's go." At gunpoint, she marched us into the garage. Emily still limped. She would not let go of her grandmother.

A Ford SUV sat next to the gray van. "Whose van is that?" Nance asked.

I shook my head. "I thought it was Tex's."

How little she'd been told.

"You." She pointed to me. "Drive. And you"—Emily—"sit in the front where I can watch you."

"No." Emily's face whitened. "I need to take care of Grand."

"Oh, I'll take care of her just fine." Nance's mouth slid into a cold smile. "I've done it before."

But you could never get her to tell you about Rawly, could you?

I locked gazes with her. "If you hurt my mother, I will *wreck* your car."

Her eyes narrowed. "Get in."

I backed out of the garage. Nance told me which way to go. I soon saw we were in San Mateo. Just ten minutes from my home. An eternity away.

In the car, we were quiet. Except for Mom, who asked Nance three more times if she was a Bad Person.

"No," Nance finally answered, not an ounce of life in her voice. "I'm your friend."

"Then why do you have a gun?"

We crossed into San Carlos. "You won't need that weapon." I glanced in the rearview mirror at Nance. "If you have your badge with you, all you'll have to do is show it. They'll let you in."

"I'll decide what I need."

At the Eddington's one-story house, Nance instructed me to pull into the driveway. No other cars were there. Surprising. No gathering of family?

We all piled out and headed for the front door. Nance kept the gun in her hand. Emily and I exchanged long glances. This was it, and we both knew it. Once Nance had the encryption key, why should she let any of us live?

"Whose house is this?" Mom gripped my hand. She looked haggard and ancient, fear in every movement.

I pulled her close. "It's okay, Mom."

Nance rapped hard on the door—a law enforcement knock. "Sheriff's Department!"

The door opened quickly. Ashley Eddington, red-eyed and worn, blinked at the sight of four of us. Her gaze took in our clothes, as if seeking a uniform. Nance fished her badge from her pocket. "Plainclothes."

Ashley focused on her. "How'd you get here so fast?"

What?

Her gaze shifted to me—and snagged there. She pulled her head back, shock, then anger flattening her expression. *"You."*

I shook my head.

"Don't worry, I've got her." Nance gestured toward her gun. "Sorry to bring her to your house, but I just apprehended her, and there's no time."

Ashley stood rooted to the floor, one hand still on the knob. Hard breaths made her shoulders rise and fall. "Get her out of here! I'll *kill* her!"

She rushed me.

I jumped to one side, trying to protect Mom. Ashley collided into my shoulder. Guttural cries spilled out of her. She pummeled my neck, my head. I threw up my arms. Emily yanked Ashley back. Nance yelled, "Hold it, hold it!"

Mom wailed.

Emily held Ashley fast. I melted toward the porch wall, palms up. "I didn't kill your husband!"

"Shut up, shut *up!*" Nance jumped between us, fury flaming her cheeks. Everyone froze. "Get inside right now, all of you!"

Ashley jerked out of Emily's grasp. "Put your gun away first. My daughter's in the house."

"And let them get away?" Nance glared at her.

Ashley backed down, tears in her eyes.

I reached for my mother. "Ashley, I didn't kill—"

"Shut *up*." Nance pushed me. "Get inside."

I stumbled into the house, Mom in tow. She hit her foot on the threshold and cried out. Emily caught her before she fell.

Ashley snarled at me. "How could you do this to your mother?"

The words tore through me.

Nance slammed the door. We stood in a small living room, not far from a kitchen. The curtains were closed, the room dim. "Ashley," Nance spoke quickly, with authority, "I need to look at your daughter's stuffed dog, Rawly. No time to explain."

"I already told you all there's nothing there."

Nance's eyes narrowed. "Told who?"

"Sergeant Wade. He called."

Emily and I exchanged a look. My daughter held her Grand protectively.

Surprise flicked across Nance's face. "Let me see it anyway."

Ashley shook her head. "Kate's sleeping with it. Rawly's her favorite toy. Her dad gave it to her."

"I *need* it." Nance bit off the words.

Ashley eyed her, disgust filling her face. "What kind of deputy *are* you?"

"She's with the terrorists who killed your husband!" Emily spat the words.

Nance whirled on Emily. "You wanna die right here?" She grabbed Mom's arm and jerked her away from Emily. Nance's left arm wound around Mom's chest, holding her tight. She jammed the gun into Mom's temple.

The rest of us froze.

Mom's eyes darted from me to Emily, her mouth open.

I brought up my hands. "Mom." I spoke with a calm I didn't have. "Don't move."

Nance held her fast. "Ashley. Get the toy."

Ashley swallowed, her eyes round. "Who *are* you?"

"Get it, please." My voice shook. "She'll kill us all. Just like they killed your husband and Morton Leringer."

I glanced at Emily. She shook with anger, fingers curling into her palms.

Ashley's face whitened. "Don't hurt my daughter."

"I won't," Nance hissed, "if you get me the dog."

Ashley turned on her heel and left the room. Her footsteps sounded against hardwood floor.

Nance dragged Mom back a few feet, her eyes on the two of us.

Mom's breath came in spurts. Her wrinkled hands were around Nance's arm, her toes pointed outward like a splayed doll. If my mother lived through this, what would it do to her fragile mind?

Rage bounced around inside of me. "Hang on, Mom. Just a minute longer."

My mother's eyes were wild. "She's a Bad Person, isn't she?"

Ashley returned, Rawly in her hand. "I already looked at it." Her bitter words were aimed at Nance. "There's nothing here."

"Cut it open."

"What? No!"

"Cut it *open*."

"Mommy?" A child's voice filtered from down the hall.

Ashley gasped. In an instant she spun, the dog dropped from her hands, and ran toward the sound.

"Stop!" Nance yelled.

A door slammed. Locked.

Ashley had left us to our fate.

For a second, Nance focused on the wall, mouth tight. I could sense the question in her mind—was there a phone in that little girl's bedroom?

Not likely.

She turned a dark look on me. "Get the toy."

I picked it up.

"Cut it open."

"Let my mother go first."

"Cut. It. Open!" Her arm tightened around Mom. My mother gave a stifled cry.

Forget my guilt about killing anyone—I would hurt this young woman. One wrong move on her part, and I'd be on her. *No* one could treat my mother like this.

"I'll do it." Emily grabbed the dog from me as if it deserved to die and stalked across the room, ignoring her hurt knee. She whirled back toward Nance, her eyes glassed with anger, neck taut. "When you get what you want—go. Leave my grandmother alone. The police want to arrest my mother anyway. And the world's going dark tonight. You'll be safe to do whatever evil things you want." Emily stomped out of sight and into the kitchen. I heard a knife slide from a butcher block.

Outside a car door slammed.

Nance stiffened. "See who it is."

No, not now. Maybe, maybe if Emily found the encryption key, Ashley would let us go. We could be so close to safety. I moved to the front curtain and nudged it back.

Sergeant Wade was sliding out of a sheriff's department vehicle.

Chapter 53

Who is it?" Nance demanded.

My heartbeat stalled. How much did God expect of me on this never-ending day?

"Who?"

"Sergeant Wade."

Fright crisscrossed Nance's face. Had she leapt over the terrorists' chain of authority in bringing us here?

"Don't make a sound." Nance kept the gun barrel against my mother's temple.

The doorbell rang, followed by a hard knock.

Emily appeared from the kitchen, a large knife in her hands. She looked at me, wide-eyed.

Wade, I mouthed.

She drew back, her gaze flicking to her grandmother.

Another knock.

What must Ashley Eddington be thinking, trapped in the bedroom with her daughter?

A third knock. We all stood, transfixed. Nance just might let us go, save her own skin. Wade never would.

It fell quiet on the porch. *Please go away.*

Vague steps on the sidewalk. Did I hear muted voices?

Silence. Wade had left.

Air once more entered my lungs. *Thank You, God.*

Nance focused on Emily. "Bring the dog in here. Get it done."

My daughter shot her a look to kill and disappeared once more.

I understood then. Since Ashley Eddington hadn't let him inside, Wade could not let his cover be blown. Nance would take the heat. Who would believe our accusations against her? Or those of a grieving widow who couldn't think straight?

Emily hurried back into the room and threw the dog on the table. She set down the knife, ripped off its red-and-white kerchief. Turned it all directions, examining it.

Nance watched, muscles tense. "Anything?"

"No."

"Cut it."

Emily snatched up the knife and plunged it into Rawly. Drew it down the length of his belly. In a frenzy she tore out stuffing, throwing it all around. I watched the knife divide and splice, knowing she wanted the toy to be Nance.

The dog's fluffy stomach revealed no hidden paper.

"Keep going!" Nance's face reddened.

Emily started on the limbs, cutting them off one by one. Nothing in the right leg. Or the left.

"Come on, come on." I muttered the words under my breath, gaze jumping from the dog to my mother. Her eyes met mine, fear-filled and spent.

"What is she doing?" Mom's voice ebbed. "Emily."

She's trying to save you. "Almost done, Mom. I promise."

Emily moved to the toy's arms. Off came the right one. She cut it down the middle, splayed it apart. Out came more stuffing.

Nothing.

Sweat beaded my daughter's forehead.

She drove the knife deep into the left shoulder, separating the last arm. Pulled it to pieces. I could feel the heat coming off her, the will to *find* something. To stuff the piece of paper into Nance's fingers and pull her grandmother into her own embrace.

The arm lay shredded. No encryption key.

A futile cry escaped Emily. She attacked the one last remaining part—the head. Off came the large bead eyes, the ears and nose. She cut up the face, pulling and yanking stuffing in a frenzy.

The head was destroyed. No piece of paper inside.

"No, it's here!" Emily threw down the knife. "It's got to be." She fell to her knees, dragging both hands through the balls of stuffing, searching with all her might. I ran over and knelt beside her. We jerked up pieces and tore them to smaller bits. Tore and tore until mere strands remained together.

Nothing. We looked around us, breathing hard. *Something* had to be here.

Emily snatched up the red kerchief once more. Held it close to her sweaty face, looking, *pleading* for tiny written letters and numbers on the cloth. Nothing on the outer side. She turned it over, eyes flicking back and forth.

She stilled.

In slow motion her hand came down. Dropped the kerchief.

"It's not here."

No. Couldn't be.

We stared at the mess. In my mind I heard Morton's hitched voice: *"Rawly."*

Nance spat a curse. "You said it was there!"

"It is! It was." My stomach heaved. What was left for us? Our country? The lights would go out here tonight. Tomorrow, in the east.

Nance cursed again. "You're *lying*."

Emily jumped up, determination setting her jaw. "Maybe it's something else to do with Rawly. In the girl's bedroom." She yanked the knife off the floor and limp-rushed toward the hall. "I'm popping that lock."

My heart squeezed. What would Ashley do when Emily broke through her daughter's door, wielding a knife? "No, wait!" I hurried after her.

"Hannah!" Mom called. I swiveled back. Pointed to Nance. "Don't hurt her! One more minute, we'll do this."

Nance glared at me. I pivoted to follow Emily.

She reached the bedroom door and pounded it with her fist. "Let me in!"

Silence.

Emily jabbed the point of the knife into the lock and turned. The lock gave way. She shoved the door open.

"Wait, Em—"

The room was empty. On the back wall—an open window. Curtains fluttering. I took in a bed, white furniture, toy boxes. A desk. Something there caught Emily's eye. She rushed to it and snatched up a small collar. "Look, it says Rawly!" She turned it over, examined the inside. Her chin lifted, victorious. "It's here!" She thrust it toward me.

There they were, a random series of numbers and letters, written with a fine tip marker. Such little things to nearly cost us our lives.

From the living room my mother wailed. Emily and I rushed toward the sound. "We found it!" Emily clutched the collar in her hand. "We found it!"

Nance let my mother go. "Give it to me."

Mom kicked Nance in the shins. "You're a *bad* person!" Rage puffed out her cheeks.

"Mom." I veered toward her.

"No! Leave me *alone!*" She reared back and screamed. The sound split the air. Anyone on the block could have heard.

"Stop!" Nance grabbed Mom and shook her. "Right now."

My mother screamed louder, her eyes squeezed shut.

Nance clapped a hand over her mouth. "I swear I'll kill you!" She rammed her gun back against Mom's temple.

"No!" Emily dropped the collar and launched herself at Nance. I ran behind her, seeing Nance's finger go for the trigger, knowing we'd never make it in time.

Mom beat both fists against Nance's side, shrieking around her fingers.

Emily knocked into them both. Nance's hand flew away from Mom's head. I yanked my mother out of her grip. Nance stumbled, still holding the gun.

The front door splintered open. Heavy footsteps pounded.

Nance spun toward Emily and fired.

My daughter thudded to the ground.

Chapter 54

At the sight of Emily bleeding on the floor, everything in me went white. My brain held no thought, my body could not feel.

Mom shrieked.

Blood rushed back into my veins. I lurched for Emily and dropped to my knees beside her. She clutched her thigh, blood oozing onto her hands. It was the same leg already bleeding at the knee. Her face was white, eyes rammed shut.

Sergeant Wade ran into the room, gun raised. He skidded to a stop and aimed at Nance. "Put the gun down."

"She came at me, Sarge, I had to shoot!"

"Put the gun *down!*"

She placed it on the floor.

"Kick it over to me."

She obeyed. He picked it up.

Was I dreaming this?

A policeman bounded in, weapon ready, followed by two men wearing FBI vests. Wade handed the cop Nance's gun. "Take her in."

Take her in?

Mom staggered to my side and bent over her beloved Emily, sobbing.

"I—o—kay," Emily sputtered. Her teeth were clenched.

The policeman cuffed Nance and led her away.

The world flowed and swayed. My brain could barely process. I could only clutch my daughter's hand, praying, pleading with Jesus. *Let her be okay let her be okay let her be okay . . .*

Wade soothed her and me, murmuring he was sorry, but I couldn't understand and had no energy to try. He could arrest me later, I didn't care. Just let me be with Emily now, let me hold my crying mother, and try to make sense of it all.

"Mo—" Emily tried to talk. "K-k-."

One of the FBI men—was he for real?—picked up the collar. Examined it. His head jerked up. "This it?"

I gave a vague nod.

"The key?"

"Yes!" As if I cared anymore. I just hung on to Emily.

Both FBI men ran out. Sergeant Wade stayed.

What was happening here?

Sirens sounded in the distance. Police came, and more police. An ambulance. Paramedics loaded Emily onto a gurney, then into the vehicle. I stayed by her side, climbing in after her. Mom wanted to come too. They tried to pull her away, but she writhed and fought and wailed, her cries piercing and high. They relented.

Somewhere along the way to the ambulance I'd seen Ashley Eddington on the sidewalk, clutching her little girl. Words flowed around her, about climbing out of a bedroom window . . . telling Sergeant Wade . . .

The ambulance door closed. It was crowded. The paramedic was treating Emily for shock. She was shaking, clammy. "Her femoral artery wasn't hit." His words burned into me. "She'll be okay."

"Where are we going?" Had I said that? I couldn't feel my mouth move. Couldn't feel my body.

"Sequoia Hospital."

Back to where we started.

At the hospital they unloaded Emily and whisked her through the emergency room doors. I followed with Mom, as fast as she could go.

Just inside the door, Mom collapsed.

I caught her before she hit the floor. I yelled for help. Nurses bustled to her side, lifted her onto a gurney and rolled her toward an exam room. Before I knew it, I was alone.

The walls of my mind closed in. I wobbled across the floor like a lost soul. Which one did I go to first, mother or daughter?

Sergeant Wade materialized. "You okay?"

I listed to one side. His strong arms caught me.

"Come, sit down." He guided me to a chair. I sat heavily. "I'm so sorry this all happened to you. If I'd understood earlier . . ."

"I'm not under arrest?" My mouth moved, but the sound was so far away. Spots crowded my vision.

Wade held my arms. "No, don't worry—"

I fought him. "Have to . . . go. See Emily. Mom."

He hung on to me. "Emily will be headed for surgery. They have to take the bullet out."

"I have to see—"

"You can't."

"But—"

"Mrs. Shire. *No.*"

This couldn't . . . "I have to see Mom . . ."

"She'll be fine. You can see her in a little while. She just needs rest. And hydration."

Me too. "She needs me."

"Mrs. Shire, *you* need you."

Weakness overtook me. I couldn't get up.

A nurse appeared. "She all right?"

"Bring her some water."

Footsteps hurried away. Came back. My fingers closed around a bottle. I drank.

My mother would need her medication tonight. It was in her suitcase. In Aunt Margie's car. Which was . . . ?

A different memory pulsed. Stuffing spread across the floor.

"It wasn't in Rawly. In his collar."

"I saw that."

"Those men—they took it?"

"Yes."

"Can they stop it in time?"

I didn't even know what time it was. Had no energy to look.

"You can bet they're trying."

"Why aren't you with them?"

"They don't need me now. You do."

Air bubbles skidded around my lungs. My thoughts ebbed and flowed, chaotic tide churning sand. "Nance Bolliver is one of them. Three men in the house. Dead."

"Where?"

"San Mateo."

"Who are they?"

"Tex. Mack. Stone."

"I mean their organization."

Full realization finally hit me. Wade had broken into Ashley Eddington's house. Arrested Nance. Saved us.

I reared back and looked him in the eye. "You're not one of them?"

"No."

My brain couldn't comprehend it. "Yes, you are."

"*Why* did you think that? Why did you run instead of calling me when that man broke into your house?"

"You told them I kept a copy of that video. They came to kill me."

A slow light dawned on his face. He shook his head. "No. Nance must have told them."

Oh. *Oh.* All the thoughts I'd had, the preconceived notions, rushed me. What had I done? I'd put my family in danger. "Is Harcroft with them?"

"No."

"But he never trusted me."

"Harcroft doesn't trust anybody."

"Only Nance, then?"

Wade pulled in a breath. "That we know of."

We fell silent. I couldn't form words. My insides jumbled and tore. I drank more water, exhaustion rolling over me. Tears fell from my eyes. I leaned over, and they plopped on my pants. "This is my fault. I *failed*."

That's when the lights went out.

Chapter 55

In the emergency waiting room the dark seemed endless. People called out to one another. Things bumped and rattled. I could hear my own breathing.

I couldn't believe it had happened. It had really *happened*.

Was this what our world would be like from now on?

What about Emily's surgery? What about Mom?

"Will you be all right?" Wade's voice, grim. "Generators should come on soon here. I need to go."

"Sure."

The lights flickered on. *Thank You, God.* I rose, demanding information about Emily. She'd gone to surgery, they said.

"But how do they do surgery when the lights are out?"

"The docs just wait for the generators. Now that power's back on, everything should be proceeding fine."

Not good enough. I wanted to tear down walls until I found my daughter.

"Mrs. Shire, would you like to see your mother?"

Smart nurse knew how to divert me. "Yes."

She pointed the way. I wound through the emergency area and slipped into Mom's room. She was lying in bed, an IV in her arm. Tugging on a nurse's sleeve. "I have to go. We have to get to Raleigh . . ."

Mom saw me—and her face lit up. "Hannah. Can we go to Raleigh now?"

A sob burst from me. Had she forgotten Emily had been shot?

Leaning over the bed, I smoothed white hair off Mom's forehead. "We don't need to go anymore."

"We don't?"

"No. We just need to get you well and home."

"What about the Bad People?"

"I don't think they'll be after us anymore." They'd gotten what they wanted. I thought of the millions of homes without power. The businesses and stores. Government buildings. *How* could anyone do this to their own country?

How long would the hospital generators stay on?

Some time later, Emily's surgery was over. "She'll fully recover," the doctor told me. "We got the bullet out. She'll have a scar, but she'll be fine. Once she's awake and in her room, you can see her. We'll keep her overnight."

The bullet, he said, had been given to police. It was evidence.

I nodded. "Tell me. How long will the generators last?"

The doctor didn't know.

Mom was admitted also—a different room. The generators held up that night, and I spent the time moving from one room to another, checking on both my mother and my daughter. At about 2 a.m., I collapsed in a chair in Emily's room.

When I awoke, a beautiful sun was shining. But the heaviness would not leave my heart.

The days that followed were full of police interviews. Sergeant

Wade took my information and filled me in on what he'd learned. Nance Bolliver had broken and confessed her part in an anarchist organization called FreeNow. Stone—the man I killed—had been its leader.

At that news, a dark justice pulsed through my limbs.

It had been a surprise to learn through Nance that Nathan Eddington was a critical member of FreeNow, creating the code that would infect the electrical grid computers. Some time back he'd apparently bought a stuffed dog for his daughter and written the key to stop the attack on the dog's collar. Her mother later replaced that hard collar with a soft handmade kerchief. But on the day before Phase 1, Eddington had turned against FreeNow and rushed the video to Morton Leringer. Eddington knew he'd soon be dead for his betrayal. But maybe Leringer could stop the impending attack. . .

"Be careful. Don't tell."

Yet another victim of homicide was found in a Redwood City apartment—Todd Nooley, also a member of FreeNow. Nooley had stabbed Eddington and Leringer while trying to retrieve the video. When Nooley failed in his task, Nance said, Tex had been ordered to kill him.

Stone had been as merciless with his own men as with the rest of the country.

The FBI task force and Homeland Security worked together in a frenzy to stop the next phases of FreeNow's plan. With mere hours to go before Phase 2, they were able to send the "abort" code into all infected computers.

Still, the western grid and the states around Washington D.C. remained in blackness.

Mom and I were allowed to go back into our home. Emily stayed with us. It was the beginning of endless days. With no heat in the house, we dressed in layers, Emily wearing my clothes. She was on meds for her pain. Amazing, how fast she recovered. I think pure rage knit her cells back together.

I chose not to go to work the first few days. I was too busy taking care of Mom and Emily. And after that, Dr. Nicholson closed his office until electricity was restored.

Our world narrowed. We fell into survival mode.

One week passed.

I drove to store after store, seeking extra candles and flashlights, but all were sold out. Many of the stores weren't even open. On my drive, I passed storefronts with broken windows, bent doors. People were running the streets at night, wild in the shroud of darkness, behaving as they never would in the light of day. Shots rang out at night, people killing, looting. Police tried to keep up with the arrests. It was hard for them to know which criminals were part of FreeNow and which were mere opportunists.

Was this what FreeNow had wanted?

Before long my car's gas tank was near Empty. We had no way of filling it. Stations couldn't pump gas without electricity.

In our town, strict curfews were set in place. The National Guard was called in. They and police worked overtime to crack down on the rising tide of violence.

A second week staggered by.

Mom, Emily, and I stayed in the house, not even answering the door unless it was for law enforcement. Reporters came, begging to talk to us. We ignored them.

I wondered about Aunt Margie. Was she safe? Staying with neighbors?

During that third week, Emily flicked on every light switch in the house, as well as the TV. Whenever the power did come back on, she wanted to know it.

Mom wandered a lot, confused and fearful. She couldn't watch TV or dance to Lady Gaga. And no amount of explanation as to why would satisfy her. She'd wake up at night, crying. Emily made a makeshift bed of blankets and pillows on Mom's floor. She wanted to sleep near her Grand's side.

The fourth week ground by.

We were rationing our food. Grocery shopping became almost impossible, even if I walked to a store. Businesses couldn't get their supplies. And credit cards were useless. We ran out of cash. Stores didn't want to take checks. No way to turn them into cash when computers were down.

In most urgent situations, the Red Cross would be there within days. But the power outage was so widespread, they'd have to move large trucks of supplies through numerous states just to get to California—on one tank of gas. And there were so many other people to help before they ever got to us.

Would they show up at all?

I prayed a lot, trying to deal with the questions. Why this? Why *us*? One minute I would thank God I'd been able to defend my daughter and mother. The next I'd be begging forgiveness for killing not one, but *two* people. Even though they were bad men, maybe I could have done *something.*

Was the world ending? Was this what the book of Revelation talked about? If so, was I ready?

Lord, You know I'm not. Please make me ready.

In the afternoons the three of us took to reading the Bible out loud. Something to comfort us. To remind us of a God who is permanent in this ever-changing, frightening world. One day in a moment of clarity Mom spoke up. "There's a book we should read." She gazed at her lap, struggling to remember. "I think it's Matthew. No, Malachi. No—Micah."

Micah?

Mom was sure.

At first it seemed a depressing choice, filled with prophecies of death and destruction. Until we came to chapter seven, verses seven and eight.

> But I will look to the LORD;
> I will wait for the God of my salvation.
> My God will hear me.
> Do not rejoice over me, my enemy!
> Though I have fallen, I will stand up;
> though I sit in darkness,
> the LORD will be my light.

At the last phrase, Mom gave a sage nod. Emily and I looked up, startled, and locked eyes. Both of us started to cry.

We clung to those two verses in the coming days. Memorized them. In the fifth and sixth weeks Emily and I repeated them to each other. *"Though I sit in darkness, the Lord will be my light."*

And I began to sense, as I never had before, God's arms around me. Yes, what we'd been through—and what we were going through now—was horrible. Awful. But the three of us were alive, by His mercy.

No matter *what* happened, our God was greater than tragedy.

The Red Cross finally came, bringing their own gas. I walked downtown to fight the lines for food and came home triumphant, lugging two bags of groceries. It felt like Christmas.

The days dragged on. All three of us were losing weight. My mother couldn't afford to lose any, frail as she was.

And then, finally . . .

After forty-seven interminable days, around eight o'clock at night, the lights and TV blared on. The lights were so bright, the sound so loud, they set Mom to screaming. Emily and I froze, not quite knowing what to do. How to live.

Then we cheered.

I hurried to comfort my mother. "It's okay, Mom, it's okay. You can listen to your music again."

She stopped, mid-screech. "I can?"

When she calmed, we held hands and stood in a circle, thanking God for bringing us through.

Mom clasped her hands and put them near her chin. "Can I dance now?"

I smiled. "All day and all night, if you want." Emily took her into the bedroom to put on a Lady Gaga CD. It was the sweetest sound we'd ever heard.

The next day, with TV news and radio and all our phones working again, we began to hear what the rest of the country had been hearing. The extent of widespread violence in all the states plunged into darkness. The cost in untold billions to our country with the economy hit. The unfolding account of FreeNow anarchists and their plot of insanity. The amazing story of three women in one family who'd saved the bulk of the nation—

Wait.

Were they talking about *us*?

Epilogue

Wednesday, December 25, 2013

"Here comes your turkey, Mom."

She'd been asking about it for the last two hours. Holding the large platter, I swept from the kitchen to our dining area and set it on the table with a flourish.

Mom clapped her palms together. "Oh, it looks lovely. Doesn't it, Margie!" Mom's cheeks were rosy, and she wore a pretty outfit of purple pants and shirt to match her hat. Which she'd insisted on wearing to the table.

My aunt grinned. "Sure does."

"I do so like turkey. And potatoes."

Emily patted her grandmother's arm. "We have potatoes for you, Grand."

Did we ever. Aunt Margie had brought sweet potatoes as well as mashed russets. Plus green beans and a dessert. Added to all Emily and I had made, it was a real feast. I wouldn't have to cook again for a week.

Emily caught my eye, and we exchanged a look—one that spoke of remembered rationing, and dark, cold nights.

I shivered.

We settled at the table and held hands to pray. I thanked God for the food, and the electricity, and the heat in our house. For our health, and Emily's healed leg. For our very lives.

We took none of those things for granted anymore.

Emily helped Mom fill her plate. As my mother picked up her fork, her face took on that blank look that came more often these days. Her fork poised midair.

"What is it, Mom?"

"Why are we eating all this food?"

"It's Christmas. Remember? See all the red and green?"

"Oh." She looked around the table. "Yes."

She scooped some mashed potatoes into her mouth.

It was about two in the afternoon. We would have eaten earlier if not for the piles of presents we'd needed to open—most of them from strangers. There were even some for Aunt Margie. And these were just the most recent. Ever since the lights came back on in April, the whole country seemed to want to thank us—in any way they could. We were so humbled by all the gifts, especially in an economy in which people were fighting to regain what had been lost as a result of the attack.

And the attention didn't end there. Emily and I had been inundated with requests for interviews—on every major TV talk show and channel you could name. We hadn't wanted to talk to anyone, but Sergeant Wade persuaded us. "Just do one or two. The country deserves to hear your story."

We'd done a full hour on *Sixty Minutes*. And another on CNN. The stations asked that Mom participate too. I said absolutely not. She remembered nothing of our ordeal. And she would likely be far too confused in front of the cameras and hot lights. While Emily and I traveled, Mom stayed with Aunt Margie.

For the most part, Mom had been delighted with the "new friends" who would stop by to say hello and thank us. If the conversation turned to That Day, she would frown. "What are you talking about?" And I'd have to steer the discussion to another topic. But then Mom would offer to play her music for our guests—and that would make her smile again.

In July, my mother received her most cherished gift of all. A signed CD from Lady Gaga herself. With a note of thanks on behalf of the nation.

Mom had played that CD every day since.

"Grand." Emily cut some of the turkey on her grandmother's plate. "Guess who's coming over in a few hours to see you. Sergeant Wade."

"Oh, good." My mother beamed. "He's such a nice young man."

Aunt Margie and I exchanged a smile.

"You ought to ask him if he has any male friends your age, Emily. You're still looking for a boyfriend, aren't you?"

Emily wagged her head. "Actually, Grand, you have no idea how many men want to date me these days. I'm kinda famous."

"Well, of course. You've always been famous to me. Doesn't mean those men are good enough for you."

"That's just the problem."

I looked to Aunt Margie. "My beautiful daughter is very picky."

My aunt lifted a shoulder. "She ought to be."

"He likes my music, you know." Mom took a bite of green beans.

Emily stuck out her chin. "Who?"

"Sergeant Wade."

"Oh, yes. So I hear."

I wasn't sure he did like her music, but he pretended to. One time he'd even danced with my mother—the only person she'd ever allowed to do that.

We'd met Charles Wade's wife and two children. Strange, to realize he was a husband and father. A man with his own personal life. We'd thought of him only in the context of a sergeant caught in the vortex of That Day. Charles and his family visited every once in awhile. And he would keep Emily and me up to date on the continuing investigation into FreeNow—as much as he was allowed.

I'd been quite incensed at the sergeant's treatment during his testimony before the Home Security Committee in September. Emily and I had spent days testifying before that committee as well. I told Chairman Morse in no uncertain terms that his attitude against Charles Wade was unwarranted. Yes, the sergeant may have wrongly perceived the pounding events of That Day in February. But so had I. Were they looking for someone to blame? Blame me. If only I'd told the sheriff's department everything from the beginning. If only I'd gone to them for help when that man broke into my house. If only I hadn't believed Tex was a real agent turned bad, and had called the FBI.

Because of my mistakes, valuable time was lost. Maybe we could have saved the western region from going dark.

The committee did not agree that I was to blame. But in the end, they did agree that Sergeant Wade was not a part of the FreeNow organization.

"Carol," Aunt Margie pointed to a bowl. "Would you like more sweet potatoes?"

"Oh, yes." Mom looked so happy. "And do we have hot tea, Hannah?"

"I'll make you some." I left my plate and headed into the kitchen.

Mom gave a contented sigh. "'He has provided food for those who fear Him. He remembers His covenant forever.'"

Amen to that. We were safe. We were together. And we were celebrating Christmas.

"You are *so* right, Grand!" Emily laughed——a delighted sound that surged warmth through my heart and lit my face with a smile.

Had Mom been playing her music, I might even have danced.

Bible Verses Quoted by Carol Ray Ballard

Chapter 1

"In God I trust; I will not fear. What can man do to me?" —*Psalm 56:11*

"The LORD is near the brokenhearted. He saves those crushed in spirit." —*Psalm 34:18*

Chapter 4

"Those who mourn are blessed, for they shall be comforted." —*Matthew 5:4*

Chapter 15

"LORD, be gracious to us. We wait for You. Be our strength every morning and our salvation in time of trouble." —*Isaiah 33:2*

Chapter 27

"The fear of the LORD is this: wisdom. And to turn from evil is understanding." —*Job 28:28*

Chapter 39

"He guards the steps of His faithful ones, but the wicked perish in darkness, for a man does not prevail by his own strength." –*1 Samuel 2:9*

Chapter 54

"But I will look to the LORD; I will wait for the God of my salvation. My God will hear me. Do not rejoice over me, my enemy! Though I have fallen, I will stand up; though I sit in darkness, the LORD will be my light." –*Micah 7:7–8*

Epilogue

"He has provided food for those who fear Him. He remembers His covenant forever." –*Psalm 111:5*

Discussion Questions

1. Have you ever made an "off-the-cuff" decision that changed your life?

2. Of the Bible verses that Carol quoted, which was your favorite? Why?

3. Can you name a time in which you misperceived the truth about a situation and based your actions upon that misperception? What happened?

4. What was Hannah's greatest strength? Her greatest weakness?

5. How did Hannah, Emily, and Carol resemble each other in their thinking and choices? How did they differ?

6. Have you ever been a caretaker for someone during a protracted illness? What was the hardest part of that task?

7. For Hannah's mom, Carol, Scripture was an integral part of her life, even when she forgot so many other things. Are there verses that strengthen and uplift you that way?

8. Could you kill someone to defend a family member? If so, how do you think doing so would affect you?

9. What do you envision your life would be like if you had to live without electrical power?

10. Why do you think God allows terrorists to carry out their attacks—sometimes on His own followers?

11. Do you think you will see another serious terrorist attack in this country in your lifetime? If so, what can you do to prepare spiritually for such an event?

12. Did you think Sergeant Wade was guilty of working with the terrorists?

13. What was the most surprising part of the story?

14. What are the different meanings of the title *Dark Justice*?

15. What did you learn from reading *Dark Justice*?